Kitty Black

a novel

LOR HILL

Matador
Unit E2 Airfield Business Park,
Harrison Road, Market Harborough,
Leicestershire. LE16 7UL
Tel: 0116 2792299
Email: books@troubador.co.uk
Web: www.troubador.co.uk/matador
Twitter: @matadorbooks

ISBN 978 1803135 557

British Library Cataloguing in Publication Data.
A catalogue record for this book is available from the British Library.

Printed and bound in Great Britain by 4edge Limited
Typeset in 11pt Minion Pro by Troubador Publishing Ltd, Leicester, UK

Matador is an imprint of Troubador Publishing Ltd

For my beautiful boys.

ONE

Kitty Black loved Scarborough. She thought the fog added a touch of mystery to the place, she thought the *tacky B & Bs* her dad talked about looked inviting, she thought the amusement arcades on the seafront were dead exciting. Jaconelli's ice-creams were the best, especially the one with the tangy lemon swirls. There was a quaint little shop called Mollie's which surely sold every ornament you could possibly want, including thumb-sized glass ducks—"Lucky Ducks"— in zodiac colours. Kitty used her dinner money to buy herself a turquoise one and a paler blue one for her Libran mum. She hoped with all of her heart they'd bring some good luck.

Kitty's dad hated Scarborough. It was his repatriation nightmare realised. It had been his third choice at the end of their posting in Singapore. 'It's *Northern*. It's *Yorkshire* for god's sake!' he'd said with a furrowed forehead.

When they'd arrived from abroad in the drizzle and mist, foghorn moaning, he'd told anyone who listened that he'd been shat on from a height, drawn the short straw; pay back for being outspoken at work. He turned his drunken wife's acceptance of the situation into hatred and within just a fortnight of arriving in Scarborough, he'd put in for expatriation. 'Anywhere's better than this dump,' he'd said. But wherever they went he was never happy. In fact, he seemed to hate most things; Kitty, her mum, his job.

Kitty liked to be away from the house as much as possible. She liked to meander through unfamiliar streets, find a bench and look down over north and south bays and watch the bobbing fishing boats head inland with their smelly hauls as squawking seagulls circled above. The breeze was fresh and sea-weedy. It felt good to take great gulps of it as it whipped her hair into her face. It was so different to the heat and smells of Singapore where they'd lived for three years; the cold blasts of wind felt refreshing. Behind her the ruins of the twelfth-century castle hugged the seaside town; to the right stood the Grand Hotel sturdy and proud with its unique shape and four towers. At the seafront she spent her dinner money in the arcades and on chips and ice-cream which she'd eat on the damp sand as she watched the donkeys earn their straw. A lone gull sometimes joined her, averting his eyes as he sidled up, hoping for a tasty morsel. It was company. None of her classmates ever asked why she missed school, if she'd been ill; no one really cared. Sometimes she'd buy a bag of cinder toffee from the market and crunch it until her teeth glued together. It tasted hollow and soulless compared to her childhood memory of it, but she always saved a chunk for her mum.

Her mum used to make cinder toffee. Kitty could easily conjure up the smell of burnt butter bubbling on the stove, could picture the golden foam spread like lava on wax paper before it cooled and crisped. Her favourite bit was breaking it into shards and tasting that first exquisite piece with its moreish bittersweet aftertaste. She could have finished every last crumb had her mum not reminded her to keep some for her brother. They loved eating sweets, her and Johnny. She missed all those times he'd come home with a white bag twisted closed in the corners and divvy up chocolate mice, Black Jacks and Fruit Salad chews on his bed. They'd balance flying saucers on the tips of their tongues until the sherbet oozed and they couldn't resist munching them. Kitty always finished hers first, she could never suck a sweet to the end. Always gave in, always greedy for the next one.

The best thing about Scarborough was Paul Scott. Kitty first noticed him striding around town in an army greatcoat and leather flying cap—so confident, so good-looking, so unavailable. She'd practically danced in front of him in her hot pants and poncho. She was a Sagittarian; showing off came naturally, and there was something about him that made her do it. He hadn't asked her out, but she'd noted a wry smile linger on his kissable lips. He'd been seeing a girl in the year above Kitty at school. Word was she'd hairy armpits and would do anything for a Toffee Crisp. When Paul dumped her, Kitty had found her missing gym kit in lost property; it had "Bitch" scrawled across the green gingham in black marker pen.

Paul had waited for Kitty outside school one day and, simple as that, they were going out. He was a Leo and protected her ferociously. She overheard him bragging to his mates it was easy pulling birds from Scarborough Girls' High, but Kitty knew he couldn't believe his luck. She caught him looking at her with such soppy eyes, it gave her a warm, fuzzy feeling.

On their first date they'd walked hand in hand through his estate in Eastfield, towards the park. Paul said he'd forgotten something, told her to wait and ran back up the street. Kitty thought he'd made a run for it. Had she said something wrong? Did she have BO? She'd tucked her fingers into her armpit and sniffed the tips. She'd detected the faint remainder of her Mum roll-on, so knew it wasn't that. She'd breathed into her cupped hand but wasn't sure she could smell bad breath even after three attempts. She'd been about to head for the bus stop to go home when a white car had screeched to a halt alongside her. It had made her jump and her heart thump wildly.

'Kit! Jump in. Quick!'

Kitty barely made it into the seat before Paul accelerated and they'd sped off towards town.

Paul loved stealing cars. He worked in a garage; he knew how to hotwire. That first one had been a Ford Escort, he'd said he liked them the best, especially if they'd red vinyl seats. His eyes had shone from the streetlights, his pupils huge; he was a speed freak. He'd lovely eyes, deepest brown and flecked with gold. He'd said hers were like the North Sea on a stormy day. He'd been sixteen then, scared of nothing and no one. Kitty had been fifteen and scared of many things, but she'd wanted to feel alive.

Kitty slid down into the footwell as they sped past the police station just in case Sergeant Martins had been about. The "Fuzz Box", Paul had called it. Sergeant Martins lived in Kitty's road. She didn't need him paying them a visit, but racing around in stolen cars had been better than sitting at home watching *The Two Ronnies* with her mum slumped drunk in her chair, her blue plastic mug of gin tucked beneath the pleat just above the carpet. Kitty had stayed in with her for so long. She'd tried to listen to the television over her mum's snores. She'd tried to ignore her mum's mumbled words which came out in the wrong order but always included *Johnny*; she'd heard it all before. She tried not to get upset when her mum cried in her sleep; she missed her brother loads too. Sometimes she felt so alone she'd cough loudly or turn the volume up to a deafening level to watch her mum jolt awake, just to get a reaction.

'S'good show—'ssn't it, Kitty?' her mum would say, and she'd be asleep and snoring again before Kitty could even answer. The realisation that her mum was more interested in the booze than her own daughter had twisted Kitty's guts for years. She wouldn't have known if Kitty was there or not so Kitty sneaked out to be with the boy who made her heart flutter.

The car skidded to a stop outside the chip shop. Heads turned in the Friday queue as Kitty ran in for a bag of vinegary chips with scraps. Paul stuck two fingers up at the hungry lads who'd leered at her bum.

'You're like a dressage filly,' the Blacks' next-door neighbour had shouted down the street after her the week before. 'You're all hair, legs and bum!' Kitty had pretended she hadn't heard the old man but had smiled to herself; heads turned to look at her. Her dad had pushed him up against the garage door but had let go when her mum had stumbled outside.

'Put him down, Bobby. He's a nutter. He should be in the looney bin!' she'd slurred. 'Keep away from that pervert,' she'd added to Kitty.

Kitty kept away from pretty much everyone, except Paul. Her dad worked away a lot—all Kitty knew was he worked for the Civil Service and when he'd gone it was much calmer, no shouting, no hitting. Kitty had become used to his anger but that didn't make the slaps sting less or nasty words less wounding. Kitty despised him for it and longed for the day she could live elsewhere, far away from him.

Bobby Black put his faith in the success of his daughter's secondary education entirely in the hands of the headmistress at Scarborough Girls' High—one Miss H. M. Lovage. Rumour had it the 'H' stood for Harriet but to the majority of pupils she was known as "Her Majesty", which was inevitably shortened to "Her Maj". With her tight perm and flowing gown she whooshed through the school corridors oozing power and fear, like a judge ready to sentence. Bobby wanted strict discipline for his daughter while he was in absentia, but Kitty had other ideas. When he was away she skived school more than she actually went. She became aware of her dad's impending disappearances when she spotted him and Her Maj taking tea in her office.

The Whisperers, who were a group of five of the best looking and nastiest girls in her year, put it about that Kitty's mum was a drunk and looked like Quasimodo. Kitty had no idea how they knew the first bit but shrugged it off in the hope the bullies would lose interest. It was rumoured Bobby and Her Maj were having an affair. Many of her parents' rows had featured other women's names; she heard them shouted through the walls, and there were lots. When she was older she realised the headmistress was just one of a long list of distractions that helped convince her dad that life was hunky dory, that his wife wasn't a drunk, and that his daughter wasn't becoming a tearaway just like his dead son.

When the truant letters arrived on the doormat Kitty got there first and binned them. The only person she missed was Mr Moore from her English class. He was one of those teachers that gave so much more, pushed you more, left you wanting more. He'd seen something in Kitty. He'd encouraged her to enter a short story competition, which she'd won. She'd read it out in assembly and everyone had clapped. With the book token prize she'd wanted to get *Portnoy's Complaint* after she'd read an excerpt in the library but hadn't thought she'd be able to hide it from her parents who'd say it was *filth,* so she'd settled for *The Lion, the Witch and the Wardrobe.*

She bumped into Mr Moore once at the shops. He pleaded with her to turn up at school more and he'd help her to catch up. She thanked him and said she would, but deep down she knew she wouldn't. She never felt she belonged there. Paul said he'd rent them a place and they'd be together forever. Kitty thought that sounded fab, but wasn't convinced it was the answer.

It would have been different if Johnny had still been alive. He'd died in 1965, just seventeen, a hit and run. A car had knocked him flying as he'd cycled back drunk from the pub on a stolen bike. Kitty had tried to make sense of it; he was an Aries after all—"born to be wild", her pocket horoscope book told her, a present she inherited after Johnny dumped yet another girlfriend. *To Johnny, my moon and stars, Jo x* was scrawled inside the front cover. Kitty's hungry mind had devoured every word of this mysterious other world and when she was happy, sad or bored she'd read it some more. It had taken Johnny three days to die of "complications" as Kitty's world turned upside down. She hadn't cried then. She'd had to prop her drunk mum up. Her dad had stood next to them at the funeral staring straight at the coffin. He hadn't joined in the singing of her favourite hymn—"Morning Has Broken"—and he'd left before the end of the service.

Kitty missed Johnny. He was still there with her. He'd looked out for her when he was alive like a proper big brother and she felt he always would. She was eight years old when he died. She'd rested her chin on his hospital bed and tried to block out the bleeps, wires and tubes pouring out of him. Her mum had gone to cry in the toilets and appeared breezily with red eyes and cups of sweet tea which sat on the windowsill until skins formed. In tough times Kitty always remembered Johnny's last words. 'Everyone has—options, Kat. Don't—mess up—like me,' he'd whispered. 'Got in with the wrong—crowd. Went off—the rails. Don't—do the same. You've got—a brain.'

He *had* got in with the wrong crowd but Kitty remembered the country boy he'd been at heart. Back then they'd lived in a small village called Horton in Somerset with cows in the field behind, hedgerows of fat blackberries lined the lanes and rivers teemed with minnows and chub. Johnny often fished on the riverbank, rod in one hand, cheese sandwich in the other. Kitty sometimes went with him until he'd chased her with the wriggly maggots, or the food ran out.

She remembered how, when she was about five, he'd crept into her bedroom late one night and gently woken her. 'Come on, Kat. You've *got* to see this! Quiet, though.'

She'd followed him down the stairs. He'd stopped to point at the creaky one, a finger pressed to his lips, the whites of his eyes urging her to be quiet. She remembers the butterflies she'd felt in her belly. It had been scary to be up in the middle of the night but she knew she'd be safe with him. He'd lifted her into her red wellies and held her hand; his yellow torch had poked out of his coat pocket.

Kitty had hoped there'd be snow. The anticipation of it had been everywhere. Everyone from the greengrocer to the Post Mistress said *it's in the air*. The greengrocer hadn't actually been green and his fruit and vegetables hadn't all been green either, Kitty had noticed. But there was no snow that night. The air was cold and moonlight lit the lane.

They'd headed down the hill, over the hump bridge and across a dewy field. Up ahead stood a massive tree with branches wide and welcoming. Johnny had flashed the light up the length of the trunk; Kitty squinted to see anything. Her brother's arm had rested across her right shoulder as he'd crouched behind her and pointed up. She'd caught her breath when she spotted something. In a jagged hole sat the biggest owl she'd ever seen. He was magnificent. He'd looked down at them with scary, staring eyes. Johnny had turned off the torch and the bird had been illuminated by the golden moon behind. All had gone very quiet except for the distant scream of a fox.

After a while Kitty had started to feel cold and clapped her mittened hands together. The string attached to the gloves inside her coat had pulled across her shoulders. Johnny had shushed her but she'd done it again because she thought she looked like a puppet and had started laughing. The huff of her breath had made her do it all the more. The owl had leant forward, spreading his huge wings wide and had flown across the field. The flapping had sounded like a rushing river.

The snow had come the next day. Kitty had opened her window to the still whiteness. Coated and booted, she'd jumped from the back door step and landed in it up to her middle. She thought *that* was even more amazing than seeing the owl.

And it had been amazing, life was amazing, her brother had been amazing. Kitty can still hear her mother's screams when the ventilator had been turned off and Johnny hadn't drawn a single breath on his own.

The options Johnny mentioned had changed. Kitty's parents had given up on her once he'd gone. It made her rage inside. Sometimes her palm bled from digging her nails in when she thought about stuff too much, or she'd pinch the top of her legs until they bruised; the pain brought her back down to earth, stopped her mind from spinning. Most of the time she tried to control it. She didn't like drawing attention to herself around her parents, tried to keep just under the radar.

Kitty was used to watching and listening; she'd learned to spot a mood change in a nano second. She could be herself with Paul. Joyriding with him gave her a taste of freedom and excitement. That first time had stayed with her. 'It's like being on the Waltzer!' she'd shouted as they'd careered down the streets on two wheels. Paul grinned as he spotted his mate Timbo at the bus stop. He aimed the car at him then pulled off a handbrake turn. The car was facing the wrong way in the road and the air smelled of burning rubber. Timbo splattered his new jogging top with tomato sauce as his burger fell at his feet, but he smiled as he recognised Paul. They had form, Paul told her; they'd met in Borstal.

'Jump in the back, Timbo!'

'Nah. Gotta be home on the next bus. Don't want no more trouble. See ya round, Scotty.' He stuck his arm out for the approaching number nine. Paul wheel-spun onto the other side of the road and then away. Kitty squeezed her eyes shut tight as her knuckles had turned white from gripping either side of her seat.

They pulled into a garage and Paul told the attendant to *fill 'er up*. In the car alongside them was a girl from Kitty's class—Denise, the ringleader of The Whisperers, and her dad. Kitty watched her dad disappear into the shop. Denise played with her hair, distractedly twirling her fingers through it; her window was wound down. Kitty stared at the girl's side profile until she looked her way, then Kitty gave her the biggest sneer, feeling empowered by Paul's proximity.

'That's for being a posh cow,' she shouted. 'Bet you can't wait to tell someone you saw me. Back to your sad life, Denny. Don't forget to do your homework. Wear your uniform. Be the same as all the others. Herded around. Oppressed. *Bitch.*' Kitty couldn't help but feel a sense of satisfaction as she watched Denise's face turn crimson. This girl, and the rest of her nasty pack, had been horrible to her from her first day at school. Paul squeezed Kitty's knee. Denise's dad returned to their car carrying bars of chocolate. Kitty wished her dad would do everyday things with her like trips to the garage, like bringing her two Flakes and a Bar Six. All her dad gave her was two fists and a piece of his mind.

Kitty had no close friends back then. She'd never been sure what the girls actually whispered about her, but thought it had been something to do with not being from Yorkshire by birth, having lived in an exotic place like Singapore for three years, and having a dead brother. It made her different. They'd probably thought she came from a privileged background by virtue of her dad's job, but it just wasn't like that. Not for her. In Singapore they'd lived within a community where they all had similar houses, gardens, schooling and *still* they'd been outsiders there. The ex-pat parties they'd been invited to saw them labelled as *pariahs* once they realised Rose Black

was an *alkie* and Bobby Black was *such a bloody angry man.*
Kitty had been nine when their neighbours' daughter Carole
had first said it. She'd announced it one day after school to
a crowd huddled around playing Jacks as they'd waited for
their school bus. Kitty had been winning.

'My dad says your family's a bunch of *pariahs!*' Kitty
had caught the glint in her friend's eyes, similar to the one
she'd noticed in her own dad's eyes recently, and realised this
accusation had been directed at her. Her whole body had
gone goose-bumpy as she'd looked back down at the game.
She'd no idea what that word meant but knew it must be bad.
All eyes had been on her as she'd slowly gathered up the metal
pieces and tiny red ball, dropped them into their pouch and
stood up. She'd turned, walked towards the bus with her face
on fire, and had concentrated on putting one foot in front of
the other. Instead of sitting in her usual place near the back
with Carole, she'd sat next to the bus escort and told her she
wasn't feeling well. Carole had got on and smirked as she'd
passed by and Kitty had leant into the escort, who'd wrapped
a concerned arm around her.

All the way on the bus journey back, Kitty had kept saying
piranha in her head; she knew what that was and it was as
close as she could get to remember the other word. When
she got home she'd run past her mum asleep on the sofa
and up to her room. Her Collins English Gem Dictionary
had told her it was indeed a bad word. It had made her feel
like a leper. Her family was different, but not in a good way.
Despite her mum's drinking and her dad's anger, Kitty still
felt a protectiveness towards her parents. They'd only just lost
Johnny. It was like losing an important puzzle piece and all
the happy things in life. Her tears were always just there and

it had made her angry that people had been saying horrible things about them. She knew they'd move away again one day, her dad kept threatening they would, and they *had* to go back to England one day as that was their home. Leaving Singapore had been a relief to Kitty and she'd looked forward to starting again.

It wasn't long before things started to turn sour in Scarborough. At senior school Kitty envied her classmates which had made her feel an outsider right from the start. She noticed and longed for those little things caring parents did: first bras bought on special mother and daughter shopping trips, not donated by a sympathetic friend (Paul's mum), who'd noticed her budding boobs; black patent school shoes that shone prettily and made their wearers surely want to get up in the morning just to put them on, instead of sensible Clarks lace-ups that looked like torpedoes; whispers about *coming on* and comparing sanitary belts and little floral bags holding billowy pads instead of handfuls of toilet paper stuffed in her knickers when a regular monthly buy was too much for her mum to remember, and Kitty was too embarrassed to ask. Her uniform got tatty and her boyish shoes got scuffed and she died inside a little bit more. Her stomach twisted when anyone stared. When they'd whispered *Pongo* one day she'd scraped together enough change from her dinner money to buy a Mum roll-on deodorant from Boyes, Turner and Burrows in town. She'd gone into their toilets, washed her armpits with a paper towel and waited in a toilet cubicle for the stickiness to dry.

By the time she met Paul, she'd got to grips with personal hygiene with no help from her parents. Using the money she collected from the empty bottles lying around the house she made sure she had a supply of sanitary towels, anti-perspirant and a discounted bottle of 4711 eau de cologne because the box was badly damaged.

After that first joyride around town with Paul, he paid for the fuel and they screeched back to the scene of the crime— Kitty guessed that's what it was as it was just around the corner from where he'd left her standing some hours previously. No one was about so he parked the car up between two chalk lines he'd made on the pavement earlier. Back exactly where it had been, as if nothing had happened.

'A gentleman thief, I am, Kit! Not many would fill up with fuel before returning it, would they?' he said, his chin tilted with pride. He grabbed Kitty's hand and they ran to the end of the road where he pushed her against a lamppost and shoved his tongue into her mouth. It tasted of vinegar and danger.

'You're beautiful and I want you, Kit.' Kitty had grabbed his arm and led him towards the park.

'I thought we were going to mess around on the swings,' Paul said as she pulled him down on top of her next to the high slide. His knees landed either side of her hips and his outstretched arms balanced him above her on the damp grass. She looked up at him through lusty eyes. 'Oh, I thought—'

'Not like this, Kit, and not yet. You're not ready *and* you're underage. But I do want you. One day.' He kissed her and held her tight. She wanted it to be special too, so instead she put into practice the kissing tips she'd read in *Jackie*.

Another time, Paul took Kitty to the fair. Eastfield Rec was alive with booming music, screaming sirens and young girls with bare midriffs hoping to catch the eye of the dodgem operator as he swung nimbly from car to car, a monkey in double denim. Kitty watched the lights from the rides turn Paul's face red then green then blue, as if there was a disco going on inside his head. He pulled her towards the big wheel queue. Heights frightened Kitty. She hoped it would develop a fault before they reached the front. A bored-looking fair man with pant-slider eyes and a stud earring held the safety bar open for them. They climbed in. Kitty studied the flimsiness of it all and worried the nuts and bolts might loosen. The bar slammed down and seemed too far away for her liking. As they ascended, Paul pointed out landmarks on that rare clear night and Kitty made the right noises, but didn't lift her eyes up from her lap. As the wheel gathered momentum, goosebumps grew on goosebumps and tears sprang to her eyes. Two girls in the cage above feigned terror, screamed then laughed hysterically. Kitty knew if she started screaming she'd never stop; she'd held in so much sorrow for so long. She thought she'd die as they came to a standstill at the top to let revellers out at the bottom; she hardly dared to breathe.

'You okay, gorgeous?' Paul pushed his feet down on the footrest and swung their cage.

'Yeah, great,' she said as she gripped the metal safety bar tightly with both hands, faint with the motion. The smell of candy floss, hotdogs and burgers had taunted her with nausea. Paul's laughter was lost to the screams from the ghost train.

It had been Johnny's favourite ride, the ghost train. He'd been the first person to take Kitty on it. She was eight and it had scared her to death. He'd laughed and grabbed her shoulders in a tunnel; she'd nearly wet herself. She thought he'd have liked Paul because they both got off on the thrill of their own freewill, living and loving every second.

When their cage reached the bottom, Kitty leaped onto the wooden platform before the fair attendant had time to help. She stumbled with jelly legs from the shock and cold. She sighed a grateful sigh when Paul draped his greatcoat over her shoulders. He cupped her face in his cold hands and gently kissed her on the nose. She tingled inside as he turned her to face the dodgems. Her eyes widened in horror. She didn't like the juddering stops in the bumper cars or the sparks overhead but didn't want Paul to think her a wimp. Her stomach was still trying to settle from the big wheel. She distracted him by turning to the coconut shy and pointing at the giant furry crab hanging overhead with all the other faded soft toys and said, 'I've always wanted one of those.' It took Paul six throws. He handed it to her with an exaggerated bow. 'For you, my lady.' She said it was too big to take on the dodgems so Paul had led the way to the helter-skelter. She watched him slalom down the ride with the crab straddling his lap. He whooped at every turn. He bought them hotdogs and ice-creams and said they didn't have to go on anything else if she didn't want to. They found a cut-through in the caravans and leant against a fence to enjoy their food.

Paul sometimes met Kitty outside school. Missing lunch to leave work early, he'd be leaning against a tree with one knee up, showing his long legs to best effect. By the time she reached him she'd: hitched her skirt up at the waistband until the top of her tights showed; shoved her Clarks lace-ups into her satchel and replaced them with her yellow clogs; dabbed pan-stick on her pimples and peach lipstick across her mouth. For the final touch she sprayed eau de cologne liberally inside her school shirt, coughing as it hit her nostrils. She always melted at his admiring look.

They'd walk, arms entwined, in their own world down road after road. Once they crossed Scalby Road and started climbing up Osborne Park, Kitty would start to feel anxious. Her anxiety manifested itself in the pit of her belly. It grew the further up the hill they got. By the time they reached the steps at the end of her street where Paul would sit on the road-sign "Leading to Walnut Grove" while she checked on her mum, the pain would be gnawing away at her. She never knew which mum would be waiting for her, devil or angel, sparring for a fight or in a deep, drunken sleep.

Once, Kitty crept indoors after gingerly turning the front door key, listening for any clues. She knew instantly if something was wrong. It had been too quiet, too still, too calm. She'd found her mum on the carpet in the front room. In one hand she still held her empty plastic cup and from the patch on her trousers, she could see she'd wet herself. Her cigarette had dropped from her nicotine-stained fingers and melted into the carpet, sticking up like a mushroom without its cap. Kitty's heart had pounded as she'd put an ear to her mum's chest. She'd detected a strong beat but wondered if it was her own. She'd held her mum's wrist, found a pulse after an age and only then did Kitty breathe out. Her mum's mouth gaped wide, a dark cave with no furniture, her false teeth secreted in her cardigan pocket. Kitty had noticed how drink had eaten her mum's features. Her baggy eyes and craggy, sallow complexion belied her age: her flat dyed red hair with its tramlines of stark white roots didn't deliver the promise of the packet in the bathroom cabinet. Panic had replaced sadness as Kitty's mum continued to lie there unaware of her sorry state.

'Mum! What have you done?' No response. She'd checked her over to make sure there was no blood or visible broken bones. She'd turned towards the window thinking she'd heard something. Paul was peering through, his hand cupped against the glass. Kitty had turned back to shield the scene, embarrassed they'd been seen. This was *her* mum, *her* world and she was used to it now, guarded it from others even. Paul had mouthed *let me in*. He hadn't been inside Kitty's house, not least because her dad would have gone ballistic at her even seeing a boy, but also because Kitty was ashamed of the state of it. There was an air of neglect: it stank of cigarettes, the carpet needed hoovering, there were dirty dishes piled high in the sink and despite Kitty's best attempts, she couldn't keep on top of it. Several days a week she'd get up two hours before school to clear up sick, and dust and hoover in the hope she wouldn't wake her mum from the sleep she so badly needed. She'd collect the washing from the bathroom, spray the vomit stains and hang out the finished load. She'd empty the bin, take the bag out to the dustbin and then tackle the dishes. On afternoons she didn't meet Paul, she'd iron as her mum snoozed in front of the television. She'd hide the clean laundry in her wardrobe if she didn't have time to iron it all—her mum had been known to attempt to iron but would wander off and things would get scorched. The taunting of the other girls when this happened to the back of Kitty's school dress was so excruciating she'd sidled along walls to avoid it.

Paul had tapped gently but insistently on the window. Kitty retrieved her mum's false teeth from their hiding place, and had gently slipped them over her gums. She'd walked to the door and let Paul in, saying too quickly, 'Mum's drunk a bit too much and fallen over, she gets lonely when Dad's away. She's breathing and everything but I can't move her on my own.' Paul had scanned the scene. Kitty had flinched, imagining seeing this through someone else's eyes: grubby slippers hung on to greying socks bursting through the stirrups of faded green slacks; her old nylon housecoat had an orange vomit stain down the front and yellowing sweat marks under the arms; she'd smelled like a tramp. She'd thought he must be wondering where the wages from her dad's good job went. Kitty knew. Lying in front of them was the sad result. Shame had coursed through her like it always did. She'd searched his face for disgust.

He'd crouched down. 'We don't need to move her and anyway, she'll be a dead weight. Get a blanket, Kit. We'll cover her over and keep her warm for now.'

Kitty had climbed the stairs two at a time and grabbed the candlewick bedspread in the airing cupboard. She'd tried not to notice the stash of gin bottles lurking at the back, but there they were—her mum's not so secret, secret. Back in the living room, Paul had placed her mum into the recovery position and Kitty's heart had melted with tenderness at his efforts. Together they'd tucked the spread around her. Kitty had picked up the plastic cup, prised the cigarette from the carpet and put them with the rest of the detritus in the kitchen.

Paul had smiled at Kitty and said, 'Okay, let's stay here this evening and make sure she's alright.' Kitty put some cheese on toast under the grill and they'd sat up on her bed and listened to records like she imagined normal teenagers did. She'd longed for her and Paul to spend time like this in her house.

'Why didn't you tell me about your mum, Kit? You know you can tell me anything.' He'd hugged her to his chest. So she'd told him about Johnny's death, her mum's drinking, her dad's violence, and had barely drawn breath. It had been easier telling him without looking at him, so she'd poked at the ladder in her tights.

'I hate my dad for hitting me and mum,' she said, and Paul had squeezed her tighter as she'd cried.

'I'll take care of you, Kit. One day soon all this will be gone, it won't always be like this.' Paul had pointed to the tatty red vanity case on the shelf above the bed and said, 'My mum's got one of those in gold—full of make-up, is yours?'

'No! My nan gave it to me ages ago,' Kitty said, grabbing it and putting it between them on the bed. She'd unzipped it slowly, using both hands as it had a tendency to catch. She'd pulled the flap back to reveal the contents. Paul had picked out a photo of Johnny, the one Kitty rarely looked at because it made her cry. Paul looked at her questioningly.

'My brother—just before he died,' was all she'd said. Paul put the photo to one side. He'd pulled out a tiny ceramic hedgehog with a black nose. It was well made, heavy with ridges for spines and exquisitely painted. Kitty explained her nan had won it in a cracker one Christmas and had swapped it for the sewing kit four-year-old Kitty got from her cracker. Paul had frowned again and Kitty chuckled as she'd explained. 'When Nan was making dinner in the kitchen, she'd watched me cup the hedgehog in my hand and whisper to it, she knew I loved it.'

'Awwww, Kit!' Paul had said without a hint of sarcasm and tenderly rubbed her knee. Next he'd pulled out a blue suede marble pouch containing Johnny's favourite onionskin swirl and a stubby piece of blue chalk. He'd held up the chalk between his thumb and forefinger. 'Did he nick cars too?' he'd asked jokingly.

'No. But he *was* killed by a hit and run.'

Paul had carefully replaced the items, zipped the case back up and placed it on the shelf. He'd reached over and held Kitty in his arms for a long time.

They'd kissed goodnight and Paul had left to catch the bus home. All night Kitty had dreamt of him—she'd seen such a kind and caring side to him. When she'd woken, her belly had been buzzing with love, which disappeared quickly once her mum's irate shouts filled the house.

Usually when Kitty checked on her mum after school, she was often just asleep in her chair or blankly staring at the television. Kitty would get changed and then run with Paul to catch the bus to his place some twenty minutes away. They drew hearts and initialled the steamy windows on the top deck, oblivious to anyone around, lost in their own world. Kitty loved these times away from home.

Sometimes when they got to Paul's house there was no one there, no car on the drive and no blaring radio from the kitchen. The Scotts had been the first to buy their council house. It was semi-detached and they'd painted their half of grey pebble-dash white. Plastic plant pots hugged the front doorstep dripping with geraniums and in amongst them a smiling gnome fished. To the right of the front door was a hanging basket which creaked under the weight of purple petunias and midnight blue lobelia. The brass letterbox was blindingly shiny. The swirly orange hallway carpet seemed so much more fun than the Blacks' plain burgundy one and reminded Kitty of a welcoming hotel. Without a word they'd run up the stairs and lie facing each other on Paul's single bed. Kitty's body would grind against his, as if magnetised to him. The feeling was delicious as they moved in rhythm.

Paul's kisses would become more insistent; she'd open her mouth wider, wanting more and more. She'd arch her back pushing his roaming hand onto her thinly clothed body, wanting him to rip her top off, mentally begging him to go further. But it was always Paul who reluctantly climbed off the bed and helped Kitty up. She'd tut with frustration, but truth be known, she'd have felt so guilty if they'd actually had sex. And she'd be in a lot of trouble if her dad ever found out.

Most times, his parents were there.

'Hey, lass. 'Ow've you bin?' Kitty loved Mr Scott. He always gave her a bear hug and she pretended to struggle for breath; it had become a ritual.

''Ow's the best looking girl in the boys' school?' he'd say and she'd laugh. He smelled of Old Spice and all things nice. Home-cooking filled the hallway. Mrs Scott's culinary skills had been honed in Ceylon during summer school holidays with her Indian grandmother. Her curries were a grand affair with a huge circular segmented dish in the centre of the dining table spilling over with sultanas, chopped cucumber and desiccated coconut. It made Kitty's mouth water and long for her mum to cook again. When the dining room table wasn't in use, on the embroidered runner was the biggest fruit bowl Kitty had ever seen. It was made of brass, and rosy apples, oranges, bananas and grapes draped from it. They didn't have a fruit bowl at home. She loved fruit though. In Singapore she'd sometimes ride her bike to the fruit market in the next village on a Sunday. The smell used to make her dizzy and the vibrant rows of reds, yellows and oranges—mangoes, pawpaw, papaya—was a feast for her eyes. Her favourite had been rambutans. They were bigger than lychees but with a red outer skin and soft black spikes. They smelled like perfume

22

and tasted satisfyingly sweet. If she had a few cents, she'd buy a small bunch and eat them with juice running down her brown arms. She hated durians. They were about the size of melons and brown on the outside. They smelled like sick and poo so she never got close enough to eat one. She thought they smelled like hell, and knew Johnny would have thought so too.

There was no shouting, no thumping, no crying at Paul's house. It was a home. There was a place set for Kitty at the table and plenty to go around. Paul's dad filled the armchair by the fire, newspaper on his lap tackling a crossword, taking it easy as his days as a postman started early. After tea, he walked their scruffy old terrier, Mitch, through the estate and across the playing field, and then settled down to the television until his snores filled the room. Kitty would rest her head on Paul's lap on the sofa as he stroked her hair and giggle when Paul's mum tutted at her husband's farts. Kitty felt so content with her tummy full of delicious food and surrounded by people who cared about her.

At home, left to her own devices, Kitty lived on crackers. There was no home cooking at their house while her dad worked away. Her mum was incapable—a danger drunkenly stumbling around in the kitchen. She'd seen it for a while now. Kitty would butter enough crackers for both of them and leave a plate on the coffee table for her mum. In the morning they'd be rancid and untouched. Kitty would tip them in the bin along with the doubled-up cigarette butts from the overflowing ashtray.

She'd watch Mrs Scott move confidently around the kitchen and desperately wish her own mum would stop drinking. She'd tried to help once. She'd gathered the hidden bottles and tipped their contents down the sink, watched the clear liquid swirl down the plughole and held her breath from the bitter stench. She'd tried to finish the job quickly but heard her mum's slippered feet drag along from the sitting room. She'd roughly pushed Kitty to one side to see the last dregs gurgle away and had turned and slapped her daughter hard across the face.

'It's only bloody botanicals—herbs, for Christ's sake!'

'It's not, Mum! It's killing you!'

'When I was having you the doctor prescribed stout. It's medicinal. It's the same bloody thing, you little cow!'

Kitty had cradled her stinging cheek and watched sadly as her mum ranted and raged with glassy, empty eyes, wishing she'd stop. But through twisted lips she'd told Kitty she knew about the new boyfriend. She'd seen them running down the road together; he looked like he was from the estate. She said she'd tell her dad and he'd be furious. Kitty knew he would be and felt powerless as her mum explained the deal: Kitty was to ferry sherry and gin home from the offie several times a week with a handwritten note and her mum would say nothing about Paul. Kitty couldn't give him up; he was her lifeline. He and his family made everything bearable; she couldn't imagine being without them.

But then one morning her dad made a grand entrance into the kitchen. Kitty was hunched over the worktop, chewing on buttered toast before school. Her mum sucked hard on her cigarette as she stared out of the window. He stood there saying nothing, waiting for everyone's attention, *demanding* everyone's attention. Kitty looked up reluctantly through the curtains of her fringe. She detected a smug look on his face, cringed and lowered her eyes.

'You'll be pleased to hear we're leaving this dump. We're off to Hong Kong,' he said as he waved an official-looking letter in the air. His tone was menacing. He wanted to be challenged. Kitty snatched up her satchel and headed for the back door.

'Did you hear what I just said, Katherine?'

Panic rose in her chest; she could feel her throat constricting. She closed her eyes and swallowed repeatedly. 'Yes!' she said, unable to keep the irritation from her voice.

He leaped forward and grabbed her arm as tightly as a Chinese burn. 'Then do me the courtesy of letting me finish. We leave in a fortnight. There's nothing keeping us here— unless you know differently, of course?'

'No, Dad,' she replied flatly.

He took his hand away. She stared at the crimson band on her skin. 'Now get out and go to bloody school,' he spat as he pushed her outside and slammed the door.

When she was safely on the path she cradled her churning belly and fought back angry tears until she was out of view. She seethed with hatred for him. She wanted to scream out loud every obscene word she knew, but neighbours were everywhere—herding children and warming up their cars. She broke into a run down the hill but tears filled her eyes and blurred the way. There was no way she was going to school but, because her dad was around, she decided to nip in for Registration, then bunk off. She needed thinking time, time to get her head around them moving away and time to work out how she was going to tell the Scotts.

At the seafront she leant against a rock on a deserted part of the beach. On the walk down her thoughts had raced and the idea to run away won. She watched a tanker crawl on the horizon; how difficult would it be to become a stowaway? Hong Kong would be no different to Singapore—Johnny wouldn't be with them, her dad would still hit her and she'd still hate him. Her mum would still drink, she'd continue to do badly at school and she probably wouldn't see Paul for years. She could find absolutely no reason why she should go. She spotted a toddler further down the beach running towards the water's edge, screaming with glee as her mum chased her and scooped her up just as the foamy waves came. That had been *her* mum once: full of life and enjoying the precious time with her children until one had died and she'd replaced him with drink. Johnny's death and his wife's drinking had turned Bobby Black into a wife-beating monster. And right there Kitty found her reason for not running away. Who'd look after her mum? She knew she was needed to complete the Blacks' unholy trinity: the bully, the drunk and the glob of glue that loosely bound them; another body to bear the blows. Their leaving sat like a misshapen stone in her guts and the only chink of light was the fact that her dad would be working shifts, as he had in Singapore. There was nothing else to look forward to. It depressed her to the point she had to distract herself by gathering up pebbles and counting them as she dropped them one by one back on the sand.

The time came when she couldn't put it off any longer. She was at the Scotts' house one evening while her dad was on a two-day course at Bletchley Park. They were all lounging in front of the television after the tastiest spaghetti bolognese—Kitty had eaten a second helping just to prolong the meal. Paul's dad awoke with a start as Mitch skidded down the hallway to the front door, barking and growling when noisy neighbours passed their gate.

'We're going abroad again, we've been posted to Hong Kong, we're leaving in ten days' time,' she said it in one breath. At first, she thought they hadn't heard her above the noise Mitch was making. In so many ways she wished they hadn't. But all three shocked faces had turned to her; even Mitch had stopped barking. Mrs Scott pulled herself out of her armchair and pulled Kitty to her. Kitty felt her kiss the top of her head. Kitty sobbed into Mrs Scott's crocheted top. Paul immediately hatched a plan for Kitty to stay behind with them in Scarborough until his dad talked him down with, 'C'mon lad. We're going to miss her but her place is with her family. It won't be forever.'

To lift the mood, Mrs Scott turned on the record player and the three of them danced around the front room to Mungo Jerry's "In The Summertime". Mr Scott watched from his armchair supping his stout until Mitch's howling along to the lyrics became unbearable and they went for their evening walk.

The night before the Blacks left for Hong Kong the family stayed in a hotel in Alma Square at the top of town. Kitty and Paul had already said their tearful goodbyes two days previously; promises exchanged to write every day, no sleep since then. Kitty spotted an opportunity to see Paul one last time. Her parents were celebrating their escape from *this godforsaken place* in the hotel bar. Drunken laughter filled the foyer as her dad bought drinks for all. Kitty listened from behind a pillar and waited before creeping out to the nearest phone box and called Paul to come over.

He was waiting for her on "their" bench in Peasholm Park, his trumpet case by his side—a present from his aunt to loosen his lungs following a bout of pneumonia when he was twelve. He played in the Salvation Army band and that night he should have been at practice. Instead they sat looking up at the star-studded sky, trying not to cry.

'I'll wait for you, Kitty. You're the love of my life. You mean everything to me.' His voice broke as he spoke these words. He stood up and from his pocket he magicked an ox-red ring box, which he flicked open with his thumb, revealing a glistening engagement ring. He held his breath as Kitty looked at his face then back to the box.

'Please wear my ring, I love you and one day I want to marry you. I'll be here when you get back.'

Kitty held back the tears, not wanting to waste a second, not wanting to leave this wild boy who'd stolen her heart. 'Yes, Paul. I love you too,' tumbled from her mouth. Paul placed the ring on her finger and hugged her to him. She never wanted him to let go.

'When you're in Hong Kong and feeling sad just look up into the sky and find those three stars in a row— they're Orion's belt. Just know that I'll be doing the same back here and missing you with all of my heart.'

Through pooling tears she spotted the stars and the love-struck couple parted.

TWO

Hong Kong was another world. It could have been Mars. Kitty was stunned by the jostling crowds of people, the noise, the smells. The heat was searing, even in the shade. Her clothes were unsuitable. In an excited sober moment before they'd left Scarborough, her mum had told her she'd have a new wardrobe with a clothing allowance of forty pounds. Kitty had imagined co-ordinating clothes just like her old Sindy doll's wardrobe: ribbed tops, miniskirts with thick belts over underwear that fitted properly, topped off with a matching mac and boots for the typhoons she'd read about. But this hadn't happened. She knew her mum had drunk away the money and it was never mentioned again.

The island was vibrant and exciting; there was a buzz about it. But it smelled awful. Kitty noticed it when they first arrived. So different to Singapore, which had felt and smelled clean. Over Hong Kong hung a fug of decaying rubbish, stagnant water and rotting fruit. She'd read about the "Fragrant Harbour" and had to agree it looked beautiful at night with its bright lights and drifting sampans. It still stank though. Insects buzzed incessantly, hands doubled as fans to swat them away. While wealthy Chinese women, perfectly made-up and not a bead of sweat on their porcelain faces, wafted elegant silk fans, Kitty felt like a heifer in a field of cowpats swishing a tail at flies.

The Blacks moved into a flat on the most southerly point of Hong Kong island – Stanley. This village was parched from the harsh heat, with skinny stray dogs roaming for food as market stallholders hollered their wares. Chinese children wearing clothes several sizes too big played marbles on the roadside. Kitty caught her breath when she saw them doing this and stopped and watched. Johnny had taught her everything she knew about marbles: which one was the shooter, which one was the fastest, which one was worth more for swaps. He'd shown her pictures in a comic once of marbles called "bumboozers" and "commies". She couldn't remember what those marbles looked like, but she'd loved the sound of the words. She wished Johnny was there to explore with.

Stanley Beach was a long stretch of golden sand onto which the South China Sea rhythmically crashed and ice-cream vendors leant against their bikes, snoozing upright when custom was quiet. The rolling waves calmed Kitty as her body browned in the balmy sun.

The best thing about Hong Kong was Gill Grant. The Grants and the Blacks moved into the same block of flats on the same day. They found themselves sitting next to each other on the school bus on their first day at school and from then on, whoever got on first would save a space with their school bag taking up the seat. Gill was short for Gillian, but Gill preferred the shortened version. Kitty told Gill her name was Katherine really, but she hated it. Gill said Kitty was a pretty name but said she thought Kat suited her better. Kitty loved it because it was what her brother had called her. She loved having Gill to go to school with and she left skiving off behind her in Scarborough.

Kitty and Gill delighted in finding out about each other. Who liked what, what they missed about the UK—Kitty: Paul; Gill: rain. Gill became Kitty's best friend in December 1972. The record clinched it. Kitty still had a faded Polaroid of the occasion. It was of the both of them—young smiling faces—grinning into Gill's dad's camera. Kitty was wearing white shorts and a blue T-shirt; Gill was wearing green shorts and a billowing orange top. She was going through her Buddhist phase and was reading voraciously about it. Kitty was holding up Cat Stevens's *Teaser and the Firecat* album, a sixteenth birthday present from Gill, and Gill had her arm around Kitty. When Kitty played "Morning Has Broken" she thought her heart would break in two.

Gill had wild crinkly auburn hair, was six inches shorter than Kitty and six months younger but looked about twelve. Her dress sense could be described as haphazard at best. She had no problem with wearing cerise, orange and red all at the same time; no thought to how it clashed with her hair. Kitty flinched when her friend approached sometimes, but at least she could spot her a mile away. Kitty soon learned that Gill's appearance was at odds with her character; she was so straight, so dependable. She had an old head on young shoulders, she was a Capricorn. They shared a love of music, clothes and boys. Their bedrooms were their dens. Gill's walls were painted white, lined with shelves of foreign novels and posters proclaiming "Existentialism is a Humanism" while Kitty's purple room had David Cassidy peering sexily down at her and her stack of *Jackie* magazines. Poems were pinned randomly around the walls, torn with a flourish from notebooks, screaming with the sense of her own poetic melodrama, and bordered with felt-tipped red hearts and gold stars.

When Kitty pranced around to Elton John, Gill sniggered and re-read T.Rex lyrics for hidden meanings. Kitty really didn't get Marc Bolan, didn't like all that wavy hair on a man and vowed if she ever had a daughter she would never call her "Debora"—with or without an "h". It was Gill's favourite song and she played it incessantly. She muttered the lyrics when she was stressed, when she was happy and when she just wanted to wind her friend up. It left Kitty cold. Marc Bolan was Gill's cultural curator; she analysed every reference, every word, every breath. But it all evened out. Kitty's Joni Mitchell phase almost drove Gill insane. Kitty loved wailing along to "Blue", deliberately missing the high notes to get a rise out of Gill. Gill said the *caterwauling* from both the artist and her friend left her hating the colour and the emotion which made Kitty laugh because she knew she was only teasing.

After homework they usually went to the beach, lolling in their bikinis—their bodies almost at the peak of teenage ripeness. They chatted non-stop and kept a look-out for boys. Well, Kitty did but Gill was less forward. She hadn't had a boyfriend yet and was still at the curious but scared stage. Kitty told her all about Paul and tried not to sound like a stuck record when she heard nothing from him. She convinced herself he must have moved on with someone else after she kept sending letters but received no reply. It made her cry to think he'd forgotten her so soon.

The beach was Kitty's favourite place; she'd always had one since Johnny died, somewhere to go and think. In Singapore it had been the rubber plantation behind their estate. Row upon regimented row of trees. Each trunk had half a coconut shell tied with wire and a channel carved into the bark leading into it. The bright white latex would drip into the cup and was collected by workers throughout the day. They never caused Kitty any trouble, just smiled at her. She'd ride there on her bike, lean it against a tree and sit amongst the bracken. The dripping rubber soothed her and the smell became so familiar, it too soothed her. Sometimes she followed an ant trail. The ants were red, seriously big and stung like hell. Her parents never seemed to notice the crimson welts on her arms, nor the fact she'd been gone hours.

At her favourite place in Hong Kong she was no longer alone. Big decisions were made on Stanley Beach. It was there the two friends became smokers, or rather Kitty suggested it, Gill dismissed it and then they did it anyway. Kitty had studied other smokers and decided she wanted some of that coolness. So they pooled their pocket money in exchange for ten Consulate *(menthol—so health-giving* they'd agreed*)*, then sat on the sand and chain-smoked five each. They practised holding the cigarettes to best effect, advised each other of their best angles, best looks. They felt grown up. It was like tasting freedom. As the sun set on another humid day they proudly declared themselves smokers. Beneath the night sky they mouthed smoke rings and listened to the rolling drag of the waves as they lay on the warm sand.

Whenever they went to the beach to smoke, Kitty kept thinking of the time she'd asked her mum to stop. Johnny had been dead less than a year. The house had become dirty

33

and smelled of cigarettes. Nobody ever visited. Before Johnny died, their home had been filled with friends and family, pop music pounding from the record player, the dining room table creaking with party food. There were no more parties after Johnny's funeral and the sound of happy laughter and music had been replaced with her parents' rows. One evening Kitty had watched her mum dragging on a fag and flinched as she'd coughed until she could hardly catch her breath. 'Please stop, Mum. It smells horrible and you might get sick,' she'd said as her bottom lip wobbled and tears had filled her eyes.

'Mind your own business, Katherine!' Her mum's eyes looked out of focus as she continued between rasps, 'I'll carry on smoking in homage to my son—it reminds me of him—if that's okay with you. It makes me feel closer to him. Now go to your room.' And she'd lit up another cigarette before the wispy smoke had left the stub in the ashtray. Kitty had looked up the word "homage" in her Collins English Gem Dictionary so as she'd know in future what it meant. Words gave Kitty comfort. She thought smoking was comforting too but wasn't daft enough to realise it was an act of defiance.

On weekends Gill swam in the tepid sea for ages. To Kitty the water was just the place to cool down between bouts of sunbathing and doing absolutely nothing, glad to be away from the flat and the fighting. When she wasn't swimming, Gill would sit next to Kitty like a resting Mexican, her body completely encased in a bright, stripy towel, her floppy straw hat pulled down over her untameable hair.

'Right. There's a blond lad behind that group over there that looks quite cute and wouldn't make you look like a dwarf.' Kitty always filled Gill in on the boy action and Gill would guffaw and give reasons why boys were a waste of space. Kitty persisted and then, finally bored by the topic, Gill would reach in her fringed bag for her latest foreign novel and Kitty would laugh and kick sand at her. Sometimes boys approached them and Gill would scarper into the sea again, leaving Kitty to wonder if Gill was so much shorter than her due to water shrinkage.

At school, Kitty became popular with boys. She'd catch their side-long glances at her curves and her face would burn. Gill told her she envied the ease with which Kitty started conversations; her own mouth dried up and she felt like the proverbial ugly sister next to her. Gill said Kitty had something, an allure that drew people—especially men—to her. She had a big smile and an easy laugh despite of, or maybe because of, the dire situation at home. Gill said Kitty's dirty laugh would get her into trouble one day. Kitty envied her friend's intelligence, her ability to lose herself in song lyrics and the way she smelled. Oranges—with just a hint of cinnamon. They joked that together they made the perfect woman.

One Saturday they were approached at the beach by a slim, well-dressed Chinese lady. Kitty realised someone was standing over them blocking the sun. She sat up and squinted at her through shielding fingers. The woman told them they were very beautiful girls, that her name was Tina and she worked for a model agency. Gill sat up and eyed Tina suspiciously while Kitty sucked in her already taut stomach, arched her back and gave the stranger her best smile. *This is it,* she thought. *Hello catwalk. New York here I come. Finally. My. Escape.*

Tina said she was looking for girls to model Elegance's new underwear range and wondered if they'd be interested.

They'd both seen the adverts on television and it was a hot topic at school. She offered a card to Kitty who'd already decided she'd be the better model—what with those extra six inches. Gill grabbed the card and studied it. "Elegance" was clearly emblazoned across it. Kitty took it upon herself to be spokesperson, being older and all. She asked when and where, and Tina told them next Saturday morning at 104 Silver Street.

'That's *Wan Chai*,' whispered Gill to her starstruck friend who ignored her and placed her left foot over her right leg, flexing her lithe limbs.

'How much?' Kitty asked Tina.

Tina smiled and said they'd each get fifty dollars, then walked across to a waiting car by the drinks shack under the palm trees behind them.

'We'll be there,' Kitty called after her, rubbing her legs furiously as cramp struck. Gill studied the card again, reminded Kitty it was in the red-light district of the island and said Tina was probably a Triad member recruiting girls for sex.

The two girls had already visited Wan Chai not long after they'd first become friends—just to see the seedy side of the island for themselves. Gill had read a book about Suzy Wong and was intrigued. What clinched the recce was their parents banning them from even putting one foot into that *den of filth,* as Kitty's dad had described it.

Kitty's tummy had fluttered during the bus and tram ride. It wasn't exactly joyriding but it had given her a buzz. They'd picked out the gaudiest flashing sign, and linking arms entered Pussy Galore. It had cost them several dollars to get in. The wizened old lady on the door had taken their money without so much as a blink. If she'd noticed Gill looked barely twelve, she'd given no indication. They'd peeped around the red velvet curtain that stank of cigarettes and hot bodies.

In the centre of the dim room was a circular stage where an oriental girl with a long plait dangling down her back pirouetted naked to "Gypsies, Tramps and Thieves" as two red tassels swung from her nipples. Young waitresses paraded the room holding up trays, teetering on vertiginous heels. Men of every nationality were sitting at booze-laden tables, lust thrusting from their gyrating groins, mouths open, eyes doleful then rolling. At one table, a girl with orange hair straddled a white man as he looked hotly into her cold, dead eyes. When T.Rex's "Hot Love" belted out of the tinny stereo system, the previously spinning girl swung her hips from side to side then bent her torso down to grasp her ankles. Everything was on display in all its naked glory. Gill had let out the biggest guffaw which alerted a bouncer by the stage who *did* think she was underage and had escorted both of them out into the muggy night.

'Bloody hell! That's "Hot Love" ruined for me now!' Gill's indignation had set Kitty off and they'd laughed all the way back to the tram-stop. Pussy Galore was a den of sex and sleaze, they decided on the bus back, Gill deferring to Kitty, who seemed more worldly-wise but not necessarily sensible. Kitty conceded that her dad's description had been spot on, and then wondered how he could possibly have known.

Saturday came and they caught the bus and tram once again to Wan Chai for the modelling session. Gill said *this is not a good idea* at least three times. Kitty looked at the yellow and orange kaftan her friend had decided on for the modelling event and told her she wasn't listening, she couldn't take her seriously in that get up. Gill looked back at her with a mock indignation.

Silver Street was grim: a stray dog licked vomited noodles from the pavement; beggars snored in doorways; rubbish collected in corners. Kitty hovered her finger over the bell to number 104. Gill shook her head. Kitty ignored her and pushed the bell anyway. They heard footsteps descending. Tina beamed at them and asked them to follow her. Gill gave Kitty one last pleading look before Kitty stepped in behind Tina and Gill followed suit. Upstairs they were shown into a windowless room strung with faded red Chinese lanterns and curtained off at one end. There was an overpowering smell of air freshener. Tina appeared with a tray holding four cups of coffee and a saucer of Rich Tea biscuits.

'Who's the fourth coffee for?' Gill asked suspiciously.

'Chang, the photographer—he's through there.' Tina nodded towards the curtain. She handed them their coffees and placed the biscuits on an empty chair next to them. Neither reached for one. *Not worth the calories*, Kitty thought and knew Gill was thinking the same. Jammy Dodgers, fig rolls or chocolate digestives would have been a different matter. Tina disappeared through the curtain with the fourth coffee.

'Drink up, we're going.' Gill made for the door as Tina came back in holding an array of bras and knickers along her arms. She handed Gill several saying, 'These are definitely your colour and I guess you're a 32A?' Gill reluctantly nodded and studied the pieces closely to hide her embarrassment of her boyish bosom. Tina then handed the remaining frillies to Kitty.

'Now, *you* will look stunning in these and they are all 34B,' Tina said. Kitty beamed; Gill tutted.

Tina told Kitty to change into whichever set she liked and said she'd be in the kitchen. Kitty swept her hair behind her ears in what she thought gave her an air of sophistication and started taking her clothes off having chosen a turquoise bra and pants to model first. Gill had her hands on her hips refusing to get changed. 'I can't believe you're doing this, Kat! Put your stuff back on and let's go.'

Kitty paraded up and down in the two-piece that flattered her curves as Gill stared at the crack in the curtain, telling Kitty she was sure she'd seen several pairs of eyes watching.

'Ready!' called Kitty and gave a twirl as Tina appeared.

Tina clapped her hands. The curtain opened and Chang appeared. He bowed and then blinded them by switching on the spotlighting. There was a red velvet chaise longue in the centre of the studio and on the far left was a double bed with a white crocheted cover scattered with circular red silk cushions.

'Please come.' Chang looked Kitty up and down as she stepped over snaking wires to get in front of the camera. Gill hung back by the curtain while Tina fussed around Kitty with a hairbrush and lipstick. Tina stepped away and nodded at Chang who started clicking his camera.

Tina urged Kitty to change into the black-net set next. Kitty came back into the room where Gill was waiting with an eye on the exit as Tina pulled the curtain back across. They heard Tina and Chang whispering.

'For Christ's sake, Kat! Let's go,' Gill urged.

Kitty said she'd just do this outfit as it made her look really slim. Gill rolled her eyes and slumped down into a chair as her friend disappeared back through the curtain which remained closed.

As Kitty posed on the bed in the black underwear for what seemed like a thousand shots, Tina entered left and suggested Kitty remove the bra. It would show the pants off to best effect, she said.

Hearing this, Gill's head thrust through the curtain as Kitty started to undo the bra clasp. 'Kat! There's two bloody Chinese pervs looking at you behind the scenes!'

Kitty heard sniggers and turned to see a side door gently closing behind the bed. Tina said it was only the cleaner and *sorry for disturbance* in her clipped English. She said she would go and pour them all a Cinzano. Gill looked at her in utter disbelief and scooped up her friend's clothes. Kitty jumped through the curtain held open by Gill and they were down the stairs and out on to the street in seconds. Kitty held onto her flapping bra to cover her modesty. They ran into a doorway at the end of the street. It smelled of pee. Kitty crinkled her nose and slipped her clothes on as Gill acted as look-out, shaking her head and rolling her eyes every time Kitty lost her balance, grabbing her friend's arm and giggling.

Kitty's attempts at joking on the bus home were met with silence. Gill stared out of the window at the sea for most of the journey but sometimes caught her friend's expression in the reflection. 'We are *NEVER* going back to that place,' Gill said sternly as Kitty quietly smirked.

'What about our fifty dollars?' Kitty asked straight-faced and sounding genuinely put-out.

THREE

Kitty longed for Gill's independence, peace and privacy. Gill's parents both worked but when they weren't, they were living the dream at the yacht club numbing themselves with pricey wine. Gill was a latch-key kid. Kitty felt sad that her own parents thought it was okay for a mother to be drunk in charge of a teenage girl; she'd rather be a latch-key kid too. Nowhere in Kitty's flat was sacred; there were no locks on any doors, not even the bathroom. Her dad refused to put them in saying *locks equal secrets*. She thought he was such a hypocrite; she thought he just wanted access to all things at all times and she hated him for it. He wanted to see everything that was going on but he also made Kitty feel invisible.

Their flat was a war zone in the intense heat of Hong Kong. When her dad was there Kitty made herself scarce, not wanting to get caught in the crossfire, but not always able to avoid it. She'd come and go, ninja-like, and often thought the Civil Service who employed her dad should earmark her for future assignments. Her mum's drinking had escalated since Scarborough, the booze delivered to the door by Mr Yeung from the local supermarket. He was just a phone call away and five minutes from their flat. Apart from the occasional hawker selling their wares, he was their only visitor.

The flat was on the ground floor; you had to pass their balcony to access the main entrance. Gill's flat was upstairs on the right-hand side as you looked at the building. Returning from school, Kitty always searched the slatted blind at their sitting room window as their school bus pulled in. It meant more to her than it should. Up and it meant her dad was home and she'd look at Gill with a frown.

'Come up to mine, let's play some records and have some tea,' Gill would say and they'd run past the balcony, past the post boxes where Kitty checked daily for anything from Paul, and escape into Gill's cool, empty flat. Sometimes the blind was down and, peering under the gap where it didn't quite meet the mosaic floor, Kitty would assess the state of her mum as Gill waited patiently outside; sometimes, beckoned by Kitty, she'd go in and help her. But they rarely spent time in Kitty's flat. Kitty continued to hope that one day her mum would stop drinking and she'd be able to invite friends in without feeling embarrassed. She'd confided in Gill and felt lucky she'd one good friend she didn't have to keep explaining everything to. And Gill *was* a good friend to have. She helped Kitty out with homework too. Instead of being in the top three in class as she'd been in Singapore, Kitty languished in the lower sets with the "Truly Unruly" (her dad's phrase), who she felt should be encouraging her as she was doing better than she had been in Scarborough. 'Did you bother doing your homework before you went out looking like a tart?' her dad sometimes asked, bursting into the bathroom as she prepared for bed.

'Yes, Dad. Do you want to see it?' she'd ask politely, trying to avoid trouble, covering her nakedness with a hastily grabbed towel. He'd sneer, make some sarcastic remark like, 'I'd be too ashamed,' and slam the door with force so the toothbrush mug would rattle on the shelf.

Kitty spent most of her home time with Gill. They had adventures. They fell in love with that crazy place a million miles from home. They liked going into the city on the wild bus ride to the markets. From Stanley to Wong Ne Chong Gap, they'd watch sampans skimming the horizon of a glistening sea, beneath a burning sun. Sea for miles, but beneath the bus at hairpin corners a sheer drop with only treetops to catch their fall. It was thrilling. Once over the brow of the hill followed a death-defying hurtle down the other side into the city, until the bus spluttered to a standstill at the depot. Bodies dripping in sweat spewed onto the pavement. Red taxis, cars, rickshaws and lorries five abreast nudged impatiently with horns blaring along Central. Trams crammed with more hot bodies pushed through the heaving masses of shoppers and office workers. Above the traffic loomed skyscrapers dangling vibrant neon signs advertising everything from soya milk to Playboy bars, loud and proud. They'd stand there for a few minutes, taking it all in, memorising it. Kitty once spotted a sign advertising the Pussy Galore Club and pointed to it. They'd exchanged a knowing smile.

On Saturdays they went to Ladder Street Market to look at clothes and records. There were stalls spilling over with handbags, scarfs and shimmering silks and then, just around the next alleyway, pungent fish heads and snakes writhing in netted baskets. Dope-dazed septuagenarians squatted in dark recesses as naked children wearing only flip flops

43

weaved between the bargain hunters and then disappeared to their shanty homes behind.

A wizened Chinese lady stirring an enormous steaming wok had gestured at them once; her words insistent but unintelligible. Kitty had been fascinated by her mouth; it was a medley of gold teeth and gaps. Realising they didn't understand, the woman had given the wok a final stir and grabbed Kitty's hand, leading them along the alley. Gill furiously mimed slashing her throat, but Kitty ignored her, still hungry for excitement. A procession of small children had followed them—possibly the old woman's grandchildren, or even great-grandchildren. The old lady stopped at a doorway somewhere behind the market and had pointed into the gloom of an unlit room to the far corner where the two friends detected movement—snuffling—and a distinct farmyard pong. Pushed forward by the giggling children, they'd made out a panting sow lying along the wall on her side feeding six piglets. Gill's expression had shown relief, while Kitty had chuckled and gently shoved her. The woman, chattering away, had scooped up one of the piglets and thrust it towards Kitty. Squealing, it had nuzzled its sightless face into the crook of her arm. She'd stroked its hot pink flesh and the children had gathered around, jumping and laughing. The woman had beamed at the girls, and rubbed her tummy in a circular motion. This pig was cause for celebration for them, food on the table and money pressures lifted for the foreseeable. Kitty and Gill exchanged a look which had needed no translation. It said *we are so lucky, we should always remember this day when things get tough.*

After their trips to the market they'd play Gill's new records and she'd model her new clothes bought with her generous pocket money. Sometimes she decided she didn't like what she'd bought after all, and if Kitty liked the tight fit, she'd happily let her have it. They sat for hours in front of the mirror in Gill's room testing make-up until their mouths were rubbed sore from the array of lipsticks. Kitty said they looked like "prozzies" after a hard night and they'd practise dance routines, gurning their overly made-up faces and pretend to be pop stars. Gill was always first to lose the rhythm, collapse in a heap until Kitty had danced herself dizzy and collapsed on top of her.

There were no secrets between them. They even knew when each other's periods were. They knew each other's fantasies—Kitty: to be rich and loved; Gill: to be rich. They'd opened up easily to each other right from the start of their friendship. Gill told Kitty that she'd been a twin, that the other one had died at birth and her mother had never got over it; the family had never got over it.

'What, like identical? Brother or sister?' Kitty was fascinated but couldn't remember what the other type of twins was called.

'Yep, sister.'

Kitty couldn't imagine two Gills; she thought surely there wouldn't have been enough brain for both of them to be so bright. Kitty saw the pain in her friend's eyes and shut up. It answered why Gill studied like crazy—an attempt to channel any affection from her parents, but it never seemed enough. It explained why Gill's mother was so cold, as if there was a wall between her and everyone else. They trusted each other with their biggest secrets. Kitty told her about Johnny and how she missed him, about Paul and how she missed him, and most of all how she missed her mum and dad. The girls

45

were bonded by the loss of precious people, each looking out for the other, each understanding their language of eye-rolls at the mere mention of their parents, agreeing that both sets sadly fell short and one day they would be free of them.

Soon Kitty was in demand for babysitting. The Australian families paid the most, particularly the pilots. She and two other girls her age in the village elbowed each other out of the way for those. There was a flat rate but always a tip on top depending on how drunk the parents were on their return. It meant Kitty and Gill spent less time together but it also meant they had more money to do things with. Kitty bought flowers and magazines for her mum—pages of fashion and make-up—hoping she'd start to take an interest in her appearance, an interest in anything other than booze. She sent away to the T.Rex fan club for memorabilia for Gill and watched her delight in adding items to her growing shrine.

Kitty spotted billboards and posters advertising a Rod Stewart concert one summer. Everyone was talking about it at school. Both girls loved him. For Gill's birthday Kitty bought two tickets. They cost a lot; Rod was hot property. They barely slept the night before and on the day of the concert they started early because they were so excited. They dressed in their newest, tightest jeans and spent hours crimping Kitty's hair and deciding on make-up as music blared from Gill's music centre. They tied tartan scarfs onto their bags, painted each other's nails white then danced around the room until the polish dried. Kitty made one last check on her mum before meeting Gill in the hallway who was dousing herself in Aqua Manda, leaving a cloud of orange oil in her wake.

The stadium was a seething mass of hot bodies. Kitty linked arms with Gill and they pushed their way through to the front, shouting *Hi!* to a few school mates in their path. Early on they decided the support act was rubbish but the atmosphere was buzzing and tension was rising for Rod. Scottish flags waved as the sun set on another stifling day. Kitty and Gill were pushed and shoved from every angle. The second Rod catapulted onto the stage the crowd screamed and surged forward. When the first chords of "Maggie May" played, a hush descended until everyone joined in and their collective voice reverberated around the stadium. When the band played "You Wear It Well", Kitty caught Gill's eye and they fell into one of their routines, swaying their hips and punching the sky at *there ain't a lady in the land so fine*. By the time they were shouting along to "Reason To Believe", Kitty and Gill were sopping wet with sweat, their clothes stuck to their skin, and their faces shone. They'd enjoyed every note, chord, riff. They were still shouting on the last bus home. Their ears rang and their excitement lasted the whole night reliving the concert in Gill's shared bed. The next day they were exhausted and hoarse.

When the chance of babysitting for the family on the top floor of their block of flats came up, Kitty grabbed it. She'd seen them around—the Millers. Tom Miller worked at her father's place and was tall with dark brown hair. His wife Pat was petite and mousey-haired. They had a daughter of five, Sarah. They were friendly and exuded an ease of style sadly absent in her own family. Tom drove a big maroon car. You could hear the engine a mile away; classy and powerful. You could hear her dad's Triumph Herald over a mile away too but that was because the exhaust had blown and he'd patched it up with tin foil. Kitty was so embarrassed. To save petrol, he always parked on a hill when they were out, even if it was miles away from where they needed to be, so that on their return he'd roll down with the handbrake off and only start the engine once he joined the road. *Tight git,* she muttered to herself every time she heard their car.

The Millers were brilliant to babysit for as they left snacks out for Kitty, and Sarah was so well behaved that Kitty spent part of the evenings catching up with homework. She felt lucky to have secured this nice little earner and Gill said she couldn't wait until she was old enough to earn some money too. Sometimes she'd come up to be with Kitty and Sarah. The Millers' flat was beautiful with jade ornaments placed just so and photos of the family laughing into the camera.

'Good looking isn't he, Gill?' Kitty said out of earshot of Sarah.

'Nah, got funny ears,' was all Gill said, tucking into a bowl of Ritz crackers.

One night the Millers returned just after midnight. Pat giggled as she stumbled into the room, tipsy.

'Thanks for looking after my baby, Kitty,' she slurred, then tripped along the hallway to bed, leaving her husband by the sofa. He sat down next to Kitty as she packed her books into her schoolbag. 'How are your exams going?' he asked, looking like he really cared.

Kitty felt his closeness, could smell his musky aftershave, was suddenly conscious of her tight jeans and even tighter cropped top. She muttered they were going well and stood to leave. He got up too. Kitty looked towards the door. Was she imagining something that wasn't there? She hesitated. He bent down and kissed her on the lips, his hand gently holding her elbow. His touch felt more intimate than it should have; Kitty felt it and her face started to glow. She hadn't expected him to do that, but it seemed to happen in slow motion. She hadn't expected to feel a charge through her body either. Embarrassed, she slung her bag over her shoulder, ran out of the door after struggling with the catch and flew down the stairs to her home. Luckily, her parents were in bed. Cocooned in her bed, she stared into the darkness replaying what had happened.

The next day Pat appeared at the Blacks' front door. Kitty's stomach flipped. Pat held out some notes and said, 'Silly Tom said he forgot to give you this! Thanks, Kitty.' She handed Kitty the babysitting money. Kitty muttered her thanks and closed the door.

'Such a lovely family,' her mum uttered as she gulped a mouthful of gin, and Kitty slunk back to her room.

In the following weeks Kitty noticed Tom a lot. He always seemed to be around and, if she was honest, she was thrilled by the attention, by his interest. Her parents rarely asked her about her exams or how she was. Until now, she hadn't noticed the sexy curl of his chestnut brown hair or his toned, muscular body. He told her his birthday was coming up. 'Fancy celebrating with me?' he asked as they sat in some shade on the roof.

'What age will you be, old man?' she surprised herself by asking.

'Thirty-six, just a number, Kitty.' She turned away as his eyes drilled into hers. She felt weird between her legs, like a fizzing bottle of Coke. He leant over and gently kissed her cheek.

The few beach parties she and Gill had been to with boys of their own age usually ended in mishandled fumbles—all fingers, tongues and beery breath. At the last one at Repulse

Bay a boy in the year above Kitty had grabbed and snogged her. It had been clumsy, sloppy and made her feel cheap. These schoolboys were just looking for anyone to use their endless erections on. Tom promised so much more than that with his concern and tender kisses, but she didn't say a word to Gill as she knew she'd disapprove.

Kitty eagerly awaited Pat's babysitting requests and for the evenings to fly by so she and Tom could have a sneaky cuddle. He started to leave little gifts for her on top of the post boxes at the entrance to the flats. She found a poetry book, dainty pots of cream perfume and single flowers made from silk—a white orchid, a yellow rose. The rose did it. It reminded her of her nan. Her lovely nan with her beloved garden. She'd once walked Kitty, aged about six, around the grounds and insisted she smelled every different colour of rose. The afternoon sun had beaten down on them as Kitty moved from flower to flower, sniffing loudly at each one. They tickled her nose and she was sure insects crawled up there too.

'Now tell me the yellow ones don't smell the best, Kitten. The yellow ones *always* smell the best', she'd said, and smiled when Kitty nodded.

These gifts from Tom made her feel special, like she mattered to someone, like someone actually cared. Then there was the note:

Dear Kitty,
I think you are the most beautiful and amazing girl I have ever met. I would like to meet you one day after school and take you out. Would you be able to arrange this?
Tom x

As she read it sitting on her bed she was worried her racing heartbeat could be heard by her parents in the next room. It felt as if she'd won first prize in a competition. When she heard her dad walk along the hallway, she stuffed the note into her bra and went back to reading the poetry book. Once he'd passed her room, she set about planning, the secret feeling all the sweeter for him not knowing.

She invented a birthday party near to school on an evening her dad was working the night shift and left a note for Tom telling him the date and time. As she slipped the folded paper into their secret place she stopped in her tracks. She noticed a blue aerogramme sticking out of their postbox. The writing looked familiar. She wanted it to be from Paul. She held her breath as she pulled it free and read the address on the back. It was from her aunt and uncle in Reading.

The day finally arrived. Kitty couldn't take in a word said by any of her teachers and every now and then a surge of excitement overwhelmed her. She looked around at her classmates to see if they'd noticed. It had taken all her effort not to let Gill in on it. She'd come so close several times but in the end she'd told her the same story about the birthday party. Gill hadn't said a word; Kitty had studied the middle distance. She felt rotten for lying to her best friend but felt in too deep now. After school in the toilets she changed into the new denim skirt and white stripy top she'd bought from the market with her babysitting wages. She walked along a bit from the gates and waited for the sound of Tom's car, trying to look casual. When she heard it she felt lightheaded and couldn't stop a big grin from spreading across her face as he pulled alongside.

She'd never been in such a luxurious car. It had cream leather seats and sax music played on the radio. It felt sophisticated. They drove for miles, beyond anywhere Kitty had been in Kowloon before. Tom held her hand over the console as the car carved its way through unknown winding roads. Finally they stopped by a beach; shingle crunched beneath the wheels, and dust clouded the carpark. There was a smart-looking restaurant with a huge wooden terrace opening out onto white sand; palm trees lined the path from the parking area.

A waiter greeted them and showed them to a table inside in the far corner. Tom propelled her towards it with his hand pressed into the small of her back, sending shock waves up her spine. There were several Chinese businessmen dotted about and a noisy family eating dim sum. Kitty and Tom sat there for hours talking, eating and drinking white wine—the waiter hadn't so much as flinched as he'd filled their glasses. To the outside world they probably looked like father and daughter, Kitty thought. She sipped her drink as if she'd been doing it for years but, truth be known, the taste was tart and unpleasant, but she didn't want Tom to think her a total child. She felt shy in his company and most of the time had to pinch herself for a reality check. The décor was stylish and expensive. Tom was putting in a lot of effort and Kitty couldn't help but feel flattered. When the waiter presented them with a platter of prawns, lobster and oysters, she could barely keep from dribbling. She'd only seen pictures of this kind of food in magazines.

As they watched the sun set into a golden orb, Tom told Kitty his marriage to Pat was over—a mere convenience— he was staying only because of his daughter and until their return to England. Kitty hung off his every word as the wine dulled her senses.

It was dark when they left the restaurant. After kissing and cuddling in the car, they made their way home, Tom driving slowly as if he didn't want it to end.

'This is our secret,' Tom said as he dropped Kitty up the road from their block so that they staggered their arrival. She lingered before cutting through the trees onto their drive, checking that all was okay; it felt like she'd been away an age. Their parking space was empty. She scanned the windows of Tom's flat; all was in darkness. The main lights were out in her flat but flashes emanated from the television. She let herself in the front door and wrapped a blanket around her mum, slumped in front of the too-loud screen. She looked up at Kitty and cried, 'My boy—my Johnny.' Kitty stroked her hair until her breathing became deep and regular. The enormity of what she'd done with Tom made her feel weak. She'd been out with a married man! She took a last look at her sleeping mum and ran up to Gill's flat. Her mum opened the door and looked at her coolly until Gill appeared and they went to her room. Marc Bolan was quietly trying to cram too many words into lyrics; Gill's school books were open on her bed. Gill went over and turned the volume up.

'*You stupid cow, Kat!* How could you? He's old! You could get pregnant. Have you thought about that?'

Kitty jumped at her friend's sternness. 'Bloody hell, Gill! You taking lessons from my dad? Calm down! It's not like that.' Kitty thought she sounded so worldly-wise, so womanly, but Gill's harsh words made her think twice about opening up. She thought Gill must have known she'd longed for someone to look at her and say, *it's you. You're the one.* Gill had barely got past first base with a boy, let alone a man; Kitty thought Gill might even be frigid.

'What on earth do you see in him, Kat? It'll end badly! You don't need this.'

'You're just jealous, Gill. Admit it! No one has ever told you they loved you and you don't want me to be happy.'

'For Christ's sake, Kat! He's an old married man with a kid who has no intention of leaving his wife. Face it!' Gill's mouth curled on one side as she rolled her eyes.

That night, Kitty climbed under the sheets and drifted into fractured sleep with images of Paul lying on top of her telling her *it has to be special* and Johnny's last words played over and over in her head: *Options—everyone has options— Kat— don't mess up like me.* In the darkest hours of the night she knew she must go no further with Tom and resolved to tell him the next day. It had all been a terrible mistake.

The bright morning light saw Kitty hastily writing a note before she ran to catch the school bus. She stuck it in their secret place before Gill came bounding down the steps. Their chatter was animated and endless on the ride to school; it was as if Tom had never come between them. They met at break-time, the first time in ages. After lunch, they sat outside and made plans for the weekend, just like they used to. In the queue for the bus later that afternoon, Kitty and Gill amused the others waiting with one of their dance routines; they were on form. 'Let's go down the beach tonight, Kit, yeh?' Gill said excitedly.

'Defo!' Kitty replied, miming smoking a cigarette and they laughed in unison.

Gill spotted him first. He was staring at Kitty from across the road, trying to get her attention. 'Lover boy's over there, Kat,' she huffed, nodding her head in his direction. Kitty thought it was a joke until she too saw him and broke away from the line, almost running into the path of the first bus as it rounded the corner. 'For god's sake, Kat!' Gill cried, but Kitty didn't turn around.

When she caught up with Tom he'd turned down a side street and was heading for his car. He got inside and slid across to open the passenger door. She stuck her head in. 'Why are you here, Tom? Did you get my no—'

'Kitty, get in before anyone else spots us!' he shouted over her.

She jumped in, cradled her satchel to her and ducked as they sped past several school buses.

'Where are we going?'

'The Peninsular. I thought you'd enjoy afternoon tea,' he said, his eyes on the road as they followed signs for Tsim Sha Tsui.

'But I left you a note, Tom,' she said, trying not to sound exasperated.

'I know, I read it. I thought we could have a chance to talk properly and enjoy some lovely cake at the same time. You'd like that, wouldn't you, Kitty? Your dad's on the two-to-ten shift, I checked, and we'll be back well before then. There's nothing to worry about, it's all sorted,' he said, patting her thigh.

Kitty thought he'd have been more upset about the note than he was but she could explain everything better during tea; maybe this wasn't such a bad idea after all, she thought. There would still be time to meet Gill on the beach too.

'I can't go in wearing my school uniform, can I?'

'No, I thought about that,' Tom said, nodding his head towards the back seat.

Kitty reached for the pink and white striped bag. Inside was a navy skirt and an oyster grey silk shirt. In a box behind Tom's seat was a pair of grey satin espadrilles. Kitty was impressed;

he'd bought all the right sizes. With his encouragement she climbed into the back and put the outfit on.

The palatial lobby had colonial columns draped with elegant ferns wafting gently beneath rotating fans, seemingly in rhythm with the string quartet by the bar. Tables were set with beautiful china cake stands holding impeccably sliced finger sandwiches and exquisite cakes that made Kitty's mouth water. Tom approached her from the desk, smiling.

'This way, Kitty,' he said, leading her past the tables and over to the lift.

'I thought we were having cake?' she asked, looking wistfully behind her.

'We are, but in the comfort of a private room where it's quiet and we can talk. Can't hear ourselves think down here.'

The room was better than any hotel room Kitty had ever seen, from the exotic wallpaper to the chandeliers and the stunning view of Victoria Harbour. The pungent smell from the huge vase of pink oriental lilies made Kitty feel lightheaded. A golden trolley holding all the sumptuous food she'd spotted downstairs was pushed into the room following a gentle knock at the door. There was also a silver ice-bucket holding a bottle of champagne with a napkin placed across the neck. The young Chinese butler bowed when Tom pushed a note into his hand, and headed backwards to the door, like they were royalty.

Tom opened the champagne as if he'd done it a million times before and when he handed Kitty a glass, she accepted it with what she considered to be the sophistication her outfit and surroundings demanded. Truth be known, she'd never tasted champagne—only gin when she'd stuck a finger in her mum's plastic beaker to find out if it really was water like she'd

56

said it was. It had tasted bitter and disgusting, making her gurn and putting her off alcohol. Until now. The champagne was as bubbly as 7 Up, but less sweet and not unpleasant.

Kitty sat in an armchair by the window and looked at Tom properly. His cream chinos, pale blue shirt and navy linen jacket looked so smart and totally in keeping with the hotel. She thought how handsome he looked. He topped up her glass; she hadn't meant to gulp but the wait in the heat for the bus after school followed by the journey here had made her thirsty. She took in the stylish décor, the finer detail, the tranquillity. This was as far from home as she could be. All around her care had been taken with comfort and well-being in mind. The thought of always living like this had previously seemed like a dream just out of reach, but was this how it could be with Tom? He'd said she was amazing and he loved her. The note she'd left that morning wasn't mentioned again.

She stood to admire the afternoon tea, steadying herself on the side of the trolley, not sure if she felt woozy or just wasn't used to her new shoes on the deep-pile carpet. Before heading for the bathroom, she took her shoes off. The door she thought was for the bathroom opened into a vast bedroom with the biggest bed she'd ever seen. The gleaming mirrors and marble in the actual bathroom took her breath away as she lathered her arms and neck with lemongrass moisturiser from an onyx dispenser and she'd delighted in finding a lock on the door.

'You okay in there, Kitty?' Tom called, sounding genuinely concerned. She realised she'd been in there ages enjoying the opulence.

'Yep,' she said. Tom was just outside the door. Kitty giggled with nervousness at his closeness. 'Wow! What a bathroom.'

Tom reached for her saying, 'I'm glad you like it, Kitty, you deserve the best.' Kitty noticed he'd taken off his jacket. His aftershave smelled warm and woody.

'Are we having tea now?' she asked, as he turned her around with her back to the bed. He pushed her gently down and started undressing her.

At first she resisted; this was as far as she'd gone with Paul. It was unknown territory but it sent tingles down her body. He kissed her on the mouth, on her neck, her breasts and her navel. Pulling her pants down, he fingered her pubic hair and kissed that too. His tongue found her vulva. She put her hands on his head in a feeble attempt to push him off but her moans begged for more.

Her body juddered as he undid his trousers. As if in a fog she said, 'Tom, please stop, I could get pregnant.' It didn't even sound like her voice; it was distant, ethereal. He looked into her eyes and rasped, 'No need, I had the snip. Years ago. God, I want you, Kitty.'

He flipped her over onto her front and pulled her until she was bent over the end of the bed, similar to playing wheelbarrows. She wanted to stop him but knew things had gone too far. She cried out when he entered her; it felt like he'd shoved a baseball bat inside. Her gasps were lost to his groans as his rhythm became more urgent. She began to panic as searing pain shot through her with each thrust and tried to squirm into a comfortable position. Beads of his sweat dripped onto her back. She clenched the bed cover with both fists as he reached a climax, breathing heavily and then squashing her with his full weight. She tried pushing herself up with her arms to move him off and get some air.

'Oh, Kitty. You're amazing and I love you,' he whispered. He finally rolled off after Kitty's fidgeting became urgent. She gingerly crawled onto the bed and he propped himself up on one elbow next to her. 'You okay?'

Kitty sucked in her lips and managed to hold back the tears. 'Think so,' she said quietly, as a single tear ran down her cheek. She noticed blood on the bed cover and was horrified.

'C'mon! Now you can have a lovely foamy bath and then we can enjoy a fabulous afternoon tea and wave goodbye to your virginity in style!'

Kitty wasn't convinced that losing her virginity was a cause for celebration. Her thoughts were confused. While he appeared to have enjoyed himself, like that was what having sex was like, she wanted to curl up in a ball and cry. She stayed in the bath for ages trying to convince herself that what had just happened was perfectly okay and that she was just inexperienced.

When she eventually walked into the sitting room, she'd plastered a sort of half-smile on her face. It was all she could manage as the burning in her pants made her breathing odd. She watched Tom's every move. He was so polite, passing everything to her and looking at her so tenderly. She wanted to go home, cry properly and recover from what had just happened, but she had no money and had to wait until Tom took them back. She only ate a mouthful of cake; it didn't taste anywhere near as good as it looked, and she'd lost her appetite.

By the time Kitty stepped through the trees to the flats she was crippled with guilt, and still felt very sore. Not once had she thought about her mum, not until the journey home as she'd changed back into her uniform. It was almost 8 p.m.

and everything seemed too quiet. The television was turned off and all was in darkness. She crept along the hallway and pushed open her parents' bedroom door. Her mum was a heap in the bed, snoring deeply. Kitty sighed with relief. Her head was banging from the champagne. She drank a large glass of water and ran a cold bath. Easing herself into it, her sobs came until she was fully bawling her eyes out. What she'd done with Tom made her feel dirty, no matter how much she tried to soap it all away. She knew Gill wasn't happy with her over Tom, but she *had* to talk to her about this, had to try and make some sense of it. *Gill!* She'd promised to meet her on the beach! Telling herself to stop feeling sorry for herself, she ran into her bedroom to find her jeans. Her fresh pants aggravated the soreness so she leaped back into the bathroom and grabbed a sanitary towel to use as a buffer. Aware of the lateness, she dashed back into her room for a top just in time to see Gill walk past her window to the main entrance. Pulling her top on, she ran to the door. 'Gill! Hi, sorry I was late—just coming to see you,' Kitty said to Gill's back, climbing the stairs.

On the last step Gill turned and with a hurt expression said, 'I'm going in now. Don't expect me to cover for you again. Your mum came up to mine looking for you. I told her you'd stayed behind to help finish a project. She fell on the stairs going back down and banged her arm. There was blood everywhere—I sorted her out, put her to bed and cleared up the mess.' And with that, she turned, stepped into her flat and let the door slam shut behind her. Kitty stood there feeling stupid, selfish and very alone.

FOUR

'I think I'm pregnant,' Kitty told Gill after realising she had no excuse for dodging swimming lessons; her periods had stopped. She suspected the extra weight she was carrying wasn't puppy fat and she had a nasty metallic taste in her mouth, although she was hopeful she was wrong.

They hadn't spoken for weeks—Kitty and Gill—not since that night Gill had walked away from her. They hadn't sat together on the school bus or met up after school. Kitty had put notes through Gill's door, devastated she'd lost her best friend, but nothing came back. She'd even gone over to her one break-time and asked if they could talk, but Gill had looked straight through her. Kitty had cried herself to sleep, except on those nights where anger stole any slumber and she raked over and over recent events, wanting to turn back time. How could she have been so foolish to sleep with a married man? How could she have jeopardised the best friendship she'd ever had? How could she have neglected her mum?

There had been no lasting damage from her mum's fall. She'd woken up confused about the plaster on her arm, which

Kitty had changed whilst making up a story about how she'd fallen in the kitchen. When her dad had returned from work later that day, Kitty heard raised words.

'Disgusting old sop! One day you'll fall over and kill yourself, then we'll all be happy.'

Kitty had heard a *thwack,* followed by her mum's yelp, and watched her dad storm past her window and drive off, crunching the gears and narrowly missing a stray dog at the junction. Her mum was sobbing on the sofa with a hand covering her left eye where she'd obviously been punched. Kitty had filled up her mum's cup with the gin hidden under the sink and held a bag of frozen peas on the wound. They'd sat and watched television together until her dad returned and told her to get to bed.

Kitty avoided Tom. He'd left notes begging to meet up again and the presents got more expensive: jewellery, show tickets, perfume, but she left them where she found them and loathed herself for falling for the expensive hotel and his charm. She sometimes spotted him waving from his flat and then he'd be walking down the drive, just to say hello. The one time she'd gone up on the roof since meeting up with him, he'd appeared. She'd run past him, face flaming, and he'd grabbed her. 'Kitty, darling. I miss you, *please* talk to me!' But she hadn't. If she *was* pregnant then he must have lied about the vasectomy. *How could he have done that?* The thought crushed her; she didn't want to believe he was a liar.

When Pat asked her to babysit again, Kitty said she was sorry but exams were coming up and she had to study— which was true, but revision proved elusive. Instead, she found herself doodling and writing angry poetry. In the exam hall she'd looked around her, wishing she was someone else, somewhere else.

'These exams are important, they decide whether or not you have a future, pull your finger out and do well, for god's sake!' her dad said one morning, echoing the headmaster's words but not quite so eloquently.

Her nerves were so bad she'd thrown up several times before running for the bus. Gill must have noticed her looking rough one morning because she turned at the bus stop and said, 'Hi,' in a quiet voice. She even saved a seat for Kitty another morning and although their conversation on the journey was stilted, Kitty hoped they'd be friends again.

Her mock exam results had been appalling; she'd scraped through only two. She'd held onto her report until her dad had demanded it and refused to leave her room until she produced it. She'd handed it over reluctantly and disappeared into the bathroom. Within seconds he'd violently pushed the door open, throwing her from the back of it onto the floor. She'd curled into a foetal position when his kicks struck her in her back and left her winded.

'You waste of bloody space,' he'd shouted, then slammed the door and left her there. She'd stared at the tufts of the bathroom mat until she was able to pull herself up onto her knees. Her mum had come in and tried to pull her up. 'Mum, it's—okay. Please go—back out or he'll be—after you,' Kitty said between gulps of air and painful flinches.

'The nasty bastard's gone out,' her mum said as she'd helped Kitty to her bed. She'd inspected the bruising after Kitty lifted her nightdress to reveal a pattern of purple welts, brought her a hot chocolate and kissed her on her forehead. They'd clung to each other like wounded animals until they heard the car return.

Soon Kitty's jeans wouldn't zip up, and her school dress became a struggle to get on as her expanding belly stole her waistline. One lunchtime a couple of boys pointed at her and shouted, 'Hey, Tank!' She pretended not to hear but it confirmed what she already feared. She knew it was only a matter of time before everyone guessed; she couldn't imagine what her dad would do to her. She'd read something somewhere about gin and miscarriage. The trouble was she couldn't remember if you were meant to drink it or bathe in it. In any case there wasn't enough of it—even in their house—to fill a bath. She wondered if the kicking might have killed any foetus, but she'd had no blood loss. It was the next day she'd told Gill, on the way to school.

'Oh, Kat!' Gill said, and Kitty couldn't avoid her friend's look of utter despair. Nowhere in that look said *I told you so,* although Kitty wouldn't blame her if that was how she felt.

'I think he lied about the vasectomy. My dad is going to murder me.' There was genuine fear in her voice as it wobbled.

'Kat, I'm here for you. I think you should tell your mum.'

Kitty thought about telling her mum, but knew it was useless. Once her dad found out all hell would break loose and just thinking about it terrified her. Gill had meant well, but Kitty knew she didn't know everything about what went on behind their closed doors. Everyone knew about Bobby Black's temper but few realised the extent of his abuse. Kitty was too ashamed to let on about the beatings they suffered, even to Gill, hiding body bruises when she could and excusing the visible ones with lies. Instead, she hid from her parents as best she could and tried to disguise her weight gain. Each day she succeeded she almost convinced herself that everything was fine. In lessons she sat watching her teacher's mouth move, not taking in one word, trying to find a solution. The French Revolution became irrelevant. She knew it was too late even for Johnny's options; her future had changed.

In the end she decided to tell Tom. She'd mulled it over a million times. If he thought she was so great and didn't love Pat then surely he'd be elated at having a child with the *most beautiful and amazing girl* he'd ever met. He'd give her a good life, she wouldn't want for anything and in the short term he'd stand up to her dad; he was strong and fit. The more she thought about it, the more she convinced herself this was the only way—she wouldn't be the first girl who'd done this to save her own skin. And anyway, once they were together she could send for her mum to come and live with them; get her the help she needed to stop drinking. It all made perfect sense.

They arranged to meet on the beach one evening. It was close to home, but that hardly mattered now; they were about to embark on a new life together. Kitty ran out of the flat, across the road and down to the sea. She spread a towel on the sand and watched and waited until he came striding along the beach to her. Her breath caught just at the sight of him; he *was* good-looking. She got up, greeted him with a smile and threw her arms around his neck.

'Can't be long, Pat thinks I've nipped out for some wine.' Tom seemed agitated and pushed his hands deep into his pockets. Kitty sat back down. He stood in front of her, blocking the evening sun until she patted the space on the towel next to her and he folded down onto his knees. He straightened the towel out around him then looked out to sea as if there was something interesting grabbing his attention.

'I wanted to see you. I've got something very special to tell you.'

Tom turned to her but wasn't smiling; he seemed to linger on her middle where her top stretched. She thought he must be stressed about work, just as her dad always was. In her head she ran through all the words she'd practised in front of her dressing-table mirror: how she loved him, how lovely he was with Sarah, what a brilliant life they'd have together now they were bonded by a baby. She grabbed his hand and looked into his eyes. 'I'm pregnant, Tom.'

Tom looked at her, pulled his hand away and pushed it through his hair. Chunks stuck out starkly on one side, giving him a crazed look, his eyes darting wildly. Kitty waited for him to say something, anything, but he didn't get the chance. Rushing towards them, slipping in the dry sand, brandishing a bamboo stick, was Kitty's dad. Tom scrambled up and raced away without saying a word. Kitty's heart sank as she watched him dart into the palm trees. Her dad stood panting and seethed down at her, 'I know all about you and him! Pat just came and told us she'd found a note from you. You dirty little tart! Get home now!'

Kitty stumbled back home several paces in front. She was raging inside. She pushed through the open door of the flat, past her mum on the sofa who squinted at her, and into her bedroom where she gave the door a mighty slam. A row started up in the front room. Kitty sat on her bed bewildered and angry. Tom had said his marriage was over; he'd called her *beautiful and amazing*. Why had he run away?

She was packing up her school bag in her bedroom one morning later that week when her mum appeared in the doorway. Kitty sucked her belly in, told her she had to get on or she'd miss the bus, that Gill was waiting for her.

'Do we need to take you to the doctor's, Kitty?'

Her mum's eyes were focused on her and Kitty could see no drink had glazed them yet. She continued busying herself with her books but the concern in her mum's voice touched her. She wanted to run into her arms and be told everything would be okay, it was all fixable, not the end of the world. She looked up at her mum and saw the yellow bruises on her arms and neck, the result of *that* evening and all Kitty's fault. Kitty averted her eyes and mumbled, 'No!' indignantly.

Her mum slid an arm across her shoulders and said, 'I think we do, Kitty, I think you've got yourself into trouble, haven't you? We've got an appointment with Dr Fernandez at ten o'clock. I'll let school know you won't be in today.'

Kitty knew a pregnancy test was the purpose of the visit and she was pretty sure what the result would be. It felt like a vice was pressing down on her head. Outside, Gill hovered with her arms by her side, palms outstretched in a questioning gesture. Kitty waved her away and she watched her head down to the bus stop. Her mum walked out of her room crying quietly into a cotton hankie.

Dr Fernandez was a smiley, smartly dressed man with hair escaping from his nose, ears and the top of his shirt. Kitty noticed he smelled of lemons and wore a big Seiko watch—a similar one to her dad's. She was acutely embarrassed as he asked her questions about her periods. When they'd first started at the age of eleven, she thought she'd been stabbed in the night when she saw blood on her sheets. She'd eventually told her mum, but her parents had opted out of the grand sex education talk by thrusting a publication called *The Facts of*

Life into their daughter's hands. They trusted the school had filled in any blanks. Actually it was Shelley Reid in 1C who'd enlightened everyone. With more information than anyone knew what to do with—delivered in a scraping-of-the-barrel vocabulary describing everything she'd ever done with boys' tongues, willies and balls; it had been an eye-opener for Kitty.

Dr Fernandez directed Kitty to the toilet to fill a receptacle. She returned holding the sample, sensing their collective hope: hope that she was just fat; hope that it was a different medical problem; hope that this was a nightmare from which they'd all wake up. *She's still a child*; she could see it written across their faces. In the taxi home Kitty's mum reached over and patted Kitty on the knee. Kitty caught her breath as tears filled her eyes; she'd ruined things for her and her mum. Not one word was spoken, just smoke filling the cab as her mum furiously chain-smoked. Once home Kitty lingered in the sitting room. She wanted to apologise for the inevitable trouble that would follow; she wanted to prolong this rare sober state with her mum.

'Mum,' she called to her in the kitchen.

Her mum didn't respond but came back into the room carrying *that* mug and a look of excitement about her. She took a slug before she fell into her chair, crossed her legs and reached for her cigarettes. 'What?' she asked as she exhaled smoke into the air, visibly enjoying the hit of nicotine and booze.

'Nothing, it's okay,' Kitty mumbled, and sloped off to her room.

Later that day the phone rang. Expecting it to be left unanswered as usual, Kitty stopped in her tracks in the hallway as she heard her mum slur, 'Th—ank you, Doctor. Yesss, okay.'

Her dad arrived home within the hour. She heard the car long before it swung onto the drive because she'd been listening out and dreading it. Kitty cowered on her bed waiting for the inevitable. Sure enough, the door flew open, banging against the wall. Her dad's twisted mouth bellowed in her face. 'You TART! You stupid bloody IDIOT! You'll pay for this! You're not fit to spit on! Only whores get pregnant at your age! Now you'll give birth to a BASTARD!'

Not only was she pregnant but his tirade confirmed her earlier suspicion; she was too far gone for a termination.

'I'm sorry, Dad, I didn't mean it to happen.' The slap across her head threw her sideways. She curled her fingers into a fist, pushing her knuckle against her mouth to still the sound of her sobs. On his way out of her room, he snatched up her radio, her purse and her shoes. She dared to breathe only after she heard his footsteps recede. When the ranting continued in the front room, she put her headphones on and listened to Cat Stevens on her cassette player and agreed it was indeed a wild world.

When Gill got home from school, Kitty ran barefoot up to her flat and thumped on the door. Gill opened it. Kitty rushed through and flung herself onto Gill's bed.

'Your dad knows, doesn't he?'

Kitty nodded through her snuffles.

'The worst is over now, Kat—they know and your dad didn't kill you.' Gill put an arm across her friend's shoulders.

'The worst is yet to come, Gill. I'm too far gone for a termination.'

'Jesus!' Gill said, squeezing her friend tighter. She moved to the end of the bed and pulled out her paisley notebook with the lovingly drawn 3D title "T.Rex Trax". 'Listen to this,

Kat,' she said in an obvious attempt to cheer her friend up. She read out lyrics from yet another of the band's songs. 'Do you think Marc means he sees his future children in the stars? Do you think he sees two or three? Is the moon his future wife?' Kitty let out a muffled groan. She wished song lyrics had been enough for her, wished she'd never met Tom and wished this whole episode could all be over.

The government machine quickly whirred into action. A black car pulled up on the drive one week later and Kitty watched from her bedroom window as Tom got in, no sign of Pat or Sarah, not one glance in her direction despite her frantic waving. Maybe Pat had been watching from upstairs? Kitty stared at the road long after the car had disappeared. She had an exhausting night battling with her thoughts. When morning sun shone on her exhausted face, she hoped that somehow Tom would contact her; she was carrying his baby, after all. Hearing a commotion outside, she peered out to see Tom's maroon car being taken away and her dad, with his hands on his hips, shouting obscenities at the driver.

Kitty had no idea what plans had been made for her; nobody said anything, and she didn't dare ask, but she no longer went to school. With no routine, she awoke feeling displaced, anxious and lonely until Gill got home. Something had to happen soon though as she was really beginning to show. One particular afternoon she looked out of her window to see the sky turn from blue to slate grey then black. She climbed up the back fire escape steps to the roof and sensed a typhoon looming. There was a cacophony of bird chatter. The wind picked up, changing from a gentle breeze to insistent swirls around her. She watched a line of palm trees arc in unison. It was becoming eerily dark too soon in the afternoon. The birdsong stopped suddenly; they'd taken cover. The rain came in fat splashes and Kitty was soaked in seconds. She heard the choppy waves from the beach; the sea was boiling up, crashing and dragging. The elements matched her mood, which had plummeted to a new depth of despair. She struggled to catch her breath in the near-hurricane wind and was blown against the shoulder-height wall. Traffic hurried home below. She knew she could end this right now. There was a white plastic stool just inside the roof door. It was for the tiny Chinese amahs to reach the washing lines. She could fetch it and launch herself over the wall; it could all be over in seconds. The roof door banged backwards and forwards like a repeated slap, distracting her thoughts. She tried to think of something worth staying for. Panic was rising and she couldn't concentrate. There had to be something more than this misery.

'Kat! Saw you from the bus. Sent home early, it was a number nine flag before lunchtime, brilliant! Let's go to mine and listen to some music.' Her words carried on the wind as Kitty stood there watching her friend tilt her face to the sky to enjoy the cool wetness until her hair and clothes were drenched.

Gill ran back to the doorway. 'C'mon, Kat!' she shouted as Kitty battled head down against the wind. She grabbed her as she got close and pulled her into the safety of the top-floor landing where everything was surreally still.

'You okay?' Kitty hadn't let go of Gill.

'Yeh. Just watching the storm—bored out of my brains—glad you've come home early. No T.Rex today though, okay?'

Gill laughed and skipped down the stairs. Kitty glanced at the plastic stool and knew she hadn't the guts to go through with it. It wasn't just about her anymore. And anyway, heights frightened her.

Three days later a suitcase appeared in Kitty's bedroom doorway. Her mum said she would be leaving for England soon and she'd help her pack. 'When am I going, Mum? Am I staying with Auntie Annie and Uncle Bert? Are they okay with it?' Kitty asked, assuming she'd be staying with her mum's sister. Her mum was half hidden inside the wardrobe door.

'Now where's that blue jumper you got from the market?' her mum asked, ignoring Kitty's questions.

'Mum! *When* am I going?' Kitty repeated.

'As soon as the flight's been arranged. Now then, we'll have to get you some more warm clothes before you leave.' Kitty knew that wouldn't happen, despite her mum's best intentions; the thought would be forgotten by lunchtime when the next few gins kicked in. It was the same story as when they'd left Scarborough, so Kitty quelled any excitement about that.

In the last few days Kitty was banned from leaving the flat by her dad; she felt powerless to argue and couldn't risk a beating now that she was carrying a child. One morning she opened her curtains and found a poster of Davy Jones stuck to the window and a line of sherbet lemons along the sill. Although the searing heat dried up the tangy insides, they were still Kitty's favourite; a fond memory from England after her and Gill had discussed what they'd missed most. She retrieved them before the flies got them. She sat on her bed sucking one after another, then folded up the poster and tucked it inside her suitcase. While her dad was in the shower, she ran up to Gill's flat. She posted her goodbye letter through the door. It had taken her three attempts to write it.

The first one got too soggy with her tears and the second one sounded far too slushy. The third one had to do. Kitty made sure to ask her to look out for her mum. Inside the envelope was a carefully folded poster of Marc Bolan from her latest *Jackie* magazine. She was going to miss Gill. The thought was unbearable.

Kitty's dad burst into her room the next morning, 'Get up! We're leaving in one hour,' he said as he banged off the air-con with his fist. Kitty pulled her sheet up to her neck and waited for him to leave. When he did, a wave of relief washed over her and her guts unclenched. She hadn't said a word, it was always the best way to be with him. The thought of just having to get through the journey to the airport and never having to live with him again felt good. She snuggled back down to savour the feeling.

'I told you to get up, you lazy COW!' Her dad grabbed her arm, yanking it until she thought it might snap; searing pain shot through her shoulder. Her mum stumbled along the hallway, propping herself in the doorway. Kitty cried out to her. Her dad pushed past his wife, thwacking into her shoulder. Kitty hugged her knees and cried as her mum gently stroked her daughter's arm.

A similar black car to the one which had whisked Tom away arrived shortly afterwards. Kitty scrabbled around for her last few belongings as her dad yelled from the front door to hurry up. Kitty embraced her mum tightly, trying hard to ignore the booze fumes, only letting go when her dad tutted impatiently and said, 'Come on! Can't believe I've got to go back there! If that fat Labour bastard gets in, the whole country's going to the dogs. Mark my words!' He climbed into the back seat without turning back to look at his wife.

Kitty slid in on the other side, dreading his company for the entire journey back to England but guessed it must be protocol that he had to accompany her.

Kitty watched her mum wave as they reversed down the drive. She looked such a sad figure in her baggy joggers and her husband's old shirt. Kitty didn't want to leave her; she knew she wouldn't take care of herself but at least she had a reprieve from the monster sitting next to her. Kitty turned and waved one last time as the car swung onto the road. Kitty knew she would comfort herself with more gin the minute she was back inside.

On the way to the airport her dad stared ahead with his fists clenched in his lap. They overtook the school bus and Kitty swallowed hard as she wished she was on it, not pregnant. She even spotted Gill. Their neighbour Cheryl was sitting in Kitty's seat next to her and they were laughing, which made Kitty feel so alone.

The flight back was uncomfortable. The only time Kitty and her dad spoke was to thank the air hostess for their food and drinks, or when she had to ask him to move so she could go to the toilet. He tutted and harrumphed so much she noticed pitying looks from fellow passengers. Their descent into RAF Brize Norton was announced twenty-three hours after leaving Hong Kong. It had felt interminable to Kitty who'd suffered cramps in the confined space for the last few hours but said nothing.

By the time they collected their suitcases and entered Arrivals, Kitty was weary and shivering with cold, her clothes inadequate and tatty. Smart people greeted friends and relatives with warm hugs but nowhere could she spot Auntie Annie and Uncle Bert.

'This way!' her dad barked, making the lady standing next to Kitty visibly jump, as he headed towards the railway sign.

Once on the train Kitty relaxed and looked out at the countryside crawling by. It looked so lush with big expanses of green and homely farms dotted about. It had been a while since Kitty had seen a cow, and the sight of them lumbering down the lane to be milked warmed her heart. Everywhere looked so quaint and welcoming. As soon as she got to Auntie Annie's she was going to write and tell her mum and Gill about everything she'd seen.

The train picked up speed and whizzed through deserted stations. Kitty dozed, woke up with a stiff neck and noticed other travellers that had since boarded. She wondered where the girl with the purple hair and bursting rucksack was going. Maybe to meet a boyfriend and run off to pastures new? Or maybe she was on her way back home to a family reunion; to be welcomed back after leaving in anger, welcomed back into the fold. Kitty wished she was that girl. The elderly lady with a kindly face opposite doing a crossword—was she travelling to or from loved ones? Was she loved? Would she be loved when she was that age, Kitty wondered. Her thoughts turned to her aunt and uncle. Her mum had given her some money so she'd bought a present each to give them—a silk pin-cushion with pig-tailed Chinamen all around the outside for Annie and a cufflink box for Bert. It looked like jade, but it wasn't. She hoped they liked the gifts and couldn't wait to see them.

It slowly dawned on Kitty that the train journey was taking too long; they'd been on it for hours. Berkshire was the next county to Oxfordshire the last time she'd looked.

Her relatives lived in Berkshire—just outside of Reading. She tried not to panic and scoured for signs. The next station they stopped at was Cullompton. Unless it was a coincidence, Kitty knew this was in Devon; her mum's dad had lived there. They'd visited when she was little. Johnny had said Grandad's house was dirty and smelled of pee; their dad had sent him out into the garden. Kitty had gone to look for him when no one was watching and had found him eating peas from pods on the vegetable patch. She asked him if he liked it at Grandad's and he'd said, *No, Cullompton's a dump!* She often asked her mum when they could go back to Grandad's in *Clumpton* as she liked it there and it had become a family joke after that. Until all family jokes were forgotten.

'Where are we going?' Kitty quietly asked her dad as the train gave a jolt and juddered to a stop. Her dad looked up from his newspaper. 'St Martha's,' he said matter-of-factly. His expression barely changed but his tone challenged her.

'What is that?' she asked, almost in a whisper. She didn't want to cause a scene but was aware that the pen belonging to the lady opposite had stopped halfway through a word.

'Umm—how can I describe it?' His eyes caught hers once again; she knew she'd walked into his trap. He was enjoying this. 'A mother and baby home, is what it is. A place where tarts go.' The crossword lady gave Kitty a sympathetic smile as Kitty felt her face burn. So she wasn't going to stay with her relatives after all, she'd got it wrong. This must have been the plan all along.

'Are there nuns?'

Her dad concentrated on an article in his magazine, as if she hadn't spoken, which confirmed her fears. They'd sent her to a convent—St Gilda's—from the age of four. She'd hated it. There were no boys so Johnny wasn't there with her. Most of the nuns were bullies and she was picked on for not being a Catholic. The children were marched to the church across the quadrant three times a day to atone for their sins, but Kitty was made to sit on the bench outside in all weathers. No one explained why she was different, made to feel different and often she'd sit there and cry until she could join the others. Her mum had stitched a dummy into the waistband of her school uniform. When the taunts got too much, Kitty would run to the toilets, shut herself in a cubicle and suck on it until she'd calmed down. That was until a girl called Amy started late in the school year. She wasn't a Catholic either so Kitty had company on the bench and someone to link arms with when the teasing got too much. She told Kitty to ignore them. She was older than Kitty, and with a friend beside her, Kitty felt she could.

'Listen to the cat-lickers!' Amy had cried as the singing inside the church reached a crescendo on one particularly bitterly cold day. They were on the bench and their lips had turned blue. As the last hymn seeped out of the stained-glass windows, the two girls had joined in "O Bread of Heaven" but substituted it with "O Bread of Devon". They'd chuckled as they'd belted it out, feigning an innocent, forlorn look when the church doors creaked open and Mother Superior led them all back to school.

The rest of the train journey was awkward. The proximity to her father was unbearable now and Kitty couldn't look at the crossword lady. She was no longer soothed by the clacking of the wheels as every few minutes the train jolted to a halt at a red signal.

They got off at Exeter St David's station. A taxi ride later and they were greeted at imposing iron gates by a nun who introduced herself as Mother Superior.

'Welcome to St Martha's, Mr Black.' Mother Superior smiled warmly at Kitty's dad but looked straight through her. Kitty fixed her face into a sneer with the right-hand corner of her mouth lifted jauntily; she couldn't resist it, wanting to set the tone right from the start. She caught the nun's menacing glint. She looped her rosary beads as if about to whip someone. Kitty knew she'd got herself into a fix but decided that celibacy and abstinence did you no favours either. *Frigid, nasty cow,* she thought. Mother Superior turned and led them down the drive. As they rounded the corner a drab, austere building came into view. Kitty shuddered.

FIVE

Silently, Kitty stood behind her dad, shifting on her aching feet and pretending to study the dusty tomes on Mother Superior's bookshelves. She wished their conversation would end. They exchanged niceties. Kitty heard the fountain pen scratch across paper; a cheque was torn from the leather wallet her dad carried in his inside jacket pocket, and finally the click of the pen top. She wondered how even a heartless bastard like him could so casually sign over his own flesh and blood.

Turning to leave, he placed a hand on his daughter's shoulder and gave her a despairing look. 'You've made your bed, now you must lie in it, Katherine.' Kitty studied her shoes. She was well aware of the enormity of her situation; it never left the pit of her guts. Getting no rise from his words, he turned and left the room with the nun. Hearing his receding footsteps, Kitty's shoulders dropped and she unclenched her fists. She desperately hoped Tom would find her and take her away from here, she hoped that wherever he was he was planning that right now.

'This way, *Miss* Black.'

Kitty followed Mother Superior through corridors, walking behind her slowly with a heavy heart and dragging her feet. They passed doors with signs saying "Laundry", "Surgical Supplies" and "Dr Wood" on them. They turned into a large, chilly room with French doors at the far end. This room had six beds on either side, occupied by girls in varying stages of pregnancy, but all bigger than Kitty and most of them looking younger than her. Curious eyes watched her make her way to the bed on the far right next to the French doors. Mother Superior waited impatiently with both hands on her hips. Kitty gripped the handle of her suitcase tighter, fixed a smile on her face, then focused on putting one foot in front of the other through the dormitory.

Her bed had a faded eiderdown of pink roses and a wooden bedside table next to it with a bible in the open recess. Above the bed was a rectangular metal framework with blue shabby curtains pushed to one side. Some privacy at least, Kitty thought. She was told to unpack her case and put it under the bed. She looked around wondering where her clothes should go.

'There are wardrobes in the next room. Find a space and then have a bath.' The nun turned on her black-brogued heels and strode out of the dormitory without so much as a glance at the other girls. Kitty shook her head and decided she'd have a bath just before bed.

'Hi! My name's Mary.'

Lying on top of the bed next to Kitty's was a heavily pregnant girl, with a mop of black curls and rosy cheeks, a book rested open on her bump. She was wearing a voluminous tent dress covered in red paisley swirls.

'I'm Kitty. Bit of a dragon, that one, I'm guessing?' Kitty's eyes looked skyward.

Mary's face broke into a big grin and, placing her book down, she swung her legs over the side of the bed to face Kitty. Her swollen belly now rested in her lap.

'Yep, she's best avoided. When you're ready I'll show you where to put your clothes, if you like?' Kitty didn't want to cause any fuss and said she'd find it while Mary rested. The others continued to watch them both, still sizing up the new girl. 'God, if I don't move soon they'll have to bloody winch me to the delivery room!' Mary puffed her cheeks out and clutched her bump.

Huffing heavily, Mary took Kitty into the next room where huge walnut wardrobes lined the walls. These were interspersed with wooden chairs holding mangled piles of plastic coat-hangers. Kitty opened a wardrobe door, delved into her suitcase, found the poster of Davy Jones and stuck it up, hoping the creases would fall out of his face soon. He was in good company with Andy Gibb and David Cassidy. Mary elbowed Kitty in the arm and gave her a thumbs up before Mary made a detour to the bathroom. Gill studied her surroundings. Walls were cracked and marked; in one corner of the ceiling were cloud-shaped brown stains. The place was drab and neglected and smelled of damp, pee and medical supplies. Kitty crouched down to her suitcase to unpack it. Beneath the top layer she found a package wrapped in pretty paper. She tore the wrapping off to find two smocked maternity dresses, one blue and one green. Her lip trembled as she held them to her. How her mum had found these, wrapped them and secreted them in the suitcase made her heart swell; she'd made sure Kitty had something new to wear.

She returned to her bed and placed the rest of her belongings into the bedside table, including her Cinderella figurine—a prize for passing her eleven plus in Singapore.

'Well done, Katherine,' her dad had said as he'd handed it over with a Timex watch strapped to the folds of the blue dress. Kitty had waited for the punchline or for the mood to turn sour but her mum had clapped and they'd had a special tea. She hadn't wanted it or her parents' attention to end, hadn't said a word for fear of breaking the spell. She'd taken Cinderella up to her room and carefully placed her inside the cupboard at the end of her bed so that it didn't get smashed. Six years on, it was next to her in the dormitory for sinful girls. She looked at it as she drifted into a deep, exhausted sleep, no longer able to make any sense of her thoughts.

She awoke to the baby kicking. It felt odd. It was the first time she'd been in a relaxed enough state to engage with the sensation. It was strange, high up in her ribcage; she struggled for breath. As she rubbed her belly rhythmically, the moving increased; they were communicating.

'Come on, Kitty! Time for breakfast,' Mary said.

They followed the smell of something unidentifiable. Kitty heard a bell tinkle in the distance and asked her new friend if that rang at every mealtime. Mary told her the bell was rung to announce a new birth upstairs. There was no bell for mealtimes. *Miss them and you go without,* she said.

In the refectory there were two long tables set with cutlery, water jugs and plastic cups. Kitty followed Mary and joined the queue for food, dished up by two dour-faced nuns wearing blue tabards over their black habits. They ladled sloppy porridge into Kitty's bowl. Kitty looked down at the splatters on her new blue dress and frowned. One of the serving nuns caught Kitty's eye and scowled at her. Kitty noted these nuns were from the same charm school as Mother Superior. She followed Mary to a table where other girls were already seated. Kitty's tummy was now rumbling with hunger, so she greedily lifted her laden spoon to her mouth. Mary stilled her friend's hand and gently eased it back down onto the table as she nodded to her right. Mother Superior had joined them and was staring at Kitty. Grace. Of course. How could she have forgotten? Just like at the convent. Giving thanks for what they were about to receive, no matter how dire. Kitty dropped the spoon noisily, placed her palms together and mumbled gibberish. The nun ended by telling God how lucky these errant girls were to be at St Martha's. *If there was a god then I wouldn't be in this state, none of us would,* Kitty thought, snatching up her spoon before the amen.

After tea Mary showed Kitty the communal lounge. There was a dusty television in one corner which was switched on for one hour each evening, Monday to Friday. Weekend viewing was thought *debauched*, Mary said; it was in the rules. Kitty thought of Pussy Galore, the club her and Gill had visited, and couldn't stop a wry smile—now *that* had been debauched. The rest of the room was filled with tatty brown armchairs. Two heavily pregnant girls chatted over the clacking of their knitting needles. Mary asked Kitty if she knitted; Kitty laughed and replied *definitely not.* As Mary turned to leave she almost bumped into a nun standing silently behind her.

'This is Sister Jude. If you ever need a cheery word or a shoulder to cry on, this is the nun for you. Sister Jude, this is Kitty.'

Sister Jude squeezed Kitty's hand, smiled at both of them and wished them a lovely rest of the day in her musical Irish lilt.

Mary led Kitty along the corridor, outside into the chilly morning and across the quadrant to the fence. Kitty wrapped her worn cardigan to her when it flapped open in the gusts of wind. Mary clamped down her dress either side with her hands after it ballooned out showing the tops of her white pop socks digging into the backs of her chubby knees.

Mary pointed to the brick church down the road and told Kitty they went there every week. 'The walk of shame,' she said with a wink. Girls who'd already had their babies knelt in the front few rows to pray and those still waiting stood at the back. Kitty asked Mary if she would have to do this because she wasn't a Catholic. Mary said she didn't know the answer to that, but not to worry as the worst bit was getting there. Kitty looked at her quizzically but Mary had already turned and was making her way back.

It became clear three days later on Sunday when they were silently crocodiled out of their dormitory, across the quadrant and along to the church. There were no whispers, no giggling from the girls. They'd been told this was a sombre occasion where they were expected to atone for their obvious sins. If they stepped out of line there'd be no food for the rest of the day. Women stopped in the street and stared at the girls; not at their faces, but at their rounded bellies. One shouted *Whores, the lot of you!* and spat in their direction. Many hung their heads in shame, but Kitty didn't, she held hers high, and looked up and down the street in the hope of spotting Tom. Once inside the building, Mother Superior scanned their faces for insubordination. The seriousness of it made

Kitty want to throw her head back and snort with laughter but she stilled that thought quickly because she didn't want to be banished to the bench outside in the biting wind. She made a point not to look at Mary, she knew that would bring on the giggles, and instead tried focusing on a serious matter. What if Tom didn't come for her? What then? When the girls at the home talked, they were all aware that if the father of their unborn child didn't want them, no other man would. What they'd done was shameful. It was drummed into them on a daily basis; their sins had found them out, they carried the evidence for all to see. The hypocrisy was not lost on Kitty as they were made to pray in front of a looming Mary Magdalene, pregnant in her teens. *Immaculate conception, my arse,* Kitty thought. Prayers ended and she crossed herself like the others and hoped with all that was holy Tom would turn up soon.

Kitty and Mary chatted often as the days passed, snatching conversations as they rested on their beds. They laughed, they whispered, they exchanged snippets of their lives. They moaned about Caitlin—the girl in the bed opposite them who snored like a steam train. They dissected their recent meals ("cockroaches and nuns' venom"), and conjured up imaginary banquets full of the rich foods of their imaginations. They soon had a cache of private looks and jokes to get them through their confinement. They looked forward to 7 p.m. on Thursdays when they were all allowed into the Television Room to watch *Top of The Pops* and jiggle their bellies along to David Essex, the Three Degrees and The Rubettes—trying to hit that high note made them sound like fighting cats. Kitty smiled to herself when her new friend changed into a capacious purple dress and blue headband for the occasion; she reminded her a bit of Gill. Mary always wore bright, cheerful clothes and had a face that matched. Kitty realised all the girls made an effort with hair and outfits on Thursday evenings. It was like a night out for them; there was an air of excitement in the dormitory even on waking. There was talk that they'd be banned from watching *Top of The Pops* soon because they were becoming *too lively*. But for now, for just half an hour a week, Kitty was transported back to her old life and the hours spent dancing in Gill's bedroom to the latest hits.

When the static stopped crackling and there was just a dot left in the middle of the screen, the girls returned to their beds bursting into chorus until lights out. A nun appeared at regular intervals and warned them to be quiet or Mother Superior would be summoned. Kitty and Mary whispered into the night. Sometimes, when emotions ran to the point of tears, one would reach her arm out and the other would find it and they'd squeeze hands.

'I was fifteen when I found out I was up the duff,' Mary said one evening as the wind howled through the French windows. 'I was too far gone by the time I realised. Are you ready for the next bit, Kitty? I'm giving you advance warning.' Kitty looked over at Mary and whispered she was. 'It was my uncle—my mum's own bloody brother.' She exhaled as if she'd been holding her breath. Kitty kept still as Mary went on. 'The bastard raped me—held his hand over my mouth until it was too late.'

'Oh my god, Mary! Your mum must be beside herself.'

'Yes, she fears I've ruined my life but I told her it was a lad at school, just wouldn't name him. If I'd told her the truth then her brother would have stopped supporting us financially and we struggled when dad died. Cancer. Riddled with it.'

Her uncle had found out about St Martha's and generously offered to pay. Mary had been glad to leave the house as he continued to bother her for sex, saying there was no worry now—she couldn't get pregnant again. She told Kitty she wasn't looking forward to going back home. Kitty shuddered.

Mary's baby was due in the next three weeks and she'd be returning to Yorkshire to continue her studies after the adoption. Her school had been told her absence was due to rheumatic fever and she was staying with relatives who lived on the coast to recuperate. She described how she'd had to wear a girdle to flatten the bump of her baby and a big mackintosh over the top once she'd really started showing.

'I lived in Yorkshire once—Scarborough. I loved it. Met a boy called Paul—bit of a wild one—got engaged at fifteen.' Kitty's eyes met her friend's and she smiled wistfully.

'I've been there! Me and Mum would go for day trips to the seaside until *he* moved in. Jaconellis ice-cream! Good times.' Both girls sat in silent reminiscence.

'Things would have turned out differently if we hadn't gone to Hong Kong,' Kitty said, unable to keep the sadness from her voice. 'It was there I met Tom. Married, he was. Said he'd had a vasectomy but he lied.' Mary's eyes opened wide in the dark. 'But I know he'll come for me before the baby is born, I'm sure of it.' Mary's eyes opened even wider; Kitty saw her friend's expression illuminated by the full moon through the French doors. Someone got up at the other end of the room and shuffled to the toilet. Each of the girls in that room had a story to tell; Kitty had heard most of them. They were all sad and shocking but they took what little consolation they could from the fact they were all in this together; no one was alone. Very few girls received visitors, especially before their delivery. The home was a no-man's-land where family ties and values were suspended. Visitors were discouraged and considered to condone their condition, so they got through this tough time by being there for each other. They were like family, like her family felt before it had disintegrated. Kitty thought about Johnny a lot at the home. He'd have been in his twenties. He'd have made a brilliant visitor with his irreverent remarks and sense of fun. She missed him terribly. She'd had to force herself to be tough with no familial support, refused to let the nuns see her fear. She thought they sounded like stuck records with their harsh words; she'd heard every insult already from her dad. Their words didn't frighten her. They seemed to revel in finger pointing so Kitty did it back but with just one finger. Every kick from her unborn child reminded her why she was there. She focused on keeping healthy for the baby, wanting a safe delivery, wanting her baby to be well, wanting Tom to turn up.

During the following weeks while Mary snoozed, which was often, Kitty watched the falling golden leaves and squirrels searching for nuts on the damp grass. She liked where her bed was; it was draughty but it gave her a view of the outside world. Sometimes she collected her coat and ventured out into the garden. It gave her the space to think. She often closed her eyes and breathed in the earthiness. She took big mouthfuls of the fresh, sharp air, so different to the smog of Hong Kong, and so quiet with just bird song and the swish of the breeze rushing through the trees. Sometimes she walked along the fence and looked through the gaps; a window to the outside world that they were only allowed to venture in, supervised, on church runs. They were told to stay away from the fence so as not to be seen by anyone. Sometimes a nun spoiled Kitty's solitude by saying she hadn't done enough chores for the week. Kitty knew the girls were cheap labour and that housework was atonement for their *unfortunate incident.* There was one girl in her dormitory who'd already had a baby a year ago and was back here pregnant again. She was referred to as "The Prozzy" by some of the nastier nuns and girls; she got no peace and seemed to have twice as much work as the others. Kitty found out her name was Sally; she wasn't a prostitute at all but had been raped on two occasions by her dad. The thought had made Kitty want to retch; her own dad was a monster but thankfully he'd not done that. Kitty knew she loved the tiny biscuits they were sometimes given for pudding and would hide them up her sleeve. Once the coast was clear, she'd drop them onto Sally's bedside table.

In the meantime, she threw herself into the work; it was exhausting but she saw it as good exercise and a distraction. Every week each girl had a list of jobs to work through. Each chore had to be crossed off and the list handed in on Friday afternoons. These included cleaning the main staircase, washing toilets, scrubbing floors and washing mountains of laundry. Kitty liked to clean the main staircase. It was the staircase reserved for guests, the few guests who visited their errant daughters or nieces and the parents who came to adopt the babies. The pregnant girls used the dank, back staircase when necessary—the tradesman's steps. Kitty didn't mind dusting and polishing the posh staircase; she loved the smell of the wax polish and the bannister came up a treat. There was a window on the landing overlooking the carpark and the farmland beyond. Sometimes she studied the cars in the hope of spotting Tom's big maroon one. She hadn't seen it so far but there had been a couple of times her heart raced with excitement when she'd heard the drone of a powerful engine. Other times, she looked out and closed her eyes as the autumn rays caught her face through the panes and she imagined lying on Stanley beach with Gill.

Kitty received regular aerogrammes from Gill. Her spirits lifted when there was one waiting for her on her bedside table. She'd climb up onto the bed and pull the curtain around her and savour reading it. She remembered one in particular. It skirted around talking about exams and teachers then told her that Pat Miller and her daughter Sarah had returned to England to be reunited with Tom. She read that line several times until her numbness turned to tears, which blurred the words. How could Tom do this to her? She'd lost her virginity to that man! She was still confused by his leaving without a word just days before her flight back but knew he'd have been given strict orders by the firm. Towards the end of the letter Gill slipped in she had a boyfriend. Kitty didn't know him, but she could feel the excitement in her friend's words describing the *fantastic* time they were having. There was no mention of the great times *they'd* had together. Kitty couldn't stop herself from feeling jealous. Gill hadn't mentioned Kitty's mum at all, which worried her. Gill finished with T.Rex lyrics squashed into the last square of space: "Oh Debora, always look like a zebra". Crotchets danced around the words. Kitty smiled at that bit. *That bloody song,* she thought. She rubbed her bump and spent the next few hours trying not to imagine the Millers playing happy families or Gill having such a good time without her.

Despite Gill's words, Kitty was unwilling to give up hope Tom would come for her. She hated herself for wishing the

Millers' marriage would fail but she saw him as her one chance to save her, her baby and her mum. Worrying about her mum kept her awake at night. She wrote a letter telling her she was being well looked after, that the place was really lovely and she'd made lots of friends. She quietly cried as she stuck down the edges of the letter ready for posting. Then she set about writing another letter.

> *Dear Tom,*
>
> *I am at St Martha's in Exeter and our baby is due at the end of the year. I don't think you've known the address before because I know you would have come. I look out of the window for your car every day.*
>
> *I miss you and look forward to seeing you soon.*
> *All my love,*
> *Kitty xxx*

She wrote the address she got from Directory Enquiries onto the envelope and stuck her last stamp on it, ready to post on Sunday. *That's why he hasn't come yet,* she thought; *no one has told him where I am.*

SIX

Kitty awoke to the ever-increasing tightness of her swollen belly and, turning to find a comfortable position, heard Mary moaning in the bed next to her, her bedside lamp illuminating her pained face.

'Kitty! Kitty! Can you get someone? I've wet the bed and it hurts, I think the baby's coming!'

Kitty swung out of bed and lumbered along the corridor to the main desk. Sister Jude greeted her with a smile and asked her if she was okay as she swiftly swiped a packet of biscuits into the top drawer of the desk in front of her. Kitty got a whiff of the sweet jam and wanted one, wanted the whole packet, then remembered Mary.

'Please come! I think Mary's having her baby.'

Sister Jude made a quick phone call and followed Kitty back to the dormitory. She pulled the blue curtains around Mary's bed which didn't block out her moans or the nun's softly spoken words. Dr Wood arrived and his deep voice issued instructions over Mary's wailing.

'Good luck Mary, I'll come and see you,' Kitty said in a loud whisper as they wheeled Mary away, then filled her mouth with the two Jammy Dodgers Sister Jude had hidden under her pillow.

By now most of the girls were awake. They'd turned their lights on to see what the commotion was, then settled back down once they realised it was just someone else's turn, relieved it wasn't theirs. Kitty lay wondering how the delivery would go for her friend and hoped she'd be fine. When her thoughts turned to the birth of her own baby she had to think about something else because panic washed over her.

Several days later, Sister Jude beckoned to Kitty from the dormitory doorway. In the corridor the nun turned in to Kitty and pressed her finger to her lips. Kitty gave a thumbs up and quietly followed her upstairs. Mary was sitting up in bed cuddling her new baby. Her eyes shone with excitement. Her cerise nightdress clashed with the yellow shawl around her shoulders and the blue blanket her son was wrapped in. Kitty rushed over and cradled them both, so pleased to see them safe and well.

'Look! Isn't he gorgeous? I've called him Jake. Would you like to hold him?'

Kitty agreed the baby was lovely although his face was wrinkled and contorted as he made strange noises. She'd no practice holding real babies, only her dolls. They hadn't squirmed, but Jake did and she was scared of dropping him. She ignored the bit about holding him because she wasn't sure how, so she plonked down in the chair next to Mary's bed. Looking around, she saw that this was a much nicer dormitory. There were brighter colours, it was definitely warmer and the bedding wasn't frayed and stained. It smelled of talcum powder, hand cream and soap. Some of the other girls in the room were sleeping, some were sitting up holding their babies, some were just staring into space. Two of the beds were empty. Kitty realised the nicer nuns worked up there; they went about their chores cheerily and placed fruit and jugs of water on the bedside lockers. There were big rosy apples in a bowl next to Mary. Mary leant over and tossed one to her and she crunched it hungrily.

'How was it? The delivery, I mean?' Kitty asked, examining her friend's face.

'Well. No sooner had they wheeled me up here, got me on the bed, told me to push a couple of times and there he was! Had to have stitches though and they sting like bloody hell.'

'Where?' Kitty asked, concerned.

'Where do you think, ya daft bat? In my whatsit! Think about it. Look at the size of him! He had to get out.'

'Was there much blood?' Kitty swallowed hard.

'Not really. Couldn't see but he was a bit slimy when they handed him to me. And there's drugs.'

Kitty's expression relaxed, not quite so terrified of her own fate in eight weeks' time. She realised Mary had gone quiet and saw that her friend was struggling to hold back tears. She reached over and rubbed Mary's hand. They didn't need to mention the looming adoption; it sat there between them like an unwelcome guest.

'Your baby box is beautiful, Mary.'

They both looked at the wallpapered box next to Mary's locker brimming with nappies, booties and a fluffy white blanket with a duck motif in one corner. The box had a robin design on it.

'Why robins? It's not Christmas?'

'Couldn't find anything with bloody storks on. It was the nearest I could get.' They both laughed. Mary's hand flew to

94

her belly. 'Mustn't laugh, might bust me stitches! Finished yours yet?'

'No. Got ages.'

The truth was, Kitty was putting off finishing her box as she knew it brought her closer to handing over her baby. The boxes had to be ready by the time of the delivery; they were to be given to the new parents—a parting gift along with their own child. They were allowed to add a present for when their son or daughter reached eighteen. Kitty wasn't even that age yet. She'd received some beautiful items: her mum had sent a yellow blanket for the baby and a pink matinee jacket for her which she wore over her nylon nightie to keep out the cold; Gill had sent a card wishing her all the luck in the world plus a white knitted rabbit with a fluffy pom-pom tail.

After hugging Mary and kissing Jake on the forehead, Kitty returned to her own bleak dormitory and inspected her half-finished baby box. It was dull in comparison to Mary's and was covered only in plain brown paper. She started to cut out flowers from the pile of magazines she'd collected and glued them on. She was glad to have something to do and it took her mind off the discomfort she was feeling in her belly. She sat back and admired her handiwork, turning it to view each side.

Over the next few days Kitty, unable to find a comfortable position on her bed, ventured out into the garden. She stopped in her tracks in the damp grass. She felt spooked, as if someone was watching her. She looked over at the tiny gap in the fence. When she got up close there was no one there. She pressed her eye to the hole in the fence and watched shoppers and drivers going about their business. Two ladies nattered at the bus stop. Kitty wished she was one of them, just doing normal things. She chided herself for being silly; no one had been watching her. Tom would have received his letter by now, but if it *was* him, she knew he'd have hauled her over the fence and into his car. She went back inside.

When the weather was too bad to go out Kitty would lie and watch the trees sway and the rain lash against the glass from the comfort of her bed. Or she'd study woodlice driven in from the rain lumber around the crack beneath the French doors—anything to distract her from feeling a bloated mess. The looming adoption hung over her like a thunderous cloud. She kept thinking of the time Johnny had thought he was adopted. She'd caught him searching their dad's desk looking for the *official papers*. She'd asked him if she was adopted too but he'd said no. He'd found a bottle of whiskey in a locked drawer; he'd discovered the key tucked inside a little notebook. He'd put the bottle to his lips and glugged the golden liquid. When she asked if she could have some he'd taken the bottle with him to the kitchen, poured a few drops into a blue and white striped egg-cup and had told her to sip it. She hadn't liked it and no matter how many times she'd cleaned her teeth, the bad taste had stayed. Her dad had obviously been secretive about drinking back then, and this memory only added "hypocrite" to the litany of nouns she had of him. Kitty had no idea if Johnny ever found any adoption papers as they hadn't spoken of it again, and she hadn't given it another thought until this day.

The following week, on 10 November 1974, while Harold Wilson governed from behind his smoking pipe at Number 10 (much to her dad's disgust), Kitty lay on a bed in the delivery room upstairs, howling like a wolf. It was seven weeks before her due date. She knew it was too early, worried that part of her baby wouldn't yet be formed (like a hole in its heart), and thought that she'd rather stay in her pregnant state. She was poleaxed by a pain so fierce she could barely breathe. She thought she was dying, that they'd missed something, that she was being ignored at a crucial time. It felt surreal, like seeing everything through a kaleidoscope—changing shapes and colours within a roaring river of pain. When one of the nuns smiled sympathetically at her, Kitty told her to *bugger off* and get her some more pain relief as the gas and air wasn't working.

'Wouldn't surprise me if there was no bloody gas in here, you tight, miserable bastards!' she shouted at the nun's retreating back, then stiffened as another killer contraction ripped through her. This went on for nine hours. The contractions intensified. She swore more. The nuns had heard it all before but they agreed this one had some life in her. Mother Superior looked in after lunch and rolled her eyes when she saw who was making all the commotion.

Kitty awoke in much discomfort in a bed opposite Mary, woozy from the medication and wondering why there was no baby next to her. There wasn't even a cot beside her bed. She couldn't remember if she'd actually had a baby and, if so, what sex it was. Mary said something to her but she couldn't make out the words. She wondered if she'd died. She looked down at her shaking hands and her teeth started to chatter. Then everything snapped into blackness.

The next time Kitty came to, bodies and faces floated around her in a fog. The familiar but blurry concerned faces of Auntie Annie and Uncle Bert came into view. They both looked a lot older than when she'd last seen them. She tried to smile at them but the effort was too much. Everything felt painful and raw. She attempted to sit up but a searing pain in her belly turned her body to jelly, so she gave up. It felt like there was a ton of wadding between her legs but she didn't have the energy to lift the sheets and look. She heard babies crying and asked where hers was.

'You have the most beautiful baby girl,' her aunt replied, as if waiting for the question. 'She's in an incubator because she's premature. She's doing fine.'

Kitty closed her eyes and tried hard to remember the birth but couldn't. She frowned.

'Now, my dear, you have been in the wars. You must rest and not worry. We're so sorry we weren't here for you before. We had no idea. Bert's been in hospital for a few months—his heart gave out. He's been poorly.'

Tricky business, these hearts, Kitty thought to herself. She'd worked out some time ago that her parents hadn't told them about her condition. Her dad would have bullied her mum to keep quiet about it. Auntie Annie confirmed as much and said she'd recently had a call from her sister, drunk and crying, telling them where their niece was. Kitty couldn't find the energy to explain she thought her dad had been taking her to them in Berkshire. He'd lied and duped her. Her aunt squeezed her hand and let out a sigh in place of harsh words. Kitty searched her aunt's face then watched as her uncle creakily stood up and crept towards the door. His heart attack had taken a big toll on him; he looked thinner and drawn. Just moving seemed an effort. Her aunt's kindly eyes were fixed on her.

'You lost a lot of blood—you caught an infection. It was touch and go for a while, dear—they had to operate.' Auntie Annie's eyes met Kitty's widening ones. Kitty lay perfectly still to hear the punchline; she knew there was more, she knew this was serious.

'They had to remove your womb, Kitty.'

Even in a drugged fug Kitty felt the unfairness. She didn't dwell on it; no point, she couldn't get her womb back now. She just wanted to know her baby was well; she needed to see her for herself. Annie told her it would probably be the next day if she rested well.

Sister Jude bustled over carrying a cup of tea with three custard creams on the saucer.

'Kitty—it means you—won't be able to—have any more babies.' Auntie Annie had waited for the nice nun for backup in case there was a scene, Kitty realised.

'I know,' is all she said as she watched her aunt retrieve the crumpled tissue from her cardigan sleeve and dab at her sad, wise eyes.

Over the next few days, and with the chirpy help of Mary and Sister Jude, Kitty grew stronger and saw her baby for the first time. She experienced a new, unfamiliar emotion. She thought it must be joy and she felt her heart might burst as she looked at the perfect person she'd created. Her daughter definitely had a look of Tom about her. She'd wondered if she would. It was the ears and nose. *We have a daughter, Tom,* she said to herself. She noted the furious expression on her baby's face—as if she had been pulled reluctantly from the womb. *She has fight in her, like me,* she thought. The baby's cupid-bow lips puckered and sucked, searching for the next feed. Kitty was flooded with love. The baby's eyes fixed unblinkingly on her. Kitty noticed two nuns watching. She struggled to muster a smile for them. She knew her gruff exterior was a way of getting through the purgatory of having a child and then having to hand it over. She *had* to be strong. She'd been saving up the good stuff for her baby. This time with her was so very precious.

She squeezed her daughter's hand in the incubator, touched the paper-thin, yellow skin. She was too small; too delicate. The tears finally fell and Sister Jude, who'd been standing quietly just inside the door, put an arm around Kitty and asked her what names she had in mind. Kitty told her she'd decided on Amy, after her friend from convent. Sister Jude wanted to know all about Amy. Kitty said she had fond memories of her. How, at breaktimes they'd escape the religious taunts from classmates and could be found by the stone wall dividing the playground and the field behind playing Post Offices. It had recesses for "letters" made from flattened Smiths crisp packets from the tuck-shop; the dark blue salt pouches were stamps and fallen leaves were pound notes. A snapped branch from the overhanging oak tree was their rubber date stamp and they'd taken it in turns to be Postmistress and serve pretend customers.

Sister Jude gently handed Kitty a breast pump and a bottle. Kitty wasn't allowed to feed her own baby; none of the new mums were. It was against the rules. They had to express their milk several times a day for a nun to do the job instead. Mary had told her it was so that a bond wasn't formed between mother and child. Kitty understood the reasoning but it hurt her physically and mentally. Her nipples were sore and cracked and stung all the time. Her whole body felt like an open wound; her young flesh had been stretched and torn beneath. She flinched when she sat down, she flinched when she stood up and she flinched from the stitches even when she lay on her bed. They were on fire. There was no comfortable position but Kitty soon discovered the best painkiller was thinking of her beautiful daughter's face. She couldn't imagine how women had loads of babies; she felt her body would never recover from this. A memory from way back came to mind. She remembered the old Indian man called Ranj who'd looked after their garden in Singapore one day a week. He'd worn a blue turban and had a white moustache that curled at the ends making him look like he was always smiling. He'd sit in the shade of their rain tree and drink tea from a flask. Kitty sometimes sat with him when she came home from school. He once took her hand in his and studied her palm.

'You will have a good life, little Kitty, and you will have a child every year,' he'd said. She thought he must have been a magician to know that, and the thought of a yearly baby had been very scary. *Well, lovely as he was, he got that wrong*, she thought as she gingerly pumped milk from her swollen breast.

When her aunt and uncle had first turned up, Kitty wondered if they could be her and Amy's lifeline, if maybe they could take them in. But once she learned how ill Uncle Bert had been and had seen him with her own eyes, she knew it wasn't an option; he needed peace and rest, not a screaming baby in the house. Auntie Annie said they would be back in a few weeks to collect her and she'd stay with them until she was back on her feet.

Kitty tried not to think if the adoptive parents had already seen Amy. It was no secret that visits happened quite quickly after the births; well-dressed couples were often spotted walking around St Martha's. If they had, she hoped they had more than enough love for her daughter and could give her everything she couldn't. She knew from the compulsory adoption day class she'd attended with Mary, papers explicitly stated that in forfeiting their babies they would never see them again. That was official. Kitty's dad had already signed hers. Kitty had read somewhere that baby girls were more 'adoptable' but in her heart of hearts she longed for no one to take Amy. She still clung to the hope that Tom would arrive soon; he must surely have received her letter by now.

Bonding with Amy was pure pleasure for Kitty, especially holding her for the first time outside of the incubator; she didn't ever want to let her go. She memorised her baby by sight, smell and sound. She knew every dimple on her body, the distinctive whiff of damp straw on her silky head, every snuffle she made. She was allowed to cuddle her for fifteen minutes a day. She'd watched Mary do it in one go with Jake, but she preferred three lots of five minutes spread throughout the morning, timed by the duty nun who'd constantly look at the fob watch pinned to her habit. If it was Sister Jude on duty then she had longer; the nun rarely clock-watched if Mother Superior wasn't around. Each time Amy's searching eyes locked onto hers, she smiled back to reassure her baby that everything was going to be alright and at the same time tried to convince herself that it would be. She wanted to remember her daughter's face forever, to have it imprinted on her brain so that one day if she saw her on a street, on a bus, in a shop, she'd know instantly that that child or woman was hers. She needed Amy to know that giving her up was the last thing she'd wanted to do, that she was truly wanted and one day—maybe— things would be different.

Kitty was acutely aware she'd created a demarcation line right down the middle of Amy's timeline: there would always be a *before* and *after* adoption. It crucified Kitty to think that this child might learn she'd been given away. She didn't ever want Amy to think she wasn't loved. She knew only too well how that felt, despising her dad even more for bringing her here to give her baby up. Each time before she laid Amy back in her cot, she kissed her eyes, her nose and her rosebud lips. She never knew when it might be the last time.

She carefully wrapped her cherished Cinderella figurine in tissue paper and placed it in the baby box for her daughter to open on her eighteenth birthday. She hoped she'd have the chance to explain the significance: Kitty got it for doing something well and Amy was her best achievement ever—perfect in every way.

It happened suddenly and slowly. As Kitty dusted the ornaments on the landing windowsill one morning, she spotted a well-dressed couple heading towards a shiny black car in the carpark. Her arms were cradling a baby in a yellow blanket. He had his arm around the lady's waist; under his other arm was Kitty's baby box. She stood there transfixed, not breathing, desperately looking for any clue that she was wrong. She couldn't take her eyes off the scene, nor could she stop the sob in her throat.

'No—*no!*' The words sounded feral. She pulled herself away, hoping she was mistaken, wanting to buy more time. She steadied herself against the bannister, and on tiptoe looked back out through the window. They still hadn't reached the car. It was definitely her baby box, her blanket, her baby. She'd imagined it must be hard to lose a child to strangers but she never imagined this searing agony. Why had no one told her it would be happening today? Sister Jude came and sat her down on the top step and muffled

Kitty's cries with her veil. She stroked her hair to calm her, then, looking furtively about her, she quickly handed Kitty a Polaroid photo. Kitty's crying stopped. Her hand covered her mouth as she looked at the picture. It was of her baby. *Thank you*. Kitty said it in her head because she just couldn't get the words out. Sister Jude smiled, her eyes crinkling at the edges; it contained sadness and hope all at the same time.

There was nothing she could have done even if she'd known what day her baby was to be taken; she'd witnessed her dad sign the adoption papers on their first day at St Martha's. Her grief and powerlessness overwhelmed her to the point she couldn't get out of bed for days; too broken to fight. She was exhausted, weak and traumatised. She felt she didn't have the right to breathe after what she'd just let happen. She couldn't be bothered to open and read the letters from Auntie Annie and Gill. A succession of nuns urged her to get up and move around, do some chores; she ignored them. Each time she surfaced and her milk drenched her nightie she turned over and slept some more. The bed next to her was empty. She missed Mary terribly and found comfort in clutching the gold chain and crucifix around her neck—Mary's heart-felt parting gift to her—and tried to block out the sound of the birth bell ringing upstairs. It now sounded like a death knell.

SEVEN

Kitty moved in with Auntie Annie and Uncle Bert in their comfortable home in Caversham, just outside of Reading. There was an ornate white water tower at the end of the road—Kitty's landmark on her many walks to clear her mind. The house was a 1950s detached with bay windows and a long driveway. Kitty's bedroom was at the back overlooking the well-kept garden and kidney-shaped pond. She loved the homely smell of the place, of home-baking and polish. The tall doors made her feel like Alice in Wonderland with their high-placed knobs. Her relatives welcomed her with a cream tea and love, with no hint that she was intruding into their idyll or an extra worry on top of Uncle Bert's health issues.

'Kitty, dear,' Auntie Annie said as they cleared away the cups and tray. 'Would you like to come to Henley with me tomorrow? There's some wonderful boutiques, you might see something you like. My treat. We could have lunch and feed the swans.' Her uncle said he'd love Kitty's opinion on *the huge range of gazebos* at the garden centre. Kitty knew he was making it up but loved him for it anyway. It was their way of making her feel wanted. She couldn't help smiling when her uncle said, 'Kitty, dear, please call us by our first names—you make us feel so old otherwise! You're like a daughter to us. We're so proud of you.'

As she settled in, she found there were days she just wanted to stay in her room. Uncle Bert whistling in the garden and Auntie Annie talking back to the radio above the whirr of the washing machine comforted her but sometimes, deep inside, a gnawing ache took over. Tears were just a blink away and the thought of going out and seeing children or prams or pregnant ladies was too much. She'd sit with her notebook, furiously scribbling her thoughts down, then translate them into poems. On those days Auntie Annie would gently knock and appear with a cup of tea, rub Kitty's shoulder and say, 'One step at a time, dear, one step at a time,' and quietly leave. When she needed to talk, they were there, she told her. Like the time her dad wrote a threatening letter from Hong Kong prophesying doom: there was no future without qualifications—she'd end up jobless and homeless, especially under a Labour government. It had upset her terribly, especially as he hadn't asked how she was or how she was getting on. She'd flown downstairs, wiping her angry tears away and shown it to her aunt who told her to ignore him and to think about herself now. She'd said her dad was *just an angry man who needed to work through his issues;* they'd gone for a drive around and a coffee until Kitty felt calmer. She received a card from her mum weeks later—one of those "Just Thinking of You" ones. It had a picture of a smiling sunshine on the front and inside it just said *lots of love, Mum xxx.* Kitty knew it would have taken effort for her mum to have done that, to synchronise a sober window, an absent husband *and* a trip to the post office. She smiled every time she looked at it.

She kept in touch with Gill, now at university in Exeter studying languages and destined for a bright future. She shared a house with two other girls who seemed to party around the clock. Gill said it drove her insane and disturbed her studies. It sounded like she was having a great time and Kitty knew her friend would do well. She wondered if she'd have made it to university had she not become pregnant, but it hurt too much to dwell on what might have been.

She didn't complete her education. She tried. She managed to secure a place at the local college but her heart wasn't in it, or it was too soon—her brain just didn't feel the same, too many distractions. She questioned who she'd be getting qualifications for and decided it wasn't for her. In the meantime she knew she had to establish a routine and earn some money to pay her way. She mustered up every bit of confidence to attend an interview for the position of bank clerk, ringed in Annie's red pen in the Situations Vacant, left strategically on the coffee table next to Kitty's seat.

On the day of the interview Kitty awoke from an unsettled night feeling sick. The thought of being under scrutiny—being judged—scared her. She always seemed to fall short of expectations.

She wore a navy pencil skirt and a paler blue jacket which Annie found in the back of her wardrobe; relics of bygone days when she was a lot slimmer. The shoulder pads fell off Kitty's shoulders but she decided once she got inside the building she'd sling the jacket over her arm.

She arrived at the imposing red-bricked building, taking a deep breath as she followed the sign to reception. She couldn't disguise her shaking hands as she signed in. She walked to the seating area on legs that felt like rubber. She picked up a magazine from the glass table in front of her but had no intention of reading it; she fanned herself with it instead.

Mrs Brown from National Westminster Bank Recruitment strode in and firmly shook Kitty's clammy hand. She was a matronly lady in a navy pleated skirt-suit, jowls heavy with middle-age and an eye that didn't blink. Kitty realised it was made of glass. She tried not to stare at it but couldn't stop herself. She'd never seen one before except on her dolls, but had heard about them in jokes. Apart from the not blinking, it was perfectly matched to the other one, the dark brown iris exactly the same shade. Kitty wondered how Mrs Brown came to have it and reminded herself that everyone had a story to tell.

Mrs Brown sat Kitty down in a small, stuffy room to take the entrance test. Kitty struggled over some of it; it had been a while since she'd done anything like this, and the room was claustrophobic. Mrs Brown collected the paper an hour later. Kitty fidgeted in the waiting room until Mrs Brown greeted her with a broad smile and congratulated her, the job was hers. Kitty beamed and suspected Mrs Brown had filled in the gaps herself because the woman had compassion—she imagined life had been a struggle for her with that glass eye and she could maybe sense something similar in Kitty.

She loved being at the bank; it gave her a sense of belonging. Answering customer queries on the Enquiries desk made her feel useful and part of a team. On the odd occasion she was asked to sit in for an absent teller, this was her favourite role. Climbing onto the frontline stool was like pulling on a comfy jumper. Entrusted with someone else's money made her sit up straight and proud—she felt worthy. The mustardy smell of the notes and coins became so familiar, it was like spending time with a good friend. Her yellow sponge pad, red rubber thimble and brown elastic bands were her tools. Her left knee rested beneath the alarm button under her desk and this, along with the bullet-proof screen she smiled at customers through, helped to make her feel safe.

At home everyone rubbed along well together. Annie had given up her charity shop work and spent more time with Bert who was really having to take things easy with his deteriorating health. They loved pottering in the garden and venturing out in the car for afternoon teas. Kitty liked life with them; she'd begun to feel comfortable and relaxed, and she could feel herself healing. Whenever she looked in the paper for flats they talked her out of it.

Over tea one evening Annie told Kitty she'd heard something really interesting on the radio earlier. The 1975 Children's Act had just come into force; adoptees in England and Wales could access their birth records from the age of eighteen for the first time in history.

'Kitty, this is exciting! It means Amy could contact you. We know you don't want to interfere in her life—and that's truly your decision, dear—but one day, who knows?' She hugged her niece tightly. Her enthusiasm was so infectious that Kitty seized that hope and tucked it quietly into her heart. She thought about it for the rest of the evening until, instead of jumping into bed, she reached into the back of her wardrobe and pulled out her old red vanity case, the zip now broken. She looked at the one photo she had of Amy and the white rabbit with the pom-pom tail, Gill's present that she just couldn't part with. They were all wrapped in the pink matinee jacket. She thought she could still smell Amy on it. She wanted that smell to last for as long it would be before she could hold her girl again.

Arriving home from work some weeks later, Kitty spotted Annie at the front window as she walked through the gate. Kitty waved but Annie didn't. Annie opened the door before Kitty had chance to put her key in the lock. Annie's face was ashen, her eyes bloodshot. Kitty thought something terrible must have happened to Bert, but was relieved to see him as she followed her aunt into the sitting room. He gave his niece a sympathetic smile which only added to her concern. They weren't their usual jolly selves and Radio 4 wasn't on in the kitchen. Annie sat down on the sofa next to Kitty and took her hand in hers.

'Kitty, dear—I've something to tell you.' She welled up and teardrops plopped from her face onto Kitty's arm.

'I'm—so sorry to tell you, my—your—mum has—passed away, dear.' She sniffed and gulped loudly, took a balled-up tissue from her cardigan pocket and dabbed at her face. 'It was—very sudden—all over very quickly according to your dad. It was a heart attack.' She squeezed Kitty's hand. *Hearts.*

Kitty couldn't think of a word to say for the thoughts hurtling around her head. Images of her mum: before Johnny's death, pretty, happy and laughing; stumbling around, shouting and unconscious on the floor from too much booze. With physical and mental distance between them, Kitty could see they'd all become trapped in a vortex of misery. *What a bloody awful way to spend the last years of your life.* And with that thought came a wave of misery which left Kitty crying noisily.

'It's alright, Kitty, let it out. It's been a terrible shock,' Annie said as she put her arm around her.

'Y—es, b—ut—I *h—ate* dad for not sort—ing things out!' she stuttered between sobs. 'Why didn't—why didn't he get—help for her—her drinking? Why wasn't he even—even—nice to her?' She wiped her nose on her sleeve before Bert handed her a box of tissues. *'He used to hit us!* Did you even know that?'

Annie gasped and exchanged a look with Bert. Bert grimaced and screwed his hands up in his lap.

'No! We didn't know that, Rose never said—but we knew about the drinking. We offered so many times for her to come here and get sorted but she always said it was fine and anyway, she wouldn't leave Bobby. We tried, I used to plead with her but she was adamant.'

'I *hate* him for treating us the way he did! After Johnny died I wanted to live anywhere but with them. It was horrible!' Kitty gasped for breath and then felt embarrassment at her outburst.

'You have every right to say how you feel, Kitty. We're so, so sorry for everything you've been through and you don't deserve any of it. There's something else we need to tell you.'

'Are you sure, Annie?' Bert piped up from his armchair. Annie looked kindly at him and nodded. Kitty wriggled back against the soft velour of the sofa and steeled herself.

'As you know, dear, there was only us two sisters. Your grandad was a bit of a drinker and a gambler. When my dear mum was diagnosed with MS, Rose had to cut her education short to help support us. We were struggling with debt and your lovely mum started nurses training. I'd always looked up to her—such a lovely, generous soul—' Annie's eyes were swimming with tears as she looked over at Bert, who nodded encouragingly. 'On her night off, she'd often go dancing with some of the other girls—that's how she met Bobby. He was a sailor, a very handsome sailor. Before long they got engaged and he went back to sea. We started making wedding plans together—Mum and Dad were over the moon for her and she was so happy.' Bert joined Annie on the sofa and put an arm around her shoulder as she calmed herself.

Kitty could see how difficult this was for her aunt, so she didn't interrupt.

'Anyway, after a late shift—someone, we never found out who—attacked Rose on her walk home. She—she—she put up a fight—lost a lot of teeth—' Kitty gasped as Annie continued. 'The thing is, Kitty—he raped her.'

'*No!*' Kitty's hand flew to her mouth.

'There's more, Kitty. Whether it was right or wrong, my parents didn't want Rose to miss out on a good future with Bobby.'

Kitty frowned.

'It was different in those days. Marrying a man with a regular income was the way to go. Anyway, they persuaded her to write to Bobby and tell him she was pregnant with his baby.' Annie left the room. Bert studied his hands as Kitty recalled Johnny's suspicions of having been adopted. He'd known something wasn't right. She felt numb with shock.

Annie came back and handed Kitty a photograph. It was of her mum and dad's wedding; she was sure she'd seen it before except this time she noticed the strategically placed posy of roses over her mum's silk-bowed bump.

Annie explained that Bobby was delighted about the baby, left the Navy and joined the Civil Service.

'Oh god, it all makes sense, Annie, but it's so bloody sad.' Kitty flew into Annie's arms and sobbed for her mum who'd lost her way and turned to booze in her heartache, and for Johnny who'd always suspected something wasn't quite right. Bert came in bearing cups of tea and Battenberg on the floral tray and set it down carefully on the coffee table, wanting to be helpful, but not wanting to get in the way.

'Do you understand the reasoning behind the li—*family secret*, Kitty? Back in those days getting pregnant outside of wedlock just wasn't on. Mum and Dad wanted Rose to have an abortion at first but she was totally against that and she could be stubborn. Believe me, at the time things were desperate—none of it was taken lightly and your poor mum was in a bad way after the attack. Apart from all the bruising, she had to have all her teeth out, the damage was so bad. Our dad had to get his act together and earn some money—it was the kick he needed to stop drinking and gambling. They liked your Bobby, they needed Rose to have a future. When Johnny arrived, your dad was besotted with him.'

Kitty sighed loudly. 'Of course I understand, Annie. Me getting pregnant was the end of the world and I can see why now—it was history repeating itself. I just find it hard to believe that Mum never told Dad that Johnny wasn't his. God knows they had some ferocious rows.'

Annie nodded. 'We never mentioned it again, not once— Bert was the only person I told.' Bert quietly picked up the cups and disappeared into the kitchen.

It was a lot for Kitty to take in. Her emotions were so mixed. *You were right, Johnny, poor Mum. No wonder she drank! How awful their marriage was based on a lie*, were the thoughts that went around her head in a loop. She went up to her room, clutched her mum's card to her heart while she cried some more.

The next day was Saturday. Kitty peered through her curtains and saw a beautiful sunny day. Bert was already in the back garden digging and planting. The radio was on quietly in the kitchen as Annie emptied the dishwasher.

'Hi Kitty, you okay? We thought we'd have a day at home today—lunch in the garden, just a quiet day. You have any plans?'

Kitty had but didn't feel up to it now. Lunch with a group of work mates no longer appealed and Sheila—number two cashier and unofficial social secretary—had been very sympathetic when Kitty said her mum had died. So Bert brushed off the patio table and chairs while Annie fussed with making coffee and pulling things out of the fridge for lunch until everything stopped and they landed in their seats in the sun. The table was laden with Bert's favourite ham and mustard rolls, cheese and onion quiche and crisps. Pride of place was a coffee cake which Annie had made the previous evening because she couldn't sleep after the day's terrible news. Her and Kitty sported red eyes and only Bert seemed to have an appetite. While he munched away, Annie talked some more about Rose. 'Your mum was known for her cakes and biscuits in our area—my goodness, could she bake! Never read a recipe—all self-taught. People would queue down the street. The lightness of her sponges was legendary, her scones melted in the mouth and her fruit cake was rich beyond belief!'

Kitty looked at her aunt's sweet face as she recalled happy memories.

'I'd leave for school in the morning and there'd be bags of flour, sugar and butter on the doorstep in the hope she'd keep on baking—she'd never accept any money from anyone. Some days I'd walk back up our street and could smell butterscotch biscuits and Bakewell tart—so could everyone else and there'd be neighbours waiting outside our door.'

Kitty swallowed hard as Annie continued. 'I was so popular at school because at breaktime I'd share out whatever she'd made.' It warmed Kitty's heart to hear this story because she had memories of this too. She told Annie and Bert about the birthday parties she and Johnny had with amazing centrepiece cakes made by her mum. Once, a ship for her brother with a sponge hull encased in black royal icing, a red liquorice plimsoll line and marzipan funnels. The portholes looked so real that Johnny had rested his elbows on the table and tried to peer through them and her parents had laughed. He was so excited he'd banned anyone from eating it until every neighbour and friend had seen it. Little Kitty couldn't resist it—it was so close to her face as she walked by and the smell of almonds was so delicious, she'd taken a bite out of the stern. Her mum had to do a quick repair job before Johnny came home. Annie and Bert laughed at that.

Kitty described how, on her sixth birthday, as she enjoyed jelly and ice-cream with Amy from the convent, her dad had carried in an iced white swan sitting on a silver cake-board; three candles glowed along each wing. On its head, above its slender neck, sat a jewelled crown made from chunks of Wine Gums, and it had an orange beak that even tasted of orange. They'd all been singing "Happy Birthday" to Kitty—Mum, Amy, Johnny and his friend Freddie, but the sight of the cake had stunned them into silence. It was just so beautiful—they'd never seen anything like it, even in the posh baker's window. There were other memorable ones she'd made: Humpty Dumpty sitting on a Liquorice All-Sorts wall; a Dalek with a silver manipulator arm made from Cadbury's Chocolate Fingers; a butterfly with sparkly pink and blue wings on a chocolate log; and a flying saucer with marshmallow aliens climbing down a ladder. None of their friends had seen cakes like it before; they were so envious. Kitty and Johnny felt very special, which made it hard for Kitty once her mum didn't bake any more cakes. Once Johnny didn't have any more birthdays cakes and celebrations became memories.

When Kitty climbed the stairs for bed that evening, she overheard the tail end of Annie and Bert's conversation in the front room.

'Poor lass. She's had so much trauma,' Bert said in a loud whisper.

'I know, love, but she's safe here, we'll look after her,' Annie replied, before the door was quietly closed.

Air tickets arrived for the flight to Hong Kong for Rose's funeral. Annie went with Kitty, who was so relieved as she really wasn't looking forward to seeing her dad. The journey seemed to take days and at the end, the dreaded landing at Kai Tak airport—a scarily short runway requiring a precision landing. On that first journey to Hong Kong after leaving Scarborough with her mum and dad, Kitty had thought the plane would crash from the moment it banked very sharply to make the descent. It had felt too exaggerated, like a sped-up fairground ride. There'd been a collective gasp from the passengers and Kitty had grabbed her mum's hands, closed her eyes and furiously sucked a sweet so her ears popped.

This time it was Annie who reached over and clutched Kitty's hand. Her aunt's head was pushed against the headrest and the colour had gone from her cheeks. She attempted a reassuring smile at Kitty but it was cut short by a burst of turbulence. When she'd started at her new school on the island everyone had talked about their arrival into Hong King: seeing the puzzle of streets below and then the drop as you passed high-rise apartments close enough to touch. You could spot families watching television or gathered around the table for a meal.

'You have to see this, Annie!' Kitty squeezed her aunt's hand but her aunt's eyes were opening for no one. Only after the plane had screeched into reverse thrust, bumped along the runway and come to a complete standstill did she attempt to peer through one slitty eye. She sat there speechless. The terror left her face once the release seatbelt sign flashed overhead.

'We made it. Thank god that's over! I don't know how anyone can keep doing this!' she said in a too loud voice, making nearby passengers chuckle as they gathered their belongings.

When they eventually walked through Arrivals at the airport, Kitty spotted her dad from a distance making her tummy churn, she was shocked to see how much he'd aged. He looked lost with his hands in his pockets and didn't raise a smile when he saw them. He didn't hug either of them, just turned and led the way to the carpark. 'This way,' was all he said, his tone flat. He drove them in the ancient Triumph Herald, conversation impossible over the drone of the patched exhaust. Annie attempted to ask him how he was but he either didn't hear or wasn't interested. Kitty smiled at her aunt as if to say, *It's okay, this is normal—it's not you. You're lovely. He's not.*

Once at the flat it was obvious Kitty's dad had gone to no effort for their arrival. Kitty distracted herself with making up their beds after settling Annie in the sitting room with a cup of tea and a box of tissues. Jetlag was kicking in and this flat—the last place her sister had been alive in—was making her emotional. Kitty's dad was nowhere to be seen until he walked through the flat jangling his car keys and said, 'Before you leave, you need to sort out the stuff in the spare room.' Then left again, letting the front door slam noisily behind him.

The spare room had been Kitty's old room. She'd hesitated to go in there until she knew her dad was out of the way. If he ever cornered her in there again, she knew she couldn't be held responsible for her actions. She stuck her head around the door and hesitated. A faded David Cassidy still smiled at her. The purple wall had been repainted white but the other walls had been left displaying brown dashes of old Sellotape where other posters and poems once hung; her *Jackie* magazines still took up the corner. When her heartbeat settled she went in. She spun slowly around and around on her plastic tulip stool to take it all in. The drawers of her dressing table were empty—apart from a dusty silk rose, a present from Tom. Her old bed had been stripped but covered with a batik throw. Her record collection was stacked beside her wardrobe—Joni Mitchell on top of Cat Stevens on top of Carly Simon. It was pretty much just as she'd left it. Kitty wondered how often her mum had come into this empty room.

There was a wastepaper basket containing her mum's make-up bag, her Scarborough lucky Duck and her glasses in a worn leather burgundy case. Next to this was a battered blue suitcase containing clothes, shoes and cuts of material that Rose often bought because she'd felt sorry for the stooped hawker who occasionally called at the flats.

Kitty held the make-up bag to her nose. It was a blend of powder, hairspray and surely a hint of gin—it smelled of her mum. Inside the bag she found a dried-up mascara, a scarlet lipstick and silver tweezers. The tweezers! She squeezed them into the palm of her hand and held them to her heart. She could picture her mum at her dressing table mirror in her bedroom in Singapore. She'd have woken from a deep drunken sleep and stumbled to the seat to take a good look at herself. She'd call Kitty who'd stand in the doorway knowing what was coming next.

'That's the last drink I'm having, Kitty. I mean it!' And she'd look at Kitty in the reflection with bloodshot eyes peering from a face badly creased and far too old for her years. She'd try to make herself look presentable. She'd open her ancient Max Factor compact and dab broken chunks of too-orange powder on her nose and cheeks then click it closed. She'd pull a comb through her brittle hair and stop in mock horror at the demarcation line between badly dyed red and bright white roots.

'Ten cents for every rotten white one you can pull out, Kitty,' she'd say as she held the tweezers above her head. Kitty would pluck away and tell her mum she was beautiful despite the mirror screaming something else. She'd stop plucking after ten hairs and comb the frizzy hair back from her face to disguise the remaining roots. Rose would smear lipstick across her parched lips with a flourish—the sign her beauty regime was over and the gin was calling. Sometimes the lipstick had worn so low that she'd dip a hair grip into the stump and drag that across her mouth.

'Do you really think I'm beautiful, Kitty?' Rose would look pleadingly at her daughter in the reflection and Kitty would look past the putty pallor, the baggy eyes and the sagging jawline.

'You're the prettiest mum there is.' Rose would take a shiny dollar coin from the top drawer and press it into Kitty's little palm. Then she'd stumble to the kitchen for that next gin she'd promised she'd never have.

Neither Annie nor Kitty could bear the thought of throwing any of Rose's belongings away. They held hands as they stared at the sum total of Rose's life, trying to be strong for each other. Kitty pulled out a pair of red leather kitten heels which she herself had loved clomping around the house in as a child, pretending to be a model on the catwalk. Annie couldn't believe her sister still had them. They'd been Rose's favourite dancing shoes as a teenager. Annie said she'd been so full of fun and laughter back in those days. Kitty turned them in her hands, dropped them on the floor and stepped into them. They fitted and still looked pretty. She put them to one side to wear to her mum's funeral the next day.

The day of the funeral was windy and bleak. Kitty lingered in bed, her thoughts bearing heavily down on her and her head sore from too much wine the night before.

'Come on, lovey. Let's do this,' Annie said, setting a cup of tea down next to Kitty.

The wind howled as the cortege drove gallingly slowly to the crematorium at Cape Collinson. Kitty sat between Annie and her dad, who stared straight ahead, his jaw set and his cheek twitching with tension. She longed for her dad of old; she'd have reached out to that one to help ease his pain. Instead, she shuddered at his proximity, wishing he wasn't there.

She watched scenes pass by in slow motion: street traders selling melons and smelly durian; a row of taxis parked under trees for a shady break; children hunched over playing jacks on the pavement; life carrying on. This life which had gone on around her mum, the life her mum had opted out of. How sad she'd died without Kitty *really* knowing her. Her mum's life hadn't really been any life at all, just lots of bad luck, wrong choices and an early death. Her parents' marriage had been based on a lie. It seemed unbelievable to Kitty that not even in her drunken years had Rose revealed that Johnny wasn't Bobby's son, not even after Johnny died. Kitty found that shocking; there'd seemed to be no holds barred during their rows. Even now the thought of those made Kitty shudder. She leant back in her seat, letting the air conditioning cool her rising rage. Annie's hand reached over and gripped hers as the urge to smack her dad in the face came and then went.

When they arrived at the crematorium, Kitty thought they must be at the wrong place. Sad and crying people congregated by the chapel entrance; she didn't recognise any of them. She hadn't expected anyone else to be going through the same misery, let alone on the same day, in the slot before or after her mum's. The sobriety of the ceremony unsettled her and jetlag made her feel wretched. The boot of the hearse opened like a scream. The coffin seemed huge and was carried precariously by six small Chinese pallbearers; even the Padre waiting in front of the funeral bier looked concerned, it was bobbing so gingerly. *Please don't let it come crashing down,* Kitty thought, linking arms with Annie as they followed her dad, who walked several paces behind the coffin, still staring straight ahead.

Reaching the front pew, Kitty couldn't take her eyes off the coffin as it was placed on the bier; it really did seem much too big. She'd once overheard a morbid conversation in the staffroom between Dave from accounts and the chief cashier, Norm, one lunchtime shortly after she'd started her job at the bank.

'Remember Abel Bassett up at Marsden's Farm?' Dave said between bites of his apple.

'Yeh! Me and my brother used to spy on him from the copse—he seemed ancient even then. We used to make animal noises at him until he waved his stick at us and threaten to call the police. We'd shinny down and run through the cows laughing. Why do you ask?' John said.

'—found dead the other day. They say he rotted in there for weeks. Rats ate his eyes and his body swelled and swelled. They had to take off the door frames to get him out!'

'*Jesus,* I hadn't heard!' John took another bite of his sandwich. They both seemed oblivious to Kitty sitting there unable to finish her salad.

Dave went on. 'My mate's dad works at the funeral parlour. He said they couldn't get the bloating down enough to fit him in the biggest coffin. They had to break both his legs and bend them in the other way!'

Now at the funeral, Kitty tried hard not to dwell on that thought; for all she knew her poor mum could be lying in there with two black eyes from the monster next to her. She jumped when someone in the pew behind touched her shoulder. She turned and saw Gill's dad; his wife was next to him and they both gave Kitty a nod. She smiled back.

Gill's dad had identified Rose's body as Bobby had been on a course in Kuala Lumper when she was found dead. Gill had tried to keep some of the detail back from Kitty but Kitty had demanded to know everything: neighbours flagged up an awful smell coming from their flat; flies at the closed windows; she'd been dead for days.

Hymns rose in the stifling air; voices too ineffectual to fill the space. Thankfully, no "Morning Has Broken". The ceremony seemed to last weeks. For once Kitty longed for the distraction of children. An impromptu yelp from a bored toddler would have been welcome, but there were no children and no distractions. Kitty heard a sob escape from her own mouth just at the start of the committal, her face crumpled, and she cried like a child.

'Get a grip! If royalty can get through these things without blubbing, then so can you!'

Annie put a protective arm around her niece, scowling at Kitty's dad when she spotted him looking his daughter up and down with disgust. His eyes lingered on the red shoes, before pushing past them and striding out of the church before the service ended. When the coffin juddered through the curtains Kitty tried to remember the colour of her mum's eyes—just something to hold on to—but she couldn't.

The wake was surreal. Strangers sprayed pastry as they made awkward small talk; few people had actually known Rose Black. Kitty wondered why they were there. Her dad wasn't at the wake or at the flat when Kitty and Annie returned later that day. Kitty put the full blue suitcase inside her own—ditching some of her own things in the dustbin to make room.

On the flight back Kitty nodded in and out of fractured sleep, too aware that her mum's ashes were in the overhead locker. They arrived jetlagged and miserable at the cemetery in Horton to deposit the urn. Kitty stood in front of Johnny's headstone and wanted to tell him his mum was there now, but the emotion stuck in her throat, rendering her speechless. Instead, she stared at his engraved name and held up her mum's ashes.

They made their way over to the office and were greeted with questions they were too exhausted and upset to cope with. Did they want a page dedicated to Rose in the book of remembrance? What would they like it to say? Or maybe they had a poem in mind? All Kitty could think about was the date on the death certificate. It was wrong, or a guess at best. The coroner had given only an estimate of the time of her death. He'd said it was impossible to pinpoint the exact time due to the extreme heat and other circumstances he didn't mention, and they hadn't asked.

EIGHT

Kitty settled into a routine living with Annie and Bert and established a bit of a social life. She loved coming home; the house was so welcoming and they seemed in no rush for her to move out. When she stumbled into the hallway after evenings out, tipsily giving Michael Crawford's signature "Ooooh Betty" routine, before tripping her way upstairs to bed, they laughed. She was like a daughter to them.

After graduating from uni, Gill came to visit. Kitty's excitement was palpable as she waited for her car to turn onto the drive. They flew into each other's arms the second Gill stepped out of the car.

'You bloody brainbox, Gill! I bet uni was great?' And Gill recounted edited tales of campus high-jinx as Kitty leant into her on the sofa, listening intently as Annie and Bert looked on. It was like they'd never been apart even though they most definitely had. And although Gill's parents had seldom had time for her, they now compensated with their bank account. They'd paid her way through her studies and were buying her a house not too far from Reading. Kitty couldn't believe her luck to think her best friend would be mere miles away from her.

It was while the four of them were having tea that Annie produced an open envelope from the sideboard and handed it to Kitty. Kitty looked at it, bemused; the addressee was Annie.

'Open it, dear, it's actually for you.'

Kitty opened it up. Stapled to the back was a cheque for two hundred and fifty pounds. It was from the Berkshire Poetry Society. The letter said that a poem had been selected and had won first prize. Kitty looked inquisitively over at Annie.

'I hope you don't mind the intrusion, Kitty, but I read some of your poems in your notebook. They were so good I entered one in a competition I saw in the newspaper.'

'Oh my god! I've won!' Kitty looked at the cheque again. 'Wow! The meal's on me tomorrow!'

Kitty was in a good place. She began to notice admiring looks from male work colleagues. Some of it was unwanted—especially from lecherous Dave from Accounts. He'd already tried it on with her behind the Kardex files. She'd elbowed him in the ribs and left him breathless. He'd an eye for anything in a skirt. The general feeling from the staff was one of pity for his wife and two daughters. When a beautiful Italian girl called Bella joined their ranks it was the start of a six-month affair and the end of his marriage. Kitty watched as it all unfolded, unable to offer any wise advice, knowing full well you learn from your own mistakes.

One busy Friday afternoon in the bank Kitty's attention was drawn to someone waiting in her queue. She was first cashier—till number one—leader of the teller pack. Norm had come down with shingles. Kitty had stepped into his shoes after a communication from Mrs Brown at Head Office saying she'd a good rapport with customers and was a conscientious worker. The man who caught her eye was talking to the person behind him and when he smiled she noticed his dimples. Then she noticed his eyes. They were the bluest blue of a summer sky, vivid and clear, as if he was blinking in reflected light. She felt the hairs stand up on the back of her neck and fumbled with the stack of notes handed to her by her current customer from the local garage. He was definitely taller than her, but under six feet Kitty guessed. *A perfect height*, was her first thought, and then silently reprimanded herself. Her face reddened as she watched him fiddling with the bags of money he held in his hands. His *ring-less* hands. He was wearing jeans and a tan leather jacket. She struggled to concentrate and had to re-weigh the bags of coins. She was aware of the Sub-Manager hovering behind her to see why she was dithering. She turned and smiled reassuringly at her boss. He loved nothing more than a lock-in if the tills didn't tally; loved taking centre stage exercising his power, breathing down the necks of clerks when they were missing meagre amounts of money at close of business. Kitty suspected this would happen this night. *Get back in your box,* she thought to herself, as her heart raced at the gorgeous man's approach.

When he finally stood in front of her till she found herself gazing into his eyes through the bullet-proof screen; her heart thumped ridiculously fast.

'Hi, I'd like to pay this in please,' he said, and smiled shyly at her. The transaction seemed to be over in seconds. She watched him turn and leave, drank in how well his jeans fitted his legs, his bum. *Don't go.* They'd barely spoken but she'd definitely felt something. Maybe it was his shy demeanour, so unassuming, so gentle. There was a calmness about him. She found it hard to concentrate for the rest of the afternoon.

Her till didn't add up at close of business and it made the Sub-Manager's day. He'd a spring in his step, a clipboard tucked under his arm and a mischievous glint in his beady eyes. They all had to stay back counting and recounting until the totals tallied. A couple of colleagues looked over in Kitty's direction and tutted in the knowledge her till was the cause of the problem, eager to get home.

Afterwards, she and some of the others went for a drink in the Boar's Head opposite, or the "Whore's Bed" as Sheila from till number two insisted on calling it. They sat there clutching their vodka and limes and Sheila cheekily asked in front of everyone if there was a particular reason Kitty's till hadn't tallied earlier. Everyone laughed at her blushes. Sheila sniggered as she asked Kitty loudly if it had anything to do with a good-looking blond man who'd made a deposit earlier that day.

This man, whose paying-in slip said he was from the local jewellers—Bright's—stirred in Kitty a feeling she couldn't shake off. She wondered if he was an actual jeweller; he looked the arty type. She thought about him constantly. She looked for him daily, but realised he only came into the bank on Fridays with the week's takings, like most of the local businesses. She had a whole week to wait.

The following Friday she watched the hands of the clock near two p.m. She'd even taken early lunch to be back at the till, make-up touched-up and hair brushed for his arrival. Between customers she watched the door. He didn't come. In his place was a spotty youth from the jewellers and her heart sank. It was all she could do to be jovial. *Where is he?* she said in her head as she pushed the stamped paying-in slips back across the counter.

The next Friday he turned up. She caught his eye as he queued, and smiled. She got a shy smile back, which made her heart jump. She found his shyness attractive.

'Why don't you ask him out?' Sheila leant over from the next till and whispered between customers.

Kitty didn't ask him out. Her feelings about this man confused her, or any man come to that. Paul had gone off with someone else the minute she'd left Scarborough, Tom had treated her shabbily and then just walked away; it just didn't seem to work out with her and men. How could she trust one again? Annie told her trust was earnt. Kitty saw Annie and Bert had a wonderfully solid relationship; they'd been together since school, they fitted together like a double-act. She wondered if there was someone, somewhere for her and if it could possibly be the man in the queue. Something struck a chord with her—she recognised a vulnerability. He seemed guarded; maybe he'd been hurt before, maybe they had that in common. All she *did* know was that every time she saw him or thought of him, she felt something buzz inside. The voice in her head didn't stop until she decided to do something about it.

One Sunday morning, with her eyes tightly squeezed shut and, after several false starts, she snapped the necklace that Mary had given her in the mother and baby home. *Desperate measures and all that,* she thought. She wrapped it in tissue. On Monday lunchtime she found herself stepping into the jeweller's shop with her heart thumping wildly. She wanted to see him. Had to see him. Wanted to be sure. It was the spotty lad serving.

'One moment, I'll see what can be done.' He took the chain.

'Could I please speak to the jeweller? This necklace is very special to me.' The boy disappeared out the back door and returned after a few minutes. Then *he* was there in jeans and T-shirt, hair tied back in a ponytail, looking at her questioningly. He *was* the jeweller! *Result,* she thought. His eyes made her melt. *He* made her melt. She smiled at him and was gutted when he didn't appear to recognise her.

'Hi, I was just wondering how long it would take you to fix my necklace? It's very special—it was given to me by a dear friend. I don't like to be without it for long.'

He looked at her and smiled. 'Hey, the girl from the bank, right?' He studied the chain. 'I'll see what I can do. Come back tomorrow lunchtime.' He turned and disappeared back through the door.

'Thanks, Matt,' the spotty lad called after him. *Matt! Kitty and Matt!*

The rest of the day passed in a blur. She counted down the hours. She could barely breathe when she stepped back into the shop, trying not to look like she'd been catapulted in. The young lad handed her a box with the repaired necklace inside; she handed him some cash but kept her eyes on the back door the whole time.

'Could I have a quick word with Matt please? I'd like to thank him personally,' she said, after what seemed an interminable wait.

'Afraid not, he's gone to lunch. Probably be back in an hour or so.'

Kitty trudged out of the shop and made her way up the High Street to the bank, scouring the crowds of shoppers, hoping to see him. She had no luck and reluctantly sloped back into work.

Days passed. One breaktime in the staffroom Kitty picked up the local paper and was drawn to the headline "Shining Award for Bright's". She read the jeweller had been selected out of all the regional jewellers for the prestigious "Cut Above" award and was hosting an open day the following Saturday; fizz and canapés for all their loyal customers. She'd been in there once; *that'll do. I qualify*, she cheekily thought. It gave her a focus in the intervening days as she planned her outfit, planned her entrance, and planned what she would say to Matt.

Saturday finally arrived. Kitty styled her hair into submission, pulled on her most flattering jeans, new top and cream jacket. She approved of the image staring back at her from her wardrobe mirror. She took a big breath and left the house. It was a fifteen-minute walk into town. Ten minutes in it started to drizzle. She hadn't thought to check the weather; hadn't thought to bring a brolly, didn't want to turn back now. By the time she got to Bright's and caught sight of her reflection, she was horrified to see her hair bouffant and frizzed by the elements. No time to worry, no time to do anything with her hair, no time whatsoever.

She saw Matt through the window chatting to customers. She steeled herself for her entrance. The wind caught the door, swinging it open too forcefully. It knocked a well-dressed man into the woman he was chatting to. Fizz splashed down the lady's immaculate green skirt suit. Kitty stood there stuttering an apology, offered some tissues from her handbag and through flaming cheeks accepted a glass of Asti from the spotty lad. He was sporting a name tag informing the world he was called Gary. Kitty noticed he was wearing an even shinier and nastier suit than the previous one. To cover her embarrassment she smiled at him. He must have thought it a cue to practise his social skills and started chatting to her in a too-loud voice, as if he owned the jewellers. Kitty was oblivious to his words. She watched the ripe spots around his mouth stretch, acutely aware that Matt was standing behind her. The well-dressed man came towards her with his hand outstretched. He introduced himself as Peter Bright, the owner. Instantly spotting the likeness, Kitty realised this must be Matt's dad. He rounded up a group of four, including Kitty, and led them out into the workshop with Matt bringing up the rear. Kitty's bum wiggled its way into the studio and joined the others gathered around a bench. Peter described how and where they sourced their stones and then turned to Matt. 'Son, show us some of your designs and talk us through to a finished piece.'

Kitty noticed Matt flash his dad a harsh look. She wondered if it might be because he was out of his comfort zone in this group situation—she hoped it was because of her proximity, but doubted it. A couple of the others asked questions. She noticed how Peter stepped in to answer them.

Moving back into the shop after the talk, Kitty chose her moment to sidle up next to Matt and say, 'That was really interesting, thank you. You obviously love your work. My name's Kitty. I'm the one from the bank. I brought my broken necklace in a fortnight ago.'

Those eyes looked into hers and he smiled warmly. 'Oh yeh, I remember you. I do enjoy my work. Don't like talking about it much though, prefer to stay behind the scenes.' He looked at her and she realised the conversation had stopped.

She was studying him, wondering if she should take a chance on him. His lips arched into a smile. The lips she wanted to kiss. She averted her eyes. 'It's your artistic temperament, I expect,' she waffled, now desperate to secure some kind of a date before she left. *It's now or never.* 'Have you tried the new café across the road yet?' she asked, hoping she didn't sound as desperate as she felt. He looked at her strangely, as if she was speaking a foreign language. She wondered if she had canapé stuck in her teeth; she'd eaten far too many.

'Um—no, but I know which one you mean. The food looks great.'

'I was wondering—if you'd—maybe like to meet for lunch one day?'

He hesitated long enough for her to think he wasn't interested. Finally, 'Yeh, could do, but when it's busy in here I don't always take an hour.'

He wasn't making this easy for her, but she found his reticence sexy, a challenge even.

'How about Wednesday, midday?' She held her breath. She settled for his wry smile and a tentative agreement. She stepped back out into the damp day without embarrassing herself any further. On the walk home, she relived the whole thing: what she'd said, what he'd said, how he'd said it. And although she was soaked to the bone she practically danced along the wet pavement. When she got back to the house Annie wanted to know the details. Kitty told her about Matt, but left out any mention of how sexy she thought he was, or how she wanted to snog his face off.

'How lovely, Kitty dear,' Annie said and relayed everything to Bert when he returned from the garden centre. They celebrated with cake which Annie made while Kitty twirled strands of hair and sat dreamily watching Bert plant nasturtiums in the back border.

On Wednesday morning during a customer lull, Kitty found herself doodling on her scrap-pad—a biro love heart on her blotting pad with both their initials inside: "KB" and "MB"; even the letters seemed right together. She told herself to stop being so bloody childish, but she couldn't help it. She composed herself as the next flurry of customers blustered through the door. Sheila caught her eye and winked.

It seemed an age before she found herself sitting opposite Matt in the designated café. Initially she thought he looked uncomfortable, but decided it was definitely his shyness as it was noisy and busy. She was secretly pleased to see that he'd arrived first and saved them a good table in the corner. They ate, they chatted and Kitty hung off of his every word like someone about to fall off a cliff. 'Gems are like friends to me. I have some real favourites like Ceruleite, Peristerite and Apatite,' he said.

'Wow! Apatite! Makes me feel hungry,' she said, and inwardly flinched at her cheesy response. She made a note to self to do some research; those words sounded glorious, and she'd use them in a poem.

All too soon the hour was up and, in her haste for a hug, Kitty lurched forward off her stool and onto Matt. He steadied her with his hands and drew her into his chest. *Those hands.* He made beautiful things out of beautiful materials with those beautiful hands. He smelled musky, like dappled forests and bracken. Walking back to the bank she pictured them lying together in the woods. Naked.

All afternoon Kitty pondered over what she now knew about Matt: he was twenty-six—four years older than her— he'd studied jewellery design at Chelsea Art College, enjoyed cooking, loved Booker T. & the M.G.'s, lived just outside of Reading in Woodley, and drove an old Escort. She smiled when he'd told her that one; Paul would have been pleased, except it didn't have red vinyl seats and Matt had looked at her strangely when she'd asked. *That's all in the past.* Matt loved ice-skating and suggested they go to the local rink. She hadn't the heart to tell him she couldn't think of anything worse—even walking on ice made her stiff like a tin soldier— but she agreed anyway because it was sort of a date and she desperately wanted to spend more time with him.

The ice-rink was busy. Kitty clung to the barrier taking sideways steps around the perimeter while Matt whizzed past, overtaking anyone in his path. He spiralled in the smallest of spaces. Kitty watched him, thrilled. Couples were laughing, holding hands, skating together to "You're The One That I Want". She willed herself to take that one step away from the edge but it terrified her. Matt beckoned to her. She held up a hand in a frivolous wave as if to say she was fine—quite happy clutching the barrier like she was going to die. Then over he came, took both of her hands in his and gently pulled her into the rink. She juddered along like a novice driver not yet familiar with biting point. He created a space around them so it no longer felt as if other skaters were aiming at her. She unclenched her body a little. Just enough, in fact, before her skates slid from beneath her. Down she went like a sack of bricks. Dying with embarrassment, she tried to push herself up onto her knees but could only do this by sticking her bum out. She could feel the damp mark on her jeans from the ice. He probably thought she'd wet herself, but she wasn't sure she hadn't. She struggled for a few more seconds until he reached over and gently pulled her up. Both spotted the drips of blood on the ice.

'Are you hurt, Kitty?'

'No, it's nothing,' she said as she clung on to him, and they headed for the exit.

On the drive back to Kitty's, once her hysteria subsided she asked Matt about his love of skating.

'My mum first took me when I was about five,' he answered, looking at the road ahead. 'I go there to chill.'

'What—literally?' Kitty watched him eventually get the joke; when he did, he turned and grinned at her. *Such a handsome face.* He pulled up outside her place, held her hand up to kiss the finger she'd sliced with her own skate, and promised to see her again soon. Kitty floated out of the car, into the house and into bed, impatient to dream about him.

Their first proper kiss was magic. It was in the park with an impromptu picnic of pasties and cream slices. When the food and the conversation came to an end they just sat in silence looking at each other. She savoured the inevitability. When her lips magnetised to his she tasted passion and promise.

After that, Kitty and Matt met regularly. She found in him an empathy she hadn't known in anyone else. She'd worried that her baggage might frighten him off, but Matt seemed impressed at her resilience. She told him everything, not just the edited highlights. It came out in one big gush: Paul, all the Tom stuff, and Amy. Especially Amy.

'I—have a—daughter.' She screwed her eyes shut and waited for the rebuff.

'Wow! How old is she?' he said with genuine interest. Kitty explained she'd be four but had been adopted. He held her hand and listened with tenderness in his eyes.

'I can't have any more. I—got ill when I had Amy and had to have a hysterectomy.' Fat blobs of her tears rolled down her cotton top. Matt sidled over and pulled her to him with his outstretched arm and held her tightly. She gulped mouthfuls of air, panicking this was just the sympathy vote. *He's not getting the subtext*, she thought. She was desperate to know if a childless union was a deal breaker. She looked up into Matt's face for a flicker of hope.

'Never had the urge to have kids. Too cruel a world to bring them in to.' Kitty couldn't believe her luck. She snuggled into his neck and told him she loved him. He held her tightly and said he would be the man she needed him to be; would be there to support and love her through everything. She'd found a keeper. Her heart sang.

NINE

Admiring glances confirmed that Kitty and Matt made a handsome couple as they walked hand in hand. Kitty loved it, loved that she'd found Matt. It was Kitty who hastened their nakedness. Matt's skin was so pale and smooth like suede, but he seemed awkward, inexperienced, Kitty thought—like her. Her one experience still made her wince, and worst of all, she was still paying the price for her stupidity. Sex with Matt was comfortable and loving and she felt he gave her exactly what she needed, what she'd *always* needed—he wrapped her in a blanket of stability.

After they moved in together, Matt brought home posies of sweet peas, or her favourite peonies—remembering her likes and dislikes. She often woke early just to look at him, taking in every detail of his beautiful face: that sexy mouth with dimples like inverted commas either side; his mass of hair the colour of hay—she'd come up trumps. He told her she was beautiful until she believed him. He said her smile lit up her face and lit up his life. He called her "Kit" after he heard the "Whole Kit and Caboodle" saying. He said Kit suited her. 'That's what you are—the whole deal down to the last kitten, my very own kitten,' he whispered to her in bed one night. She purred into his neck but didn't tell him that someone else called her that name once.

Matt knew everything about Kitty; she'd told him all there was to know. They'd shared their stories and found common ground on which to build a future. She'd found the love she'd been longing for, treasured it with all of her heart, showered Matt with the affection and adoration that had remained dormant since she'd handed Amy over. Their future was like opening a new book—all that hope and possibility. She found his kindness and thoughtfulness endearing, making him easy to love. She sighed in his presence. Her heart lifted when she heard his key in the door.

Romeo and Juliet? Maybe, maybe not. They had their differences. Their first was over where they would live together. Matt favoured the more bohemian side of town while Kitty preferred upmarket cul-de-sacs rubbing alongside middle-aged couples whose broods had left the nest and were now enjoying life with fewer stresses. She couldn't cope with lots of children constantly around.

They eventually compromised with a Victorian semi in a tree-lined avenue that housed everyone from a semi-professional musician with an interesting succession of girlfriends, to a couple who opened their home as a spiritual centre to anyone who could afford the extortionate fees in a quest to *find themselves*. Gardens came alive each morning to the buzz of birdsong, replaced in the afternoon with the hum of mowers, the shrill of strimmers carving out perfection and the satisfying smell of fresh-cut grass.

The second Kitty saw the house she wanted it. It was love at first sight. It had an air of neglect about it. Russian ivy dripped over the doorway, red and orange with summer. There were rusty patches on the railings where the black paint had flaked away. The spots of rot on the elegant sash windows seemed to look at her pleadingly; curlicue trims drew her towards the front door as the wild lavender stroked her legs. An apple tree sat in the overgrown garden in the back, the branches weighed down by fat green beauties, and plums hung like Christmas decorations above dense brambles in the corner. She *had* to have this place. Matt agreed it was a good one. She dragged Annie and Bert over to see it; they loved it too and insisted on helping with the deposit.

Matt sold his place and moved his belongings in without taking up much space. Kitty had been shocked when she'd first visited him in Woodley; it had been so sparse— minimalist in the extreme. Few books, no photos, his prized skates. She was amazed that someone could live so simply and decided he was just very self-contained, very tidy. A huge removals van arrived with Kitty's belongings; she wondered what on earth could be in it. Bert pulled up behind and beckoned her over as the removals men opened the back doors.

'Annie and I thought you might need a few things. Don't worry, it's not our taste!' he chuckled. 'On your shopping trips with Annie she made a note of things you said you liked—we just bought a few, nothing much really.' And Kitty's mouth fell open as she watched a succession of beautiful shabby chic pieces of furniture bob their way into her new home: two matching dressers, a dining room table with four matching chairs and, most excitingly, a red leather three-piece suite. Kitty hugged her uncle until he cried out for air.

Kitty and Matt differed over décor which led to DIY stand-offs lasting far too long. Kitty liked colour while Matt preferred clean white spaces. They agreed to allocated walls. Matt visibly flinched at Kitty's brash choices, while she stifled mock yawns at his expanses of blandness. His earnest pedantry at getting the lines between white emulsion and white gloss just so drove her to mockery, but secretly she found it endearing; she loved that he cared about attention to detail. Occasionally his inflexible need for order bleached out Kitty's freer side, which she found odd; he was the arty type. Although she needed stability she also craved spontaneity now and again. The more she thought about it the more she thought they could work through it in a love conquers all kind of way.

They clashed over holiday destinations too. Matt wanted to camp in damp Devon fields while she wanted salsa, sangria, sightseeing. They ended up doing a bit of both—meeting their differences somewhere in the middle. She teased him about his packing. He covered for every contingency: a waterproof; two jumpers for chilly evenings; a Swiss Army knife for any eventuality. And the performance of the suitcase weigh-in! He weighed their luggage several times until he felt the device wasn't lying. Returning home from holidays he'd systematically unpack everything—half his suitcase unused. It made Kitty chuckle.

Eventually they discovered a mutual love of foreign holidays. They sipped rioja on balmy balconies and terraces, they talked about unimportant things until the stunning sunsets silenced their words. They languished next to hotel pools and watched swifts swoop low; they lay on beaches browning their bodies, dozing to the sound of the rhythmic waves, content to do nothing. On dismal days back at home Kitty would imitate the fruit seller with cries of *pineappp-le, coconu-ut, baa-naana* and they'd smile at the shared memory of the jolly fruit man as he'd heaved his heavy basket across the sand. They collected mementoes: shells from yellow beaches, prints capturing freedom from routine and memories of serene hours spent together lazily entwined and oblivious to anyone else.

There was a single sticking point and each time the subject was raised, it went like this: 'Kit. Why won't you contact the authorities and find out where your daughter is?'

'How many times do we have to go over this, Matt? I've told you. I've no intention of turning Amy's life upside down now—I've caused enough damage.' And the rest of the conversation she'd finish in her head—*and I don't need anyone's advice on the matter. Thank you.* Matt knew she kept an old suitcase in the wardrobe and sobbed on certain dates; he'd first seen her through the crack of the door, then held her in his arms as she'd cried.

They bore their childlessness bravely, showed a united front, saying they were unable. It was the truth, after all. Friends and acquaintances looked at them inquisitively but neither offered any further information. *I already have a child,* screamed inside Kitty's head, *her name's Amy!* They steered clear of playgrounds with chubby toddlers squealing with glee on swings and slides.

From the start Matt made it clear he didn't want to get married, saying he hadn't been impressed with his parents' marriage; they'd set a bad example. Kitty wasn't okay with this although she certainly understood the parent bit. She secretly hoped he'd change his mind one day and they'd be together *until death us do part*. She'd already seen the ring she liked in Bright's. It was one of Matt's creations. She cooed over it each time she visited the shop. 'If I was ever to get engaged, that's the ring of my dreams,' she'd say and look at Matt hopefully.

It became apparent to Kitty that Matt was a bit of a loner before they met as most of their friends were her friends to start with. They socialised with Jane and Andy Barker the most—Andy worked at the same bank as Kitty and they'd hit it off on a course they'd attended when Kitty first started her job. He and Jane had married two years before Kitty and Matt got together. Kitty thought he was a great guy. One of those people who would do anything for you if you asked, but also good fun. He overstepped the mark once by tipsily kissing her at their work's Christmas party but had apologised profusely once they returned to work after the holiday.

Kitty found Jane a bit obsessional about her appearance. She looked like Claudia Schiffer on a good day and Olivia Newton-John on a bad one, which to Kitty's mind was a brilliant state to be in—she'd have given her right arm to be *that* pretty. Jane moaned about the way she looked even though she had the loveliest face, and eyelashes that could swat flies. Kitty and Matt discussed this and decided that Andy couldn't have been giving his wife enough attention. Kitty thought she had plenty of attention from Matt; he told her daily he loved her and regularly complimented her. She wondered if Jane secretly fancied Matt. She'd spotted her playing footsie with him and playfully touching his knee when Andy was out of the room. It didn't really bother Kitty, instead she felt a sense of pride that other women found her partner attractive; she knew she could trust him. She also spotted Matt's glowing pink cheeks, not from the wine like the rest of them—because he hardly drank—but from embarrassment. She sometimes got the feeling he tolerated their social life for her sake; he enjoyed the cooking and preferred staying behind the scenes in the kitchen saying he was happiest there, creating.

The couples met up about once a month at one another's place and enjoyed a combined effort of a meal put together by the two men who fancied themselves as chefs; Matt's mum had taught him to cook and he was always looking up recipes. He followed them to the letter which drove Andy to distraction, who'd tell him to *just chuck everything in, mate*, especially when he'd had a few drinks. Matt would take the ribbing from him as they were all friends. Kitty tried persuading Matt to meet up with Andy for drinks occasionally but her words seemed to land on deaf ears.

Kitty and Gill picked up where they'd left off once they ended up living a mere few miles from each other. Gill's career path had taken an interesting twist when she told Kitty one day that she'd secured a job working for Magnate Airlines as an air hostess.

'A *trolley-dolly? You?*' Kitty said, tongue in cheek.

Gill actually worked for a private airline that demanded top-notch multi-lingual staff. Gill fitted the bill perfectly and Kitty was pleased for her. It gave her friend the opportunity of worldwide travel and a constant stream of lovers. She'd been a late starter but boy, she'd made up for it.

When Kitty first introduced Gill to Matt she sensed a tension, a bit like two cats circling each other and you're just not sure how it's going to pan out—friends or foe. Keen for her friend's approval, Kitty phoned Gill afterwards for feedback.

'You love him?' Gill had asked. Kitty hesitated at her friend's directness, but then had replied she did, he was a good fit and one day she'd like them to be married.

'He's alright—but marriage, why?' Gill replied, but Kitty knew she was holding back. Gill started to say something else but stopped. Kitty knew her friend would prefer her to be with someone more adventurous, someone who at least challenged her on some level; she'd said as much before Matt came along. They'd got tipsy one evening and Gill had asked Kitty why she always settled for men who were beneath her. Kitty had called her a snob. Although they were close and had once been a lot closer, Kitty reminded her they weren't the same person, that she wasn't the same carefree girl she once was. The fact of the matter was that Matt was just what Kitty felt she needed in her life at that moment—he offered stability, and she wanted that more than anything. It meant everything to her to live in harmony with someone, no matter how cheesy it sounded, even in her own head. Existing within her parents' battlefield had made her crave the complete opposite for a very long time.

'Okay, Kat. Just remember—familiarity breeds contempt. Don't know why you need to even live with him. You'll soon get bored of his stamp collecting—or whatever he does,' Gill smirked, and Kitty raised her eyes. 'Or is it bell ringing?'

'Won't be asking you to be chief bridesmaid then!' Kitty said, only half joking.

'Absolutely not! Marriage is for losers, Kat. Just have a bloody good party.'

That evening, Kitty had asked Matt what he thought of Gill.

'Well, she thinks a lot of herself, doesn't she?' Kitty had been shocked. She'd never heard him speak like that before.

She'd mulled it over and decided that the two people who loved her the most managed to just about get on and she'd settle for that. When Gill was in the country, Matt made himself scarce, leaving them to their gin and gossiping. It worked okay.

Kitty and Matt had something else in common too. They both had uneasy relationships with their dads. She learned that Matt had left home four days after his eighteenth birthday, a fortnight after his mother, Grace, died of stomach cancer. Matt told Kitty that on her deathbed she'd asked him to look after Peter, that his father's bluster was all a front and that he wouldn't cope very well after she'd gone.

During chemo and radiotherapy, Grace's role as mediator had been more in demand than ever as the two men were thrown together for longer periods of time. Maybe Grace had hoped that with her out of the equation they might find common ground, that all those years of sullen moods and exasperation would be a distant memory. But the loss of his mother had been more than enough for Matt to cope with and his relationship with his father, such as it was, disintegrated, he admitted to Kitty. Tensions rose and father and son tried to exist in the same house but it became untenable. Peter gave Matt a lump sum to put down a deposit on somewhere decent and upped his salary to afford a mortgage while he was left to grieve in peace. It had been the only viable option for the family business to continue. The deal was that Matt continued working at the jewellers, they'd try to get along for the sake of the business, and agreed to keep one Sunday a month for lunch together. *Quality time* was how Peter put it to his son.

'My dad isn't easy to get along with either,' she told Matt during an evening on the sofa together, sipping wine.

'I got that feeling some time ago, but how come?' Matt asked.

'Well, after my brother died he was just so angry and would hit out at me and Mum. It was bloody awful. They started rowing so much—especially in Singapore where we ended up after Johnny's death. He even broke my mum's jaw once.' Kitty saw Matt's expression turn to shock.

'Bloody hell, Kit. Must have been horrible for you!'

'Yeh, it really was.' Kitty's stomach lurched at the memory. She described how she'd been trying to block out their fighting that night by playing records on her portable record player. The Monkees were on at the time, singing about that last train to Clarksville. But even their "doo doo doos" couldn't mask the almighty crash. Seconds later she'd heard her dad's car drive off. Quickly she'd pulled the needle off the record. The house was too quiet. She'd found her mum lying on the floor with blood oozing from her head onto the tiles, the coffee table on its side; cigarette butts littered the floor. The television was lying face down amongst a kaleidoscope of broken glass. Kitty hadn't known what to do first until she heard her mum mumble *amblance, amblance.* She'd raced to the phone and called for one. Terrified her mum might die, Kitty had knelt down by her and stroked her shoulder for an age until blue flashes lit up the window. Her mum had gone quiet and still. The ambulance crew had spoken kindly and told Kitty that no, she wasn't dead but she would have to go to hospital because her jaw was broken and it needed to be mended.

'Did your dad come back?' Matt asked.

She explained she'd stayed with neighbours for the next few nights until her dad had come to collect her and said her mum was home from hospital—no hint to anyone that his own fists had caused this. Kitty had been so pleased to see her mum again that she'd climbed onto her lap and hugged her. Her hair had smelled of hospital—a mix of Germolene and scabs.

'Funny what you remember, isn't it?' Matt sighed loudly. It felt good to talk about it, but Kitty knew her childhood normal was rarely the same as anyone else's. She could tell by the horror in people's eyes and the hesitation in choosing their next words for fear of damaging her further. Matt was no exception; he'd looked at her as if he didn't know her. Adept at smoothing things over, she'd said it was okay—her mum's recuperation afforded them a welcome breather, a holiday from all the fights. She was good at putting a breezy slant on her history once she sussed out she'd shared too much.

'Why didn't they split up?' Matt persisted.

'They talked of divorce once—or rather, my mum used to scream the word at my dad lots of times. When I asked her about it one day, she'd said I'd have to choose which one to live with. I immediately thought *neither*—if that was an option. Nothing came of it though and we limped on. It was hell. If I annoyed him in any way he'd slap me. Hard. There was no pleasing him. In the end it was easier to take it and hate him.' She gave a sad shrug. 'We haven't spoken in ages. Did your dad ever hit you, Matt?'

Matt looked at her thoughtfully. 'No, but he can be bloody awkward,' was all he said.

When Kitty and Matt began living together, she made sure the deal about Matt and his dad's monthly rendezvous was kept. Her relationship with her own dad was non-existent but she wanted to do all she could to help the one with Matt's. Every fourth Sunday she cooked a roast and kept the conversation buoyant during the meal. After the meal she made herself scarce. Sometimes it worked and she heard them talking, but more often than not she heard raised voices and Matt would appear in the kitchen minutes later, cold and unapproachable. There was something that jarred in Matt and Peter's relationship that Kitty just couldn't put her finger on.

Kitty liked Peter. His work ethic was something else and, unlike her own dad, he seemed to take the initiative in trying to sort things out between him and his son. At least he was aware there was a problem. He paid Matt an excellent wage, was extremely generous towards the couple, could be relied upon in a crisis. When Matt's old Escort died, it was Peter who stepped in with a replacement the very next day, without a second thought. It was just frustrating for Kitty that she had to jump through hoops in persuading Matt of the fact he had a great dad.

After Peter's visits Kitty always ended up thinking about her own dad. Their relationship had worsened on his return to England. At first he wouldn't talk to her and had put the phone down before she'd finished her opening line, leaving her hanging. She discussed it with Gill, who, in a hesitant moment said, 'This may sound harsh, Kat—but do you actually need him in your life? Ask yourself that.' Kitty had given it much thought. She knew she still felt very angry towards him, but she needed to hear remorse over his abysmal treatment of her and her mum. After talking it through with Matt she decided she had nothing to lose.

She presented herself at his house in Devon. She just pulled up outside, walked up the path with her heart pounding furiously and pressed the doorbell. She was taken aback by the general shabbiness of the place; it was the worst one of the terrace. It was a while before he answered but she knew he was in, had noticed the curtain move upstairs and for a minute she wondered if he'd leave her standing there. And there he was, looking gaunt, tired and a lot older than the last time she saw him at her mum's funeral. He held the door open and let her through, huffing and tutting. He walked with effort. The house was grubby and smelled of mushroom soup.

'Hello, Dad. How are you?' She surprised herself with her familiarity but also couldn't ignore how clipped the question sounded or how much she'd started to shake with anger.

'How do you think?' His answer was unsurprisingly terse. She walked into the sitting room and stood with the backs of her legs against the furthest easy-chair. He came in and looked at her with his arms folded across his chest. 'What do you want, Katherine?' She met his gaze, hesitated for a second until words formed.

'I want us to talk.'

'About what? How you brought shame on our family? How you went with a married man and didn't think twice what it would do to your mum and me?'

Kitty ignored the urge to leave and slam the door violently behind her—she wanted answers and she was no longer afraid of him. He'd been a bully and she had things to say. 'I'm well aware what happened, Dad. You made our lives bloody hell!'

Bobby clutched the back of the sofa. He looked down at his feet; his knuckles turned white and his jaw clenched.

Kitty continued. 'I hated you after Johnny died. What gave you the right to even lay a finger on me—or mum? How *bloody dare you* treat us like that? You should have found help for Mum and—*and*—'her words were hot and furious—'I was nine, just *nine* when Johnny died and you left me to my own devices. Who does that? I died inside too when I lost my brother but you were the adults, the bloody parents, and you left me! Was it any surprise I got into trouble? *Really?* And even at the end did you ever once think to help me, support me rather than shunting me off to that hell-hole nunnery and handing my child, *your grandchild* over to bloody strangers? No! *You fucking bastard!* You had all the choices and I had none. *How fucking dare you!'* Kitty drew breath and looked at him defiantly. He looked back at her with a furious expression. If she'd sworn at him like that in the past she'd now be cradling a throbbing head. 'Go on, then! Hit me! Only *this* time I'll fucking retaliate and you'll need an ambulance, just like Mum did when you broke her jaw!'

He walked out of the room and into the kitchen.

'Yeh, *walk away!'* She was shaking with fury; her skin felt like it might rip apart. Resting her hands on her temples, she could feel her blood battering through her body. She heard him clattering cups and saucers. She closed her eyes until the red mist lifted. She glanced over at the front door again. Too easy to walk out and just forget this whole sorry mess. She continued standing there, mulling over what to do next. She breathed out, unclenched her fists and went to find him.

He was holding onto the sink, staring out of the window and quietly crying. His side profile was a map of lines in the afternoon rays and a nerve in his cheek twitched. He heard her come in and for a second she saw his jaw attempt to set into its stubborn, jutting way but it wobbled and hung beneath his trembling lips. For all of his anger and for all of those horrible years, not once had Kitty ever seen him cry. It stopped her in her tracks. He composed himself, looked up at the ceiling as if formulating words and went back into the sitting room.

They each took a seat. Kitty noticed how stuffy the room was and longed to open a window but didn't want to spoil this moment. She could tell her dad was struggling for words.

'You should *never* have had to go through what you did, Kitty. It's all my fault.'

She saw the pain etched on his face, heard the agony in his voice and let him continue.

'You're right. We *did* neglect you, me and your mum. I couldn't forgive her, you see—'

Kitty pursed her lips and wondered where this was going.

'He wasn't—mine—you know. Johnny. Johnny wasn't—my son. She told me the day after his funeral. I'd no idea. I loved him like my own—I worried deeply when he started mixing with the wrong crowd of boys. I, I—wanted—my son to have a good future.' He couldn't stop sobbing now. Kitty reached over and took his hand in hers; it felt cold and bony. His rheumy, sad eyes looked into hers as he practically whispered, 'Did you know any of this, Kitty?'

After a long pause she admitted, 'Annie told me after Mum died.' He put his head in his hands. It seemed an age before he lifted his head up. Kitty stayed quiet and still. There was snot on his top lip and his eyes were bloodshot. 'I made life hell for everyone from then on. I know I did. I was *so* angry. Your mum's drinking was spiralling out of control in Singapore. I thought going there would have eased the pain of losing Johnny—fresh start, but the heat and the unfamiliarity of everything just made it worse. It sounds pathetic, but I was too ashamed to get any help—if my work knew about Mum's problem they'd have sent us all back to the UK. I didn't want that either.' He studied his hands and looked at Kitty pleadingly, a tear rolling off his nose. 'By the time you hit your teens you were becoming wayward—your mum said a lad was sniffing around in Scarborough. We took the posting to Hong Kong thinking it was for the best—and the worst happened. When you fell pregnant—it was like you were your mum. You were carrying—a bastard. It was happening all over again. I couldn't—I just couldn't have a baby in the house, it would have reminded me every day of Johnny. I just couldn't do it. Your mum begged me to let you stay. God rest her soul.' He looked so miserable, like he had nowhere to hide and nothing left to give. *'Please forgive me, Kitty,'* he rasped.

Kitty could clearly see her dad was a broken man. The giant of a father she'd once had was now a slight and fractured shadow of his former self. She knew there was nothing to be gained from perpetuating this. There was a long pause as she chewed over the right thing to say.

'Dad. I won't lie, it *was* awful and I bloody hated you.' Her dad's expression didn't flicker as she continued. 'But bad things happen. We've lost half our family but we're still here. We've got—each other,' were the words that came out of her mouth, and the ones she never thought she'd hear herself saying. They held each other in a tight embrace.

Kitty made them a sandwich and they talked some more. She told him all about Amy and showed him the one photo of her, his granddaughter. He clutched it like it was precious and fragile. More tears slid down his cheek. She filled him in on Annie, Bert and Matt. She stayed with him until after darkness had fallen, until finally his sobs subsided, until she thought it was safe to leave him on his own. It felt as if a huge weight had been lifted and it gave her plenty to think about on the drive home. Before she'd started this trip she'd known it could have gone one of two ways. She pulled in and looked in the rear-view mirror once she'd rounded the corner. Her face looked like it'd been in a fight, red and puffy, but a thankful smile danced around her lips.

By the time Kitty and Matt had gone to bed, she'd told him everything and felt so relieved at having taken a chance on seeing her dad. She thanked Matt for giving her that final push; it was what she'd needed. She felt they could now start to make up for the time they'd wasted.

Her dad visited them at their house and Kitty was pleased at how they were with one another; she was amazed at how far they'd come. He met Peter. They all had a meal out and the two dads would meet up for a drink whenever Bobby came to town and Kitty and Matt were busy. Kitty felt a warm glow inside as it added another facet to their lives which had been sadly missing.

One Saturday Kitty and her dad went on a mission to *try and put things right* (his words). It was Rose's birthday and they decided to pay their respects. Her dad hadn't visited the cemetery since Johnny's funeral. The last time Kitty had been was to leave her mum's ashes. She'd intended to return regularly, but hadn't.

She drove them through the gates of Horton Cemetery, past looming stone angels guarding crumbling headstones with faded names, and the deliberate light-hearted chatter of the journey stopped. The mood became sombre; the scent of the flowers in the back suddenly became pungent and heady.

From the corner of her eye Kitty saw her dad's shoulders rise and fall but kept looking straight ahead to the visitor's carpark. As she turned off the ignition, her dad's crying seemed too loud in the silence. She began to wonder if this had been such a good idea after all. She could feel her own emotions rising as fat tears filled her eyes and her stomach somersaulted. Taking a big breath, she reached over and patted her dad's bony knee beneath his best twill trousers then retrieved tissues from her handbag. They blew noisily into them and exchanged tearful smiles.

'Come on, Dad,' Kitty said as she grabbed the two bunches of lilies on the back seat.

They walked arm in arm towards the garden of remembrance, down the path lined with sentry-like yew trees as "For Those in Peril on the Sea" drifted eerily on the breeze. Gardeners were out in full force in the landscaped gardens and the smell of freshly mown grass hung in the air. Kitty tried not to stare as a dark crocodile of mourners filed into the chapel behind a small white coffin draped with white roses, accompanied by the mournful beckoning of the pipe organ. She saw the couple at the front holding each other up as their nightmare continued to its finale. The hearse drove silently to the back entrance to lay out the floral tributes and teddies that hugged the tiny casket.

Kitty and her dad stood in front of Rose's plaque; it had taken ages to find it. So many names and so many dates, but they found it just before Kitty was about to go and ask at the Enquiries Office next to the chapel. When she read "Rose Ivy Black" it felt as if someone had punched her in the stomach. Images of her mum in her checked apron, tucking her in at bedtime, waiting for her and Johnny at their gate filled her mind. When they became unpleasant—of the drunken mum she'd rather forget—she turned and looked over to the far corner where a lone yew tree stood, where Johnny's grave was. Half their family was here, she realised. She felt overwhelmingly sad but tried with all of her might to hold it together for her dad who seemed to dissolve into tears every few minutes.

Kitty handed one bunch of flowers to her dad who placed them in a line of vases beneath the wall. They looked elegant next to wilted chrysanthemums, bald roses and plastic windmills. They stood back not saying a word until her dad started talking, but not to her. She left him to it and walked slowly across the grass to the chapel. A man with sad red-rimmed eyes held the door open for her, then left. She was alone as she read the open pages of the book of remembrance. She found her mum's name; the exactness of the calligraphy was mesmerising. "He Wishes For The Cloths of Heaven"— Kitty's favourite poem—looked so elegant, so right with its swirly curlicues. Her mum was gone but Kitty's gift to her was encapsulated in every word of these tender lines.

She walked out into the cemetery and saw only sadness in the rows and rows of the resting dead. She stepped aside as a frail man approached and as he drew closer she realised it was her own dad. She showed him the book of remembrance and stood next to him as his tears dripped onto the glass case.

They linked arms and went over to Johnny's grave where they placed the remaining lilies in the vase in front of her brother's headstone. They stood there with their own thoughts until Kitty could bear it no longer; her head was dizzy with grief.

'See you back at the car, Dad,' she whispered and stiffly strode back to the carpark, putting one foot in front of the other. Once inside the car she leant back against the headrest. She closed her eyes in the hope her thoughts might stop racing, but they didn't. Image after image of her mum lying on the floor with her jaw broken; Johnny in that hospital bed, dying a little more with each bleep; and her cradling a rattling head after yet another blow from her dad. She realised she'd underestimated the emotional toll this trip would have on *her*, let alone her dad, who she spotted in the rear-view mirror reluctantly heading back to the car. He climbed into the passenger seat without saying a word. She noticed his hands shaking as he clasped them in his lap.

They drove back in silence. By the time they were sipping tea in his sitting room, he seemed calmer, more at peace with himself, and Kitty's mind had stilled. They recapped the events of the day, how well the plaque and headstone were bearing up, how well tended the cemetery was and how right it was they'd gone together.

Soon it was Christmas. Kitty took the brave or reckless step (she couldn't work out which) of inviting her dad, Matt's dad plus Annie and Bert over. She planned for weeks; it took over her every thought until her work colleagues were finding forgiveness hard for any more of her silly mistakes and more lock-ins. When Helen sniped she was running out of valuable shopping time for her family, Kitty knew she had to focus and stop her incessant chatter about decorations for the tree and matching napkin rings.

The house was fit for a magazine spread with a drinks cabinet worthy of a five-star hotel and enough luxury foodstuffs to feed their avenue. Initially it was tense between her dad and Annie. Kitty made it her mission to keep drinks topped up, and diffuse any potential aggro. She'd previously asked Matt to monitor conversations while she was preparing the meal, but it proved too much for him. He slunk into the kitchen with a sheepish look on his face and assumed the role of chef, gently pushing Kitty out the door and back into the minefield.

The cracker-pulling, the silly riddles and jaunty paper hats all helped to make their Christmas a memorable one. They were all like kids when the Quality Street tin was handed round; gasps of delight at all the brightly wrapped sweets and that unctuous smell guaranteed to make your mouth water. Bobby made a big song and dance removing a penny toffee from his denture; Annie smiled conspiratorially as she poked at a chunk of hazelnut under her bridge.

When they'd all left and her dad had climbed the stairs to the spare room humming "Deck the Halls", Kitty clutched her mulled wine to her chest and exhaled a relieved sigh. The day had been a success. All her planning, stressing and organising had been worth it in the end. There'd been a sticky moment when her dad had got a bit too gung-ho about Margaret Thatcher during the Queen's speech, but Kitty had given him a look which had silenced him, leaving a weak smile on his face. Peter and Annie had hit it off immediately, which was great, because when the effects of too much whiskey hit him, Annie had been a captive audience hearing all about his wonderful Grace.

Matt came in from the kitchen and kissed her on the cheek. 'Well done, love.' They snuggled on the sofa and he told Kitty that while she'd been out in the kitchen, Bobby had said he liked the way Matt spoke to Kitty, he liked his gentle ways. He said she deserved only kindness and made Matt promise he would look after her and never let her down like he once had. Kitty's heart swelled when she heard this. She told Matt she hoped one day he and Peter would enjoy one another's company just like her and her dad were now able to.

Before her next planned visit to her dad, he phoned and cagily asked if she had any recipe books. 'Of course,' she told him. He asked her to bring some with her. She was intrigued by his request and finally got out of him that he wanted to try and make the spaghetti bolognese and lemon meringue pie her mum used to make. They'd all loved these, and especially Johnny. Kitty promised to bring the ingredients and make the dishes with him.

'Don't tell anyone though, will you, Kitty?'

'Not if you don't want me to, Dad.'

'I wouldn't want anyone thinking I'm a poof or anything.'

TEN

Kitty loved working at the bank and felt confident and at home being there. Customers would call in—not to change any of their personal details—but to tell her their beloved pooch had been put down or to hand over bags of harvested fruit from their gardens. The hulking great Securicor guard who did a bullion pick-up twice a week always winked at her and, if she wasn't behind the desk, asked of her whereabouts. She was liked by staff and customers; it gave her a real sense of belonging.

She'd attended every training course Mrs Brown had sent her letters about. Kitty liked being at Head Office too. Mrs Brown always greeted her warmly and asked how she was. There was only one course Kitty couldn't make; she'd had a heavy cold, but she'd phoned Head Office to explain. A fortnight later she was serving a customer on the Enquiries Desk when she spotted the Head of HR swish through the lobby. Within the hour Kitty was summoned to the Manager's office which panicked her. She'd only been in the Manager's office once and the last time Mrs Brown visited, Dave had been dismissed for *inappropriate behaviour* (feeling another girl up behind the Kardex who'd taken it further, unlike Kitty).

'Kitty, hello!' Mrs Brown offered her outstretched hand and smiled warmly, her eye still and unblinking. 'Please take a seat,' she said as she took up the manager's chair, who was on another exotic holiday. Kitty swallowed loudly and watched as Mrs Brown studied an opened folder.

'Now then, Kitty. You've been here a while now, how do you feel you're getting on?'

'I love it here,' Kitty said in a barely audible rasp, fearing her job was about to be snatched away as this was no planned appraisal.

'Yes, yes—it shows and your appraisals have all been excellent. How have you felt about the temporary responsibility of First Cashier?'

'Hmmm—I love it but I know I've caused a few lock-ins,' she gabbled.

'No more than anyone else, my dear.' Mrs Brown turned over a page from inside the folder. 'So the idea of being permanent number one cashier here at this branch doesn't send you running from the building? No desire to move elsewhere?' Mrs Brown smiled her jolly smile and blinked her good eye. Kitty let out a surprised squeak, shuffled in her seat to compose herself and said, 'I'd love it. I love it here.'

'Good, good! Consider the job yours from the first of next month.'

Kitty's grin spread from ear to ear. '*Oh my god!* Thank you, thank you, Mrs Brown! You won't regret this!'

'I haven't regretted a day since you started, my dear. You are a credit to National Westminster Bank—long may it continue.' She stood, shook Kitty's hand and held the door open. 'Now get back to that queue of customers and I'll get the formal documents in the post.' Kitty practically danced along the corridor to the bank hall as she absorbed the good news.

As well as the promotion, Kitty was looking forward to celebrating her and Matt's tenth anniversary of living together. She hoped he'd ask her to marry him; he'd been secretive lately. She watched his face closely when they agreed to a meal at their favourite restaurant, but she must have caught him at a bad time as he was looking weary and was a bit curt with her. She knew the extra hours were too much for him and wished Peter would organise some cover soon.

They met after work at Antonio's. Kitty arrived first wearing a black dress, heels and new matching underwear. She wiggled as she walked; she felt the business. Everything was going right—the promotion, the house was looking fantastic and she loved Matt with all of her heart. They seemed to work so well together, barely ever rowed and had an excellent quality of life. She still hoped he might be hiding a ring, *the* ring. She'd tingled with excitement for weeks just thinking about it. She wondered if his shortness with her recently was just a double bluff, but wasn't absolutely convinced he was capable of such deception. She'd called Gill in the hope that, despite her and Matt not being best buddies, he might have involved her in something as big as an engagement. However, the moment was a little spoilt when Gill asked how "Miserable Matt" was. Kitty tried to ignored it.

'What's the celebration?' she'd asked Kitty, and Kitty knew she wasn't pretending—could tell instantly. She couldn't blame Gill for forgetting the anniversary, she was barely on terra-firma much these days; her job was so full-on. So Kitty didn't let that dampen her spirits; she realised it was actually a step too far for Matt to include Gill in anything.

'Our tenth anniversary of living together.'

'Oh yeh, I remember now—was just polishing the medal I was going to give you,' Gill chortled.

'Well, familiarity hardly bred contempt, did it, Gill?' Kitty asked sarcastically.

'Only joking!'

Kitty couldn't bring herself to mention her hope of an engagement, didn't want to cope with a sarcastic retort, but Gill gushed about Kitty's promotion and said they'd go out together to celebrate.

Kitty phoned her dad the same day and told him what she was hoping for. He'd gone quiet and then asked if Matt was *the one.* She'd laughed and said yes, he made her very happy. Her dad said she was lucky, he seemed a good chap, *bit quiet* but if that's how she felt, she should hold onto someone so precious, ending with, 'But most of all, Kitty, you must take care of yourself. Never forget that.'

Kitty sat at their table in the restaurant sipping water and watching the door. Matt finally appeared but wearing his work clothes—jeans, grey polo shirt, grubby boots—and looking flustered. Kitty was surprised at this; he usually took such care with his appearance. She could see he'd lost weight; she hadn't noticed this before. He repeatedly hoisted his jeans up by the belt.

'Sorry, Kit. Work was manic—didn't get chance to change.' He pointed towards his grubby shirt, then hid his dirty nails in his palms, and sat down sheepishly. Kitty reached out for his hand across the table and gently stroked the fine cuts on his fingers made by his jewellers' tools. While they waited for their drinks to arrive she pulled out a card from her handbag. She handed it to him, impatient for him to open it, having scoured so many card shops for just the right one. It was exquisite, with hearts, doves and ribbon. She'd lovingly written one of her own poems in turquoise ink. Inside, there were two tickets for a weekend in Paris, staying at a top hotel, no expense spared. Matt hesitated as he read the words, then handed her a smaller card from within his inside jacket pocket. His expression was apologetic. *He's playing with me*, she thought, *any minute now he's going to burst out laughing and show me the ring.* She studied the card. It had a picture of yellow roses on the front and inside the printed words told her he was glad to have found someone as special as her.

'I was going to get you some flowers—but the shop was shut by the time I left work. Sorry, Kit.'

Kitty couldn't remember the last time he'd bought her flowers but didn't dwell on it, still holding out for the "surprise". The prosecco arrived. They watched the ritual uncorking, the pop and fizz, the flourished pour. The waiter looked from one to the other and Kitty beamed back at him. Matt fiddled with his napkin. Kitty thought he was nervous about the job in hand—a proposal. He was not one for public demonstrations of affection. She decided she wouldn't prolong his agony once it was out there, that was for sure. The waiter left. They clinked glasses and wished each other a happy anniversary.

Their starters arrived. Kitty looked to see if the ring was hiding beneath the garnish decorating the three scallops resting on pillowy mounds of pea puree. It wasn't, but she chewed each mouthful carefully, just in case. She realised that she'd been smiling for so long her face was aching. Matt was shovelling in pâté, oblivious to anything going on around him. She took her growing disappointment to the ladies' after the first course and gave herself a talking to; *plenty of time yet!* Matt was sliding his mobile phone into his inside jacket pocket hanging on his chair as she returned to their table. He smiled at her and reached for her hand but fumbled, nearly knocking her glass over. She caught it before it toppled and checked to make sure the ring wasn't drowning in the bottom. It wasn't. Her favourite spaghetti vongole arrived. She discreetly prised wide each clam shell. Nothing. She watched as Matt twirled and stuffed in his spaghetti bolognese like he hadn't eaten for a week; sauce splattered his chin. She moved her food around her plate with the stylish silver fork, barely eating.

When he'd finished his dish, Matt looked at her pleadingly and she pushed her plate towards him. He finished that too, then slid her cleared plate back across the table; the empty shells laughed at her. He hardly said a word. She asked him if he was okay. He replied he'd been battling a headache all day and really couldn't manage a pudding. And then it finally dawned on her. She realised there was no ring, no proposal and no bloody dessert. She tried to block out the happy laughter coming from couples at tables all around them. She stared at the sauce stain next to her placemat; it looked like a splodge of blood on the pristine tablecloth. The waiter cleared their table and mimicked a sad face when they refused dessert and coffee, but gave Kitty a knowing wink. Matt paid the bill and they left.

When they arrived home, Kitty noticed the landline blinking red. She listened to three voicemails from Annie asking her to call urgently. She'd left her mobile off in the restaurant; she hadn't wanted to spoil what she'd hoped was going to be a romantic evening. She worried something might have happened to Bert. She turned it on and saw four missed calls. Just as she was about to call Annie on the landline, the phone shrilled into life, making her jump.

'Kitty? Is Matt there with you?' Annie sounded breathless.

'Yes, hi Annie. What's up?'

Her aunt's voice now concerned her. It sounded different, over-emotional, fractured. 'I'm sorry Kitty—but there's some—really bad news I have to tell you.'

Kitty steeled herself. 'Go on, Annie. Please.'

'Your dad's had an accident. I'm afraid he—he's—*dead*. I'm so *sorry*, dear.'

Annie's words hung in the stillness of the room. Matt appeared when he heard the phone hit the desk. Kitty had her hands over her ears, her body still, her mouth trembling. He picked up the phone, spoke for a few minutes and then replaced it in its cradle. He turned to Kitty and clenched her to him which muffled her sobs.

'Kit. I know this is hard to take in—but I'm here for you. We'll get through this, love.'

She looked up at him, wanting to believe him. Hot salty tears trailed down her face and into her mouth. She felt so lost.

'I need you to be strong. Suicide is awful. I'm *so* sorry.'

Kitty was stunned. Her body stiffened. Annie hadn't mentioned that word. Kitty had pictured her dad falling off his push-bike and cracking his head as he already had several times after resolutely refusing to wear a helmet. *Stubborn bugger*, she'd thought at the time. She'd pictured him stepping into the path of a car—distracted by the shopping list he'd inevitably forget once he entered the supermarket, and would rush back to the car to retrieve. She'd thought of him falling off a ladder as he cleared leaves from the guttering, too tight to pay for a handyman to do the job, and his back giving out. Those were *accidents.* Annie said it had been an *accident.* Suicide wasn't an accident; it was an intentional act. Her thoughts raced. She'd only spoken to her dad days previously about the anniversary meal. He'd seemed fine. What had happened in those intervening days? She tried hard to make sense of something that made absolutely none whatsoever.

Matt left it until the morning before breaking it to Kitty the details of her dad's death: that he'd hanged himself from his loft in the early hours of the previous morning. She couldn't take it in, not after they'd made peace with each other, not after everything. They all should have been celebrating her and Matt's engagement, but there was no engagement to celebrate, and Matt was making arrangements on the phone for her to see her dead dad.

Bert had given Matt the details: Bobby had left a note addressed to the police before he killed himself. He knew the Meals on Wheels lady would be delivering the next day— she'd found the note and called the police straight away. His body was taken to the police mortuary.

Climbing the steps into the Police HQ was surreal. Kitty had to keep reminding herself to breathe; she was on autopilot. She had tired, bloodshot eyes after restless sleep and her head pounded. Matt hesitated to hold her hand. She wasn't sure if she wanted Matt to hold her hand; she felt as if she was inside a bubble. He did in the end but let it go again to talk to the overly jocular desk sergeant. When Matt announced who they were, the policeman became sombre.

A young female officer appeared and led them down into the bowels of the building. They passed through brightly glossed corridors with posters urging everyone to beware of thieves and pickpockets. Down a flight of stairs they went, where the décor became stark and clinical, the atmosphere very still and noticeably colder. Kitty grabbed Matt's hand tightly and breathed deeply. The officer stopped in front of a metal door declaring "MORTUARY". She saw Kitty's look of panic.

'It's okay, dear. You should go in. He just looks rested.'

Matt gently led Kitty into the room. The officer directed them to a curtained cubicle off to the left. The temperature had plummeted further and a familiar, yet unidentifiable, smell hung in the air. She racked her brain, the distraction welcome. It came to her; biology class, dead rats in jars, formaldehyde. The officer pulled the curtain back. It took Kitty a while before she could lift her gaze from the floor, she was so scared of what she might see. In the second when she did scan the recess, she saw nothing other than whiteness. She desperately clung to the hope this had all been a mistake, a nightmare from which she'd soon wake up, but Matt's sharp intake of breath forced her to look to into the far corner. The whiteness ended and her dead father's neck began. Edging slowly closer, she saw the wrinkled skin was a deep mottled purple, darker still at the Adam's apple and at a shockingly weird angle. Kitty wondered why the officer had lied. Why had she duped her into coming in here to see this horrific scene? Why had she said he looked *rested?* Her dad's handsome face was far from rested. He looked worn and defeated. A broken heart, a broken neck, a broken man. A giant slain by his own hand. Her hands covered her mouth to hold in her shocked sobs and to stem the nausea rising in her throat.

The rest was a blur. She couldn't recall speaking to Matt again, couldn't recall retracing her steps and leaving the building, couldn't recall launching herself out onto the pavement. She sucked in mouthfuls of air as if they'd dilute the images she'd just seen. Why had she needed to see her dead dad? She hadn't thought it would be like that, she hadn't thought about it at all.

She headed down the high street. She kept walking until she started running, not stopping until she came to a park. She knew it once she got there. The ornate pagoda in the middle of the pond. Parson Park. The one she'd gone to with her dad to feed the ducks when she'd visited him. She headed for the nearest bench. She was numb to the playful activity around her. She leant her head back and closed her eyes, trying hard not to cry in public, but failed.

She jumped when Matt rested his hands on her shoulders and then sat down next to her. She knew he'd noticed her make-up was all cried off. She knew he saw the raw vulnerability that he'd told her many times made him fall in love with her; how lovely she looked without the *greasepaint.* She felt as far from lovely as was humanly possible. From his coat pocket, he pulled out a white envelope and placed it in her lap. She recognised the writing.

'The sergeant just gave it to me, Kit.'

Opening it she read:

My dearest Kitty, your forgiveness for my appalling behaviour over the years means the world to me. You did not deserve to be treated so badly, my precious daughter.

I'm very proud of all you have achieved. You have inherited all of the finest qualities of your mum who I miss every second of every day. I wish I could have her back to put things right.

Three months ago, Dr Riley confirmed my worst fears. The pain in my back is pancreatic cancer. The prognosis is bleak. I can't cope with this alone and I do not want to burden you and Matt.

I hope, one day, you will be able to find it in your heart to forgive me for what I am about to do. I know you will be shocked and sad. Please try to understand, I just cannot face this.

Know my love for you goes on. With all of my heart I thank you for the good times we enjoyed and for never giving up on me. I truly did not deserve your forgiveness. I cherish many happy memories of our latter years together.

Dad xxx

Kitty's tears dripped onto the words. She'd always admired her dad's writing, so neat and elegant, the rounded script of a diligent student. Just like the one she should have been. Wiping her eyes with the back of her hand, she passed the note to Matt.

'They said to give this to you, Kit.' Matt gave her a clear plastic bag from his pocket. Inside was her dad's Seiko watch.

She clutched it in her hands. As Matt read the letter she watched a group of children on the spinning roundabout. Their heads were thrown back by the force of the spin and they laughed loudly at the sky as they whizzed around. A dog lurched after a catapulted tennis ball, skidded to a halt, returned it to its waiting owner and stared at it to be thrown again. A mother hurried past pushing a wailing pram with baby paraphernalia spilling out from a Mothercare bag on the tray beneath: nappies, bottles and toys rattled along. As the world passed Kitty by she tried to imagine how wretched her dad must have felt in those early hours to consider taking his own life. She tried to imagine how desperate he must have been as he tied his own noose. The image of him slipping it around his neck, jumping and hanging from the rafters of his loft was too much to bear. Beyond miserable. She recalled a conversation from years back. It had been her new dentist just after she'd moved in with Annie and Bert. She dreaded going to the dentist, always had. Dragging her feet childishly towards the chair, fear consuming her, the dentist had caringly asked her how she felt.

'Like I'm going to the gallows,' she'd said.

Presumably, to distract her, he'd launched into a history lesson. 'Too many people to hang during the Revolution—not time efficient. It's not the rope that kills you, it's the weight of the body—causes strangulation. Doesn't work every time. Sometimes can take up to twenty minutes. And that's why the French brought in the guillotine.'

Why did people tell you these things? She at least hoped what her dad had done had been quick. She thought about the unfairness of it all, how they'd only just repaired their relationship, the lack of time she'd had to adjust to his death. She tried imagining her life without him in it, but was distracted by the scudding clouds and instead searched for familiar shapes, something to cling to in her confusion. She could smell mown grass and it reminded her of their visit to the crematorium; it hadn't been that long ago. Now she was the last family member standing. The responsibility dizzied her. How was life still carrying on? Birds sang, children played, dogs barked. She knew Matt looked at her several times as if wondering how she would ever get over this. She wondered too.

As soon as they got home and Matt was out of earshot, she called her dad's landline.

'731042, Bobby Black speaking.' He sounded so alive. There was no subtext to chew over; it all sounded quite normal, not desperate, not like someone about to kill themselves. *Kill themselves.* She phoned the number several more times the next day. On compassionate leave from work and no customers to distract her, she did all the things that grief demanded—over and over again.

Kitty and Matt's holidays after her dad's death were disastrous. It felt to Kitty as if his corpse had been strapped to the roof-rack as they drove to Yorkshire, Cornwall, the Lake District or wherever Matt thought would be a distraction. They even went to Greece but Kitty said on the very first day that every cypress tree looked like a hanging body; her dad's hanging body. She wasn't interested in anything; getting up was too much of an effort and the relentless sun felt an insult to her grief. She'd spent the rest of that holiday in bed in their hotel room; Matt had stroked her and ushered the cleaning maid away.

Back home, Matt held her when she woke distressed from horrific nightmares. He came home from work to comfort her when she called him, crying in the middle of the day. He begged her to get help. He left leaflets around the house. As soon as Gill landed in the country he called her to come round. Kitty would open her eyes and see her friend next to her bed, jetlagged and beaming despite desperately needing her own bed. 'Want me to read you some poetry, Kat—promise it won't be T.Rex?' Her chuckle fizzled out with Kitty's distant look but Kitty was comforted by her friend just being there. The smell of her. The orange and cinnamon, but now with a classy hint of vanilla. Hugely expensive perfume put together on one of her trips to New York, Gill said, but not paid for by her. She'd winked. She'd brought a beautifully packaged scent back for Kitty. It smelled divine, Kitty agreed. It had hints of violet, neroli and money. It sat in her bedside drawer, untouched.

Outside of Gill and Matt she'd only confided in a couple of recently bereaved people. They hadn't understood. They went into great detail about hospital visits, what the doctor had said and how exhausting it had been sorting through their loved ones' clothes. Kitty wouldn't have dreamt of interrupting with how she couldn't get rid of an image of her dad hanging from a rope, still questioned what she could have done to prevent it, still wished she could have been at *his* hospital bedside. It was too divisive; people who weren't in the know thought death was death, but she begged to differ, silently.

It was Gill who finally persuaded Kitty to seek professional help; she knew someone who knew someone. Kitty contacted a bereavement group one evening because she didn't know what else to do with herself. It was a support group for those affected by suicide. After the first session, she waited for Matt to get home. He was working later and later but she wanted to tell him how it had gone. She said she felt guilty finding consolation in others' horrific tales but couldn't help it. They were so shocking: the wife whose day started happily enough with a trip to the post office. It ended with discovering her beloved husband's brains sprayed around their Sanderson co-ordinated bedroom, a shotgun lying across his lifeless body, a suicide note on his desk revealing massive debts. Or the lad who ran through the woods looking for his twin brother after a frantic call from their parents. He saw the dangling legs first, swinging in the breeze from a sturdy fir tree. As he attempted to get him down he tried not to look at the purple face with the tongue sticking out grotesquely from one corner of his brother's mouth, and the bulbous, lifeless eyes. Or the husband who jumped in front of the fast train to London at Reading Station. He was badly mangled but didn't die. It was eight months before he gained enough strength to stab himself in the throat with hospital cutlery; his uneaten cottage pie on the tray in front of him splattered with blood and not ketchup.

The bereavement counsellor taught Kitty coping strategies. 'Your stress bucket over-floweth, my dear,' he'd said after she told him about Paul, Tom, Amy and her parents. He showed her breathing exercises and distraction techniques. He told her to be kind to herself, to stop blaming herself for events she couldn't have prevented. He said grief was often compounded by losing the remaining parent: that no matter how old you were, or what the circumstances, the bereaved could feel abandoned, orphaned. Kitty identified with everything he said. She wished she'd come sooner.

And although the loss of her dad didn't go away, she gradually learned to build her life around that gaping wound. She realised she could go a whole day without crying; without feeling the aching loss. And then a week. Then two. She dealt with the guilt she'd felt at hating him. She did that by trying to understand that in his own way he'd been desperate to stop her following the same path as her mum and Johnny. Even though he'd failed, he'd meant well. If there had been anger management classes around in those days, he would have been too proud to go anyway, she knew that much. She tried to focus on the good times they'd enjoyed but every now and then a wave of misery would take her—it could be a song or an overheard snippet of conversation which would hit home that she was no longer anyone's daughter—or sister—and she would feel lost again, like the world was just too big. But she *was* a mother. That thought kept Kitty going. She would always be a mother and one day she knew she would hold her daughter again.

Kitty returned to work once the worst of the grief dissipated. She was welcomed back into the fold. Kitty and Matt enjoyed a honeymoon period. Matt surprised her with flowers. He took her out for meals. They talked about a *proper holiday* and no one was more surprised than her when he suggested a trip to Hong Kong. He thought it would be cathartic for her and the more she thought about it, she felt so too. She loved him for his thoughtfulness.

Matt's face was a picture as they landed at Kai Tak airport—she never tired of watching family members' disbelief as they touched down on the short runway. She was excited about showing him where she'd once lived and so much had happened. Gill had given her a list of places to visit; things had changed since they'd lived there—distractions from the heavy stuff was a good idea, they all agreed.

She'd forgotten how it had been in Hong Kong: the smell, the thundering traffic, the frustrated outrage of everyone. It was a minefield walking anywhere; pedestrians seemed to aim themselves at you, no room to manoeuvre. They travelled by bus to Stanley—the journey had hardly changed, and Matt was agog. It *had* to be by bus. There was no other experience like it—no theme park ride came close. The hairpin bends had him gripping the rail and gasping as the sea shimmered beneath sheer drops. Kitty smiled at him, remembering her and Gill's reactions as teenagers. She studied the side of his face as he watched outside rush by, the harsh light catching the salt and pepper in his hair. His eyes had lines she hadn't noticed before. She was finding the first growth of white hairs in her roots and at the temples, and while it made Matt look distinguished, it made her look like she was aging quicker. But the fact of the matter was—time was ticking on.

They got off the bus a stop before the flats where she lived on Stanley Village Road. Everywhere was so much more built up and there were few white faces around. Kitty held Matt's hand as they walked up the drive. It seemed so different, but also familiar. It felt surreal to think this tiny corner of the world still existed, and had continued to exist, while she'd built another life thousands of miles away.

Their old balcony was full of pots with browning, parched plants, and the railings were rusted and neglected. Since the handover, these flats had been returned to the locals, no longer living quarters for ex-pats. Kitty looked up to Gill's old flat—it too was in a similar state of disrepair as was Tom and Pat's on the top floor. It all looked so sad and tired. Standing there with the traffic thrashing past behind her, Kitty recalled her dad's anger and wondered what the neighbours must have thought. There was no blind at the window like there used to be, but through the open door she could see the same mosaic floor. But time had dulled the memories and there were no more tears to be lost on them. They sat on the beach where her and Gill had wiled so many hours away. Matt said her description of it was far better than the reality. Everything looked neglected; to Kitty it was still wonderful.

They travelled on Star Ferry over to Kowloon to her old school, but couldn't find it. They went to the night market and Kitty showed Matt the street food she'd dreamt about since leaving Hong Kong; Chinese food back home just couldn't compare. The punch of ginger as you lifted chunks of honeyed chicken to your lips, the moreish taste of sweet and sour grouper, heavenly shrimp dumplings that dissolved on the tongue. Matt eyed the food and sanitary conditions suspiciously which made Kitty laugh—Gill had done exactly the same when they'd first arrived, but that had changed when Kitty had told her to get over herself.

She took Matt to Wan Chai. Walking through streets of high-rise offices spewing workers out into the late sun she lost her bearings, couldn't begin to place where Pussy Galore once was. The rows and rows of gaudy girlie bars had been replaced with just one short pounding strip of clubs. Kitty ran towards the pulsing beat of Queens; it had the loudest music. Matt held back. 'Come on, Matt! Let's have some fun. I could murder a cold beer, couldn't you?' She paid the entrance fee and pulled a reluctant Matt behind her; Madonna's "Vogue" vibrated through their feet. Not until she saw the mass of gyrating men on the stage did she realise it was a gay bar. Glistening bodies in micro-shorts, leather and fishnet vests writhed to the beat. While Kitty and Matt sat on black vinyl stools at the bar and ordered two beers, they watched the throng of men dance like no one was watching. Kitty was transfixed. Conversation was impossible. It felt like they'd gate-crashed a private party, until she noticed there were two other couples like them just watching and enjoying the atmosphere.

After another round of beers, Matt commented it was getting late, but Kitty ordered more drinks. She knew Matt was concerned about her; it had been an emotional trip, but she said she was okay now. After one more drink and a final trip to the men's room, he told Kitty it was time to go and they stepped out into the sticky night. The relative peace outside was a relief to Kitty's ears. Matt was quiet on the way back to the hotel and was asleep by the time she came out of the bathroom. The manic city and heat had taken its toll. Her lovely gentle man was exhausted from the brash, thrashing world she'd once called home; it was a lot to take in. She climbed in beside him and let the drone of the air-con lull her into a deep, heavy sleep.

Kitty spent the remaining days in the places she'd once loved, next to the man she loved, and hoped that he'd loved this journey as much as she had. He said he had. She found a silk kimono for Gill in the palest blue. Matt balked at the price, but Kitty bought it anyway. On their last evening they watched the sun make its leisurely descent over the harbour and saw the vibrant lights of the skyscrapers take over their watch. They sat in a smart bar, sixteen stories up, and sipped on cold martinis.

'Would you like something to eat, Kit?' Matt studied her face. She replied she didn't. The drink had worked its magic; she didn't need anything else. She tipped her head back and closed her eyes to savour the crooning tones of "If You Don't

Know Me By Now". She missed Matt reaching into his jacket pocket and lifting out a burgundy ring box. So his, 'Will you marry me, Kit?' took her completely by surprise. He wasn't on one knee but he was leaning forward on his stool with the ring box open as he looked sincerely into her shocked face. A halo diamond platinum ring surrounded by micro-pavé stones twinkled at her. *The* ring. She'd loved that ring for so long. It was so simple yet perfect. Tears sprang to her eyes as she replied, 'Yes! I really *do* want to marry you.' The bar staff clapped and deposited an ice-bucket with champagne in front of them. The ring fitted perfectly. Of course it did; he knew her jewellery measurements off by heart. It sat on her finger like it was meant to be, like it had always been there. It was the perfect end to their holiday. They said goodbye to the crazy city reflected in the water before them. They kissed on the way back to their hotel and Kitty said a silent *thank you* for all the things that were going right in her life.

ELEVEN

Kitty came rushing back from a weekend at Gill's after an early morning call with Matt. He hadn't contacted her the previous evening so she'd called him as soon as she'd woken up. They had an unspoken rule that if either was away overnight, they always phoned before bed or first thing in the morning. Or both. The phone had rung for ages. She thought she'd misdialled. She tried again, trying not to panic but knew it was odd. He eventually picked up but didn't speak. She heard strange noises. She pressed the phone to her ear trying to make out what they were. He was crying and inconsolable. 'I'm on my way, Matt,' she said. She scribbled a note for Gill and drove straight over. She ran through the house and, sensing no movement downstairs, took the stairs two at a time. She found him lying on the bed. His face was bruised, expressionless, his eyes like steel. She sat down next to him, gently took his hand in hers and stroked it. She struggled to understand what could possibly have happened; the house didn't look disturbed. Maybe there'd been another burglary at the jewellers. The last time, according to Matt, Peter had been held at gunpoint. The thieves left with a sizeable haul, but no one was hurt. That had been a long time ago, way before Kitty had met Matt.

'What's wrong, Matt? What's happened?'

'Nothing,' he answered flatly, his breath sour. Kitty stopped stroking his hand and looked at him in disbelief. Was that it, *nothing*? Her eyes widened.

'I'm okay—really,' he rasped.

'You're obviously *not* okay, Matt, you're bruised to hell.' She tried to keep the impatience out of her tone. 'How did *that* happen?'

His eyes filled like pools as he stuttered, 'A couple of—y—yobs attacked me. I'd— gone for a walk along the canal. They t—took my wallet. The police know. My dad knows—couldn't manage work. Please don't t—tell anyone else, don't want a f—fuss, Kit.'

They sat there in silence for what seemed an age despite the questions running through Kitty's head. Matt looked everywhere but at her. She couldn't push him any further; she could feel his pain, *see* his pain. She gently coaxed him out of bed, into his dressing gown and downstairs. He moved gingerly so she knew his injuries were not confined to his face. They sat in the kitchen drinking tea until he limped to the sofa where he stayed for the rest of the day, slumped, staring at the TV. His dad called in unannounced with a box of cakes which Kitty couldn't resist. He was horrified at the state of his son. While she left them alone to talk she grabbed the meringue and busied herself in the kitchen. Before Peter left, Kitty asked him if he thought Matt was really okay. He said he was, that the injuries looked worse than they actually were and work was the best place for him. The distraction would do him good and *stop him from feeling sorry for himself.*

The next morning Matt returned to the jewellers, reluctantly, making himself late and with an attitude Kitty could almost touch. She worried he wasn't up to it. Gill phoned for an update when Kitty returned home from work. She asked again about what had actually happened to Matt and then said, 'Well, that's odd, isn't it, Kat?' She barely waited for a response from Kitty before she went on. 'I've not heard of any attack down by the canal and I can't find anything in the paper about it. It was the night you stayed here, right?'

Kitty had been in the middle of sorting out the laundry box. There was a mountain of housework to get through and her day at the bank had been long and exhausting. She replied, distractedly, 'Yep. Matt said he'd reported it. They took his wallet, rotten bastards. Not heard anything yet though.' She cradled her phone in her neck as she separated colours from whites, then spotted the time and said she had to get on as Matt would be back for tea soon.

Things changed between Kitty and Matt after the attack. Some subtle, some not. Like flakes shaken in a snow globe, their life seemed somehow all over the place, but Kitty hoped it was temporary. She asked more questions about what had happened. 'It's just awful, Matt! Please don't go down by that canal in the dark again, will you?'

Matt assured her he'd no intention and was *over it now.* 'Kit—it was just one of those freak incidents, wrong place wrong time.' He said he'd kissed his wallet goodbye and the injuries were almost healed. *Time to move on,* but his clipped words only worried Kitty more.

It was about this time Kitty received a visit from Bert. Bert without Annie. He stood on the doorstep looking ashen. Kitty ushered him in, hugged him warmly but was really concerned when he didn't reciprocate. She put the kettle on and instead of him following her into the kitchen with his usual chatter, he disappeared into the sitting room. She placed his tea on the table next to the sofa along with a plate of chocolate digestives. He was as still as a statue.

'It's Annie, Kitty!'

'What, Bert? I thought I hadn't heard from either of you for a while.'

His hands flew to his face as he said, 'She has cancer, she hasn't got long. Only found out yesterday when she collapsed in the garden. They've kept her in hospital, the Royal Berks,' he whispered.

They went to the hospital together later that afternoon and it was to be the last time Kitty got to see her lovely auntie as the next day she slipped into a coma and died. Within a fortnight Bert had died too; the coroner's report had said *myocardial infarction,* but the general consensus was he'd died of a broken heart. It was the cruellest blow for Kitty to lose two of the kindest people she'd had the pleasure to know and who'd helped her at a time when she'd truly needed help.

She read out "He Wishes for the Cloths of Heaven" at their joint funeral—stumbling over the last line, feeling like she was going to faint until Matt quickly strode over and helped her back to the pew. They'd never trodden on her dreams; quite the reverse, but those last words got her every time. Matt stayed with her throughout the wake and spoke pleasantly to Annie and Bert's surviving friends. He passed around egg and cress sandwiches and poured copious cups of tea for those who couldn't make it to the refreshment table. He even spoke pleasantly to the vicar which convinced Kitty everything must be fine with him as he was an even bigger atheist than she was.

However, in the weeks following the funeral, Matt became moodier and would disappear for hours. 'Just off for a walk,' he'd say, and the door would slam without waiting for a response from Kitty. She always jumped at the uncharacteristic noise and then silence fell around her like a stone wall. Left alone with her thoughts, she'd try to get stuck into something but found herself clock-watching. After a couple of hours, she'd go upstairs to the spare bedroom and peep out of the window. When she eventually spotted him coming back up the avenue, she'd run back downstairs and strike a casual pose on the sofa, pretending to watch TV. Other times he'd mutter, 'Going skating,' with the usual slam of the door, and she would hear his car pull off the driveway. He began to lock the bathroom door whenever he had a bath. This used to be their "catch-up" time. Armed with mugs of tea, Kitty would perch on the loo with her knees to her chest while Matt reclined, their chatter and laughter rising with the steam. Now a no-go area.

'You okay in there?' Kitty would call through the door in the hope he'd open it and let her in. He rarely even answered her.

She noticed he'd developed a facial twitch—just above the faint arc of his right dimple which seldom indented these days. Whenever she asked him anything his mouth pulsed, like it was deciding whether or not to break out into a smile.

Sex became a one-way street where Kitty felt she was forcing herself on him, but the more she thought about it, it had always been like that. She'd read somewhere that in every relationship there's a dominant one and male libido ebbed after age twenty. Matt was more than twice that. She told herself to be more patient with him, not pressure him. She settled with holding him which he submitted to rather than returned. Now, when she woke early and looked at Matt she had a sense of unease; she wondered where *they* had gone. She knew things weren't right and it bothered her enough to dread bed. Many nights she stared into the darkness resisting sleep to avoid the crushing reality on waking. She wondered if he was depressed, unhappy or just no longer in love with her. Whatever it was, it was devastating and shaped her every thought. She'd no idea who to talk to. If she went to their GP and asked questions for *a friend,* she knew she'd be eyed suspiciously. If she spoke to Gill or Peter they'd become impatient and say he was fine. If she took anyone at work into her confidence she risked opening up her private life and she knew that was a definite no-no. As great as some of her colleagues were, and as much as some of them loved telling all and sundry the minutiae of their lives, she just couldn't trust anyone enough. She wished Annie or her dad were still alive. Annie would've been kindness itself and offered up so much of her worldly wisdom. Her dad could have given her another man's perspective; maybe she'd missed something she just couldn't see. In the end she begged Matt to talk to a professional.

'I'm fine,' he said, his clipped words cutting her to the core.

She wasn't a snooper but suddenly felt drawn to the pockets of his coats. The act racked her with guilt. After a couple of false starts when she was interrupted by the phone going or the doorbell ringing, she eventually got on and did the deed. She found nothing other than a couple of crumpled receipts for innocuous items and felt immense guilt for doing it.

In the face of Matt's disinterest in helping himself, Kitty found a counsellor online, phoned and explained the situation to him. He said if she could get Matt to call then he'd speak to him; see if he could help. She explained to Matt at the first opportunity what she'd done. His eyes turned cold, his right cheek started twitching and he slammed out of the house. Shaken and upset, she'd left the details on the kitchen table and jumped in the car to Gill's who offered little sympathy but huge glasses of expensive wine.

Neither Kitty nor Matt mentioned the fact that their engagement had turned into an indefinite one with no wedding on the horizon. Some days that bothered her. Maybe they both needed the commitment. She wanted to broach the subject but each time she got close his expression stopped her. He was so unapproachable these days that Kitty's guts churned with despair. Some time back she'd suggested attending a wedding fayre at the Roseate hotel in town, but he'd shown no interest and said he was busy, so she'd gone with Gill. She'd *ooh*ed and *aah*ed at the teetering tiered cakes, quizzed the music man about wedding waltzes and sat in the back of pristine limousines. Gill had humoured her, sampled all the cocktails and laughed at anyone who mistook her for the bride. On the way home she'd snoozed in the passenger seat and belched champagne burbs at regular intervals while Kitty had listened to love song dedications on the radio.

Matt had smirked at the wedding paraphernalia leaflets Kitty held out as he made himself a cup of tea in the kitchen that evening. In that moment she realised he didn't want her as a wife. She was no longer anyone's daughter, niece, or sister and it was looking likely that no one loved her enough to want to be with her forever. Her heart felt heavy and the only thought that kept her from running to the hills was that she was someone's mum.

TWELVE

The day of Amy's eighteenth birthday arrived. Kitty greeted the grey morning hanging with tiredness from a restless night. *Where had all those years gone?* How many times had she thought about contacting the Adoption Contact Register? Maybe a million, but decided a million times more she couldn't go through with it, couldn't disrupt a life that might be happy and settled, wasn't strong enough for rejection. That day when her daughter could legally contact her had finally arrived. If Kitty could bottle all the love and heartbreak she'd felt through those years she'd present it to her daughter and say, *here's what I feel for you, what I have always felt for you. Don't ever question for one second my love for you.*

Kitty couldn't settle, couldn't relax, just in case Amy contacted her. Her relationship with Matt had become mechanical at best. While he was absent in the evenings she'd too much time to analyse things. Looking back over their years together she could see how grief had made her selfish after her dad's suicide; it had taken the spark out of their lives. She'd tried hard to breathe new life into *them* once she felt less fraught, less broken, but it all felt so one-sided.

Amy's birthday was a Tuesday. Kitty had booked the day off of work some weeks ago, fobbing off anyone who asked about her plans. Lately she studied every female teenager who queued to be served—hoping it might be Amy even though, deep down, she knew it would be highly unlikely. Matt got ready for work, brought Kitty a cup of tea in bed and left the house without kissing her goodbye. She thought he must have forgotten what day it was, despite her mentioning it just the day before. *It's early,* she told herself, *he'll remember and ring later.* She knew she'd pull out the blue suitcase from the back of the wardrobe. It was as if it was calling her, but going through those things so early in the day would only upset her. She got up and went into the kitchen to distract herself. She saw Matt's breakfast dishes left by the side of the sink. The bin was overflowing, and rage rose up inside her. They used to share the housework. She switched on the radio and foraged for coffee. While the percolator hissed into life, she heard Bill Clinton talking on the news and then "Don't Let the Sun Go Down On Me" played.

Her mobile rang. The "Let's Dance" ringtone felt incongruous this day. It was Gill.

'Kat, hi! Just thinking of you. You know I'd be with you if I could. You okay?'

'Sort of—thanks. Wish I was in Oz with you. What time is it?'

'Tea time. In a bar—in St Kilda—not drinking tea!' Kitty heard the bass thump of jazz funk in the background. Gill's crew members were laughing and making the most of their down time.

'Keep your chin up, Kat. Don't get sad. I'll be back in a few days. We'll talk.'

'Thanks, Gill. Look forward to seeing you. Take care.'

Kitty looked in the fridge for nothing in particular but nothing grabbed her. She wasn't hungry really, just wanted comfort. She noticed Matt's sandwich box on the top shelf, saw the grains of rice, red peppers and peas from the previous night's supper pressing against the clear plastic. She decided to go into town and hand him his forgotten lunch; it would be better than moping around the house. If he didn't want the leftovers then maybe they could go out for a bite to eat. The thought cheered her up.

By 11 a.m. the crowds of shoppers had lifted Kitty's mood, dragged along by their rush to splash cash. She made her way down the high street to Bright's and saw Gary replenishing the window display. His white-gloved hands waved at her; he looked like Marcel Marceau.

'Matt forgot his lunch,' she said to his back as she walked through to the studio.

'He's not here, Kitty—said he was just popping out.'

'Oh. Okay. I'll stick this in the fridge then and leave a note on his desk.' Kitty stepped into the pokey kitchen and put the sandwich box on the top shelf of the fridge. She crinkled her nose at the smell of sour milk. She tipped the curdled contents of a carton down the sink and binned it. As she opened the drawer under Matt's desk looking for a pen, something shiny caught her eye. It was a gleaming silver "K"—about twenty centimetres high—lying in a nest of white tissue paper. She held it in her hands and studied it. There was a hallmark on the back. She loved it. She wondered if he was going to give it to her as a birthday or Christmas present. She knew exactly the right place to put it once he'd given it to her. She carefully placed it back in the paper and closed the drawer. She'd say nothing to him. She didn't want to spoil the surprise. She scribbled a note telling him where his lunch was and said cheerio to Gary.

She decided to walk to Prospect Park; it was only a couple of miles away and the exercise would do her good. It was usually busy at the weekend but today the kids were at school apart from a couple of toddlers and their chatting mums. She found an empty bench over by the pond and watched the ripples on the water as ducks slid in and out. Trying to block out the sound of happy children, Kitty wondered if Amy was thinking of her. She mentally listed all the generic milestones she'd missed with her daughter: the first teeth, the first steps, the first words. Someone else had enjoyed those—that well-dressed couple she'd spied from the window that awful day. She heaved a sigh of sadness and got up.

She made her way towards the toilet block. She needed to go before heading back. She should have gone back at the shop really. As she crossed between the parked cars she did a double-take behind a silver one, then peered inside. She'd thought as much. On the back seat was Matt's scarf. It was Matt's car. She wondered why he'd be here and looked around. She couldn't spot him. She carried on to the toilets and decided that if she found him after then they could maybe have a coffee somewhere together.

As she reached the top of the grassy slope she stopped in her tracks. Matt stepped out of the men's room. She was about to call out to him but thought twice because she thought he looked odd. Furtive. She leant against the graffitied side wall and watched him stride back down the hill, get in his car and pull away. As she stepped toward the ladies', a man with a shaved head wearing running gear came out of the block. She jumped with fright. He smiled at her and ran off in the opposite direction.

Leaving the park, Kitty stumbled home feeling cold and uncomfortable. She'd no idea why Matt had been at the park and felt sick at the distance between them. What had stopped her calling out to him? she wondered. Why did they no longer share things? She thrust her hands into her pockets and headed on.

Once home, she grabbed a hot drink and went straight to the suitcase. Such precious things, they were still in pristine condition, as if she'd just left St Martha's. There were also letters from Mary. They'd written to each other over the years, recalling memories and updating one another on what had been happening in their lives but hadn't met up. Kitty flicked through the ribboned bundle. The postcard of Rievaulx Abbey ruins caught her eye. She slid it out re-read it. *GUESS WHAT, KITTY! I'M IN LOVE! I'M GETTING MARRIED! TO A FARMER!* Kitty smiled as she read Mary's huge, excited words. The wedding invite had arrived the following week but Kitty had declined, feigning illness, and sent in her absence a chubby china robin perched on a branch—a nod to Mary's baby box, a nod to their shared history. They continued to exchange letters; neither phoned for fear of intruding on a life that maybe didn't know their secret, but Kitty knew Mary would make a robust farmer's wife in the Yorkshire Dales. Staring at the postcard now, she wondered how Mary had fared on Jake's recent eighteenth birthday. Had she sobbed her heart out at the image of him opening the present lovingly wrapped by her all those years ago? Maybe Jake had been in touch with his mum; maybe Mary hadn't told her new husband about him. Kitty made a mental note to write to her friend; it had been too long. There was something more pressing she knew she had to do; the time had finally come.

Inside a notebook in her handbag were the contact details of the Adoption Agency. She'd opened the page so many times the ink had faded. She fetched it and held her mobile phone in her other hand. Slowly she keyed in the number and waited. Engaged. She counted to ten and tried again. This time a female voice asked how she could help. Kitty's heart pounded. Panic rose in her throat so that when she tried to speak only a squeak came out. She clicked her phone off. She dropped back on the bed, drew in deep breaths, exhaled then sat up and tried the number again. The same voice answered. Kitty sat up straight and tried to keep the panic from her voice. 'Hel—lo? My name is—Katherine Black. I—I gave my—my—daughter, Amy—Amy Black up for—for—for adoption in 1974.' The voice on the other end didn't interrupt or hurry Kitty along, which Kitty was grateful for, or she thought she might lose her nerve. 'I'd like to—find my—daughter now please. She's eighteen today.' The last few words came out in one gushy breath. Kitty waited for what seemed an age before the voice said she'd have to check their records and if Amy had recently contacted them they'd get back to Kitty for documentation. Only then contact could be arranged, the kind lady explained. Kitty thanked her and sat there as relief flooded her veins like a junkie's fix. She'd finally done it. God, it had been scary but now it felt so good. She just had to play the waiting game, but she was used to that.

It was late by the time Kitty sealed the envelope and stuck a stamp on the letter for Mary. She looked at her watch and gasped when she saw just how late. She wondered where on earth Matt had got to but wouldn't call him. He got tetchy when she did that these days and accused her of checking up on him; she didn't want him coming home in a bad mood—after all, she had some good news to tell him. She had some *great* news to tell him. By the time she climbed into bed she was exhausted and needed a hug after her eventful day. She looked over at Matt's empty space. He always seemed to be absent these days—even when he was there he wasn't really. Usually sleeping. Their relationship seemed one of polite evasion. Where had the passion gone, the easy conversation, the tender touching in passing? She put those thoughts out of her head; tiredness wasn't the time to dwell on these things. She yawned and snuggled down under the duvet. As she drifted off she heard Matt climb the stairs, heard him wash and then brush his teeth. She felt him slip in beside her. She reached for him but he'd turned over and had already slackened into sleep. She turned over too, distancing herself from his snores and fell asleep thinking about Amy.

THIRTEEN

Two years into the new millennium. It was a bittersweet year for the queen. Up and down the country, royalists celebrated her Golden Jubilee, but were also mourning the death of the Queen Mother. Kitty missed talking to her dad about this; he'd been a keen royalist. There was a street party in Kitty and Matt's avenue. Neighbours sat side by side in the extra day's bank holiday sunshine, waving flags, getting merry and eating red, white and blue cake. Kitty sat next to a lady called Dolly who wore a blue and white checked minidress with a bright red boa around her neck. She turned out to be one half of the couple who ran the spiritual centre a few doors down from their house. *She's certainly found herself*, Kitty thought. Dolly's loud slurred words carried down the length of their trestle table; her shockingly short dress revealed bony mottled legs when she stood to raise yet another toast *To Lizzzzzie!*; her exposed décolletage had seen much tauter days. Dolly's unsubtle leers and come-ons to Dave, the semi-professional musician sitting opposite her, made him splutter on his cider. He sprayed the contents of his mouth over quiches and cheese sandwiches. His goth girlfriend next to him flashed her black kohled eyes at Dolly in warning, but she was drunk and oblivious to the girl. When music blared from tinny speakers, Kitty watched Dolly dance like someone shot, alone. Whether it was the wine or just the happy atmosphere, Kitty jumped up as soon as Shakira's "Whenever, Wherever" started playing. Her hips swayed to the beat and she playfully pulled Dave up to join her, not even thinking twice about his pouting girlfriend who'd been sitting in sullen silence since Dolly's unsubtle innuendo. They gyrated and jiggled. Kitty gave her best rendition of a belly dance while Dave bent backwards imitating limbo under an imaginary bar until the many pints of cider got the better of him and he landed in a tipsy heap. Kitty shimmied over to him, pulled him up to standing. They clasped hold of each other and continued to list unrhythmically to the rest of the song. When the music stopped, they both laughed and tripped back to their chairs.

When darkness fell, Kitty returned home and was surprised that Matt still wasn't back. He'd gone into work to finish an urgent set of cufflinks for a client's wedding, he'd said. Kitty had hoped he'd have returned for at least one drink with her before it got too late. They'd argued that morning. Kitty had woken early and reached out for Matt's warm body in the dark. Sleep left her immediately when she realised he wasn't there. He'd come home late the previous evening and had got up way too early. By the time he'd come back from his walk—*needed some air*—Kitty was sparring for a fight.

'You don't want to marry me, do you, Matt?' Their eyes locked and he was first to look away. 'If you did want to marry me then we'd have organised something way before now.' She couldn't help herself—she told him she'd seen him at the park that time. She said it with an accusing tone. He shook his head and turned away, muttering he liked to get some exercise at lunchtime, but not before she spotted a cagey look cross his face.

'Are you seeing another woman?' The words left her mouth before she'd time to consider them.

'Of course not, Kit!' he said indignantly and wrapped his arms around her, pulling her close.

'We're not as close as we used to be, Matt. All this overtime is taking its toll on you, on *us*. Do you think we ought to think about counselling?'

He pulled her closer and eventually said, 'Kit, love. We don't need all that American claptrap! It's for couples who are breaking up. I'm *definitely* not talking to a stranger about our sex life.'

Kitty stopped herself before the sarcasm had a chance to leave her mouth, but thought *well that subject would be over in seconds.* His stubbornness rankled, she tried again.

'Do you want us to get married, Matt? Yes or no?'

His response had taken so long that his silence felt like an insult. She looked at him pleadingly one last time.

'One day—maybe.'

She wondered how he could be so cold. She ran upstairs and shut herself in the bathroom just as the front door slammed. Their row had made the decision easy to go to the street party alone, and it had been fun, but now the reality of the bad vibes between her and Matt returned.

It was very late by the time he silently climbed into bed. Kitty was still awake. She knew she could easily start the morning's conversation back up again, throw the lights on and demand to know what he meant by his hurtful words, but they both had work in the morning. Before she drifted off she was faintly aware of a scent. It wasn't the Givenchy she'd bought him for his last birthday. Perfume? Just the thought of Matt with someone else was too much to bear. They'd been together so long. He'd said he wasn't being unfaithful. He wasn't in the habit of lying to her, why would he start now? Because of all the overtime, she couldn't remember when they'd last spent quality time together. Actually, she couldn't remember when he'd last showed an interest in her *or* her days. Before sleep stole her thoughts she decided they must make time for each other—at the weekend, once he came back from work on Saturday. She'd tell him about taking the first steps to find Amy. She snuggled into his back and drifted off.

The next morning Kitty decided she must have dreamt that smell on Matt. In fact, she wondered if it had been Dolly's perfume on her. She'd spent most of the evening drunkenly draped over Kitty wailing that her *bastard husband* had left her for *a pissing child*. She'd thought at the time that if she ever behaved like that in public, then someone please shoot her. Matt turned over in bed and hugged her. He apologised for missing the party and said he'd make it up to her. Her tummy fluttered with love for him; he'd beaten her to it to put things right between them. Before he left for work he took her hands in his and told her he loved her then kissed the top of her head as she munched on cereal in the kitchen. He waved as he reversed the car off the drive. Kitty felt like the worst person in the world for suspecting him of anything; how could she have accused him of seeing another woman? She left for a busy day at the bank.

She called into Gill's before going home after work. They

chatted generally—work, clothes, new eateries—until Gill told her to spill.

'Matt and I had a bit of a ruck the other day, it's fine now,' Kitty said, smiling. 'I think we got into a bit of a rut, what with both of us working and Matt having to do so much overtime, but we've sorted it.'

'So there's no one else involved or anything?' Gill's question surprised Kitty.

'No! Absolutely not, Gill. Living together for so long isn't easy, you know. You've got to work at it and keep things fresh. We rarely go anywhere or do anything because he's always so tired. We're sorting it.'

'That's good then, Kit. So when do I need a new outfit for the wedding?'

Kitty studied the ring on her finger and hesitated before replying. 'Ummm—he's not sure he wants to marry me now.' She could feel Gill's exasperation.

'Kat. If you're locked into the same narrative, change the bloody book!'

Bit harsh, Kitty thought, but said nothing. She didn't want them to fall out. They'd been having similar conversations for a while now. Kitty said that Matt was going to make it up to her so there was nothing to worry about, then made her excuses and left.

Matt returned early and presented Kitty with flowers, kissed her on the cheek and prepared them a meal. They huddled on the sofa under the fur throw and watched rubbish television. They made love for the first time in ages that night and they became them again. Kitty felt disloyal for discussing her unfounded concerns with Gill and resolved to think twice in future before blurting.

She went to work without a care in the world the next day. She had butterflies about how well the previous evening had gone. She asked her boss if she could leave early that day. She booked a table for them in the swish new restaurant in town and at lunchtime called into the travel agent's and picked up holiday brochures, excitedly poring over them in the staffroom as she ate her sandwich. The rest of the day flew by and before long she was putting on her jacket and looking forward to going home. *This is going to be an evening to remember,* she thought as she waved a cheery goodbye to her colleagues.

On the drive back, Kitty decided she'd have a quick bath before Matt arrived home—she'd texted him telling him about the booking and for the rest of the journey she thought about what she was going to wear. She stepped out of her shoes and flung her coat and bag on the kitchen counter. She took the stairs two at a time as she unbuttoned her shirt and leaped into the bedroom.

The sight that greeted her made her stop as still as a building, not moving, not breathing. They hadn't heard her. They hadn't heard her because they were going at it like dogs. Matt and *someone.* Matt and *another man.* Both on their knees—Matt in front, grasping the headboard with both hands and making sounds she'd not heard for a very long time and *whoever* slamming into him from behind. The stranger's face was red and screwed up tight with sheer intent, his bald head glistening with sweat. They still hadn't heard her because as she stood there watching in surreal disbelief, unable to turn away, they both reached a noisy, juddering orgasm.

'Hi,' she said in such a tiny voice after all the noise of their sex. She hugged her unbuttoned shirt to her.

They turned towards her in unison. Their eyes opened wide.

'Oh, Christ!' The stranger leaped off the bed—*their* bed—grabbed his clothes and ran past Kitty and down the stairs without a word, but still panting. She got a good look at his face and realised she'd seen him before. It took a while to remember because he'd had clothes on the first time she'd seen him. Running gear. Coming out of the toilets in the park that day.

Matt sat up, clutching their Cath Kidston throw to his chest, his face flaming with guilt. He said nothing for what seemed an age. Kitty wished with all of her heart that he'd smack himself on the forehead in some cartoonish way and admit he'd just made a terrible mistake. He didn't.

'Kit—'

Silence.

'I'm so, so sorry. I know you're shocked—I never meant to hurt you.'

She stared blankly at him.

She told him to get dressed and come downstairs. For one panicky moment she thought she was going to be sick. She breathed her way through it, until the room stopped spinning and she could move forward. She carefully went down the stairs, holding the bannister, trying to steady herself from the shaking that was beginning to rack her whole body. As if in slow motion she glanced at her reflection in the hallway mirror. She saw the colour had drained from her face and her eyes were glazed—giving her the look of a trauma victim.

By the time Matt came down, the bomb inside Kitty's head was ready to explode. Her temples pulsed. She wasn't sure if either of them would survive the blast. He stood in the kitchen doorway, now fully dressed, his face also pallid and probably the saddest she'd ever seen him. He sniffed back tears. He made no attempt to approach or hug her. He looked pleadingly into her eyes but his shoulders sagged and there was an utter hopelessness about him. Kitty swallowed hard and tried to put out the lit fuse. She spotted the partially full bottle of red from the previous weekend but resisted pouring herself a glass. A tense silence hung between them. After several stops and starts, she spoke first.

'I *knew* there was something wrong. I had no idea it was— *this*. No wonder you wouldn't come to couple counselling.'

It was a long time before he said anything.

'I'm sorry. There was no saving us, Kit.'

The words landed like a heavy weight dropped from a height. Kitty hoped desperately she'd misheard. His expression told her she hadn't.

'You became distant after your dad died—unreachable. I felt lonely. I never wanted to hurt you. You've meant the world to me. I kept it completely separate from you. From *us*.'

Kitty felt fireworks explode in her head. Bloody great cakes of them. She suspected if she looked in the mirror now, there'd be clouds of smoke above her. She wondered how many times he'd rehearsed those lines; probably been practising them since she quizzed him about seeing another woman. She unscrewed the cap from the wine bottle, threw it against the tiled splashback, sloshed wine into a glass and gulped thirstily at it.

'You bastard! You're blaming me for you sleeping with *men*? You're *gay* and you're trying to blame me?'

She really didn't want to know the answer to her next question, but couldn't help herself asking, 'How long?' Her voice was loud and trembled with fury.

He didn't reply. He looked down at the floor. In that moment she knew he'd always known.

'You've been doing this for *over two decades?*'

Matt remained silent, his head bent. His index finger absentmindedly traced the marbled pattern of the work surface. He sighed and finally raised his gaze to Kitty.

'I wasn't sure.'

'Oh! So you thought you'd practise until you were. And use me at the same time?'

'It wasn't like that, Kit.'

'Why the hell did you ask me to marry you, Matt?'

'I thought it would make everything right, everything— normal. It's hard to explain, Kit.'

She looked at him in disbelief. Her whole body shook with such anger that she wanted to hurl herself at him and do some damage. Instead, she placed her hands on her hips and spat, 'Who was *he?*'

Matt studied his hands. 'His name's—Kevin.'

'And where did he spring from?' She didn't even attempt to keep the sarcasm from her voice.

'Met him on my walks down by the canal—s—some time ago. We—we met up a few more times since then.'

Kitty shook her head and lurched for more wine, slamming the bottle down loudly. 'Meet to do what, exactly?' she said, then fixed her eyes on him as she brought the glass to her lips.

Matt's face reddened. 'You don't need to know this, Kit.'

'*Yes, I bloody do! Keep talking.*'

'Sometimes—just talk. Sometimes—just hold each other.'

'*Talk? Hold each other?* That's what *we* do, Matt!'

He stared at the floor tiles. She took another big swig

of wine. It was having no effect and her imagination was running wild at the frugal information he was giving her. He lifted his pained face. His eyes turned to ice. His face now wore an expression she hadn't seen before. In that moment she remembered she'd read how the first things you loved about someone became the very things that you disliked in the end. His face no longer looked handsome, no longer a source of wonder, but instead an irritation—ugly even, with a sneer.

'Who are you to be homophobic, *Katherine Anne Black*? You're hardly in a position to judge anyone after what you got up to. Or have you conveniently forgotten the affair with the married bloke and the illegitimate kid? Who are you to be so bloody sanctimonious? No one else would have taken you on if I hadn't!'

The words landed undiluted by a response from Kitty as she reeled from their force. Her mouth fell open; she breathed in sharply and peered at Matt through eyes that were now slits. Her breaking heart smarted from the contempt in his voice. She'd never heard him speak to her like this before. She'd never heard this kind of venom coming from her Matt. It was a while before she could reply.

'How *dare* you! I *don't* have a problem with anyone being gay. What I *do* object to is when the person who professes to love me and has been my partner for *decades* says he's *gay*, says he's been sleeping with *men* behind my back and then I catch him in the act. It's all the lies and deceit, the duping me into thinking he was someone else. *That's* the problem, Matthew *bloody* Bright.'

Matt bit his lip; his eyes darted around the room as if looking for an escape. Kitty stared at him for a response. It seemed surreal that just that morning she'd been on the till at the bank chatting with customers, dispensing cash and looking forward to a great evening with her fiancé—a normal day. Matt should have been working too, and getting excited about their date this evening instead of *that*.

'I knew you'd take this all the wrong way, Kit.'

Exasperation silenced her. He was trying to make this seem like a reasonable situation that she was failing to grasp, like she was an idiot. Gaslighting. Before she could formulate a reply he started to walk out of the kitchen. She bore into his back.

'Who are you, Matthew Bright? Do you seriously think you can do this to me and then walk out? Just like that? You—*of all people*—know what I've been through. You know I'm not strong enough for this. You know everything about me. *I trusted you.* We have a good life together.' Her tears were hot and angry.

'Kit, I—'

'No! You listen to me. For some time now I've felt rotten. You've pushed me away. I thought you just needed space so I let you have space—and time. But you were doing *that*. And now—*now*— *when I'm nearly fifty*, you decide you're done with me?'

Matt stopped in his tracks but wouldn't look at her. He said nothing more which only added to Kitty's fury. '*And the Oscar goes to*—the bloody liar and cheat in the corner. So much for promising my dad you'd look after me and never let me down.' She knew she sounded like a spoilt brat but couldn't help herself. She took the stairs two at a time to the spare bedroom, threw herself onto the bed, and cried into the duvet. Outside she heard a car alarm go off and a dog barking while inside her whole world had tipped on its axis. Matt—the man she thought she knew so well, knew every contour of his body, knew what he liked to eat and when, the man who'd held her so tenderly after her dad died, soothed her on Amy's birthdays, listened to her when she'd a bad day at work, cooked all those wonderful meals—did all of those things just to disappear now? Cease to exist? She didn't know how she was going to give it all up.

She went over and over the previous evening when they'd seemed so close. She became stuck in the last moment her life had made any sense to her. She heard the front door close, clutched the duvet to her and gave in to another wave of sobs. She knew there was no coming back from this. She knew he couldn't just flick a switch. *I've lost him,* she thought in despair, and the saddest thing of all was that she now knew she'd never had him in the first place. She'd always found it hard to believe those women who suspected nothing when their partners played away. How could they not know? Now she was one. If there had been clues they'd slipped by unnoticed, hidden by lies. And there were more lies when she *had* confronted him. He couldn't pretend any longer, couldn't be the other half of them; they'd ceased to be. Kitty and Matt. Their story. Nearly a quarter of a century in the making: page after page, photo after photo, dream after dream all gone in one day. And now, the explicit scene she'd witnessed earlier between her man and another man would stay with her to her grave.

She was still lying there when Matt returned. She was on her back staring at the ceiling as he stepped into the room. He hesitated then perched on the edge of the bed and placed his hand on her arm. She wanted to reach for him and nuzzle into his neck. Instead she shrugged him off. They stayed like that, stiff and awkward, for several minutes.

'I'll pack my bag and go. I'm—so sorry, Kit.'

Every bit of her wanted him to stay. She desperately wanted to hear him say it was a blip, a one-off, a mistake from which they'd recover. In her head the words *please give me another chance, I'll be anything you want,* screamed out. But even in the depths of desperation she was too proud to say it. Knew it was useless anyway. Knew in her heart of hearts that he couldn't continue like this any longer. His pain was clear to see. She felt the universe would surely come to a standstill without him in her life.

'Yep, you best be going, Matt,' she said, forcing herself to sound nonchalant.

Matt gathered his things and crept back downstairs and out of the door. When it clicked she felt completely undone, like her limbs had been torn from her. She wondered if there was any humiliation greater than this. For years their relationship had been solely Matt's invention. She placed her hands over her face. This was what loss felt like. It rose like yeast from her soul and gnawed into every sinew. She had no idea how she was going to get through this.

Peter turned up days later. He stood on the doorstep looking concerned, sheepish and embarrassed. Kitty realised immediately he knew about his son being gay, probably had known all along. And suddenly it dawned on her why his and Matt's relationship had not been easy.

'I'm sorry, Kitty. I thought it would all work out. I was hoping it was just a phase Matt was going through.'

'You *knew* about this but never thought to mention it to me?' Her temples banged like drums.

'Grace never knew either. By the time I realised, she was going through chemo. She had more than enough to cope with.'

The silence between them seemed to last a lifetime. She didn't want to disrespect Grace's memory but so many questions raced in her mind.

'So—how *did* you find out, Peter?'

He took a while to answer. He kept looking at her and then at the ground. His eyes pleaded with her to understand. 'I came back to collect some things for Grace and found Matt—and a friend—in— bed together.'

'What friend? *He didn't have any friends,*' she demanded.

'They were friends at senior school. His name was Kevin. *Is* Kevin. Grace cooked tea for them a couple of times many years ago.'

And it was only then that Kitty felt the room spin as she remembered the silver "K". It hadn't been meant for her at all. Matt had made it for Kevin.

FOURTEEN

Kitty packed the rest of Matt's things up some months after he left. She binned the bedding from *that* awful day, dragged the mattress down to the bottom of the garden and set fire to it, finding a strength she didn't know she had. The bed had been an anniversary present from Matt's dad. She couldn't remember which anniversary, but it was a generous present for a sex life that had sadly dwindled in her and Matt's last few years together. They'd replaced the mattress at healthy intervals just like the adverts advised, but you'd have needed a microscope to spot any stains; there was a distinct lack of action towards the end. Super king-size beds were a luxury Matt's dad enjoyed on his swish holidays and it afforded Matt enough room to move without touching Kitty. Time and space, she'd innocently thought.

She ordered a new mattress and new bedding and when it arrived she moved back into their bedroom. She stuck pictures and cards on his white walls. She tried to get used to the solitude. The TV or radio blared through the house most days. Cooking for one was too sad; she lived on cheese and crackers, comfort food from her childhood. Sometimes she added a glass of wine or two, just to take the chill off. She tried going out but it was hard. There were couples everywhere. It cut her to the quick. An earworm repeated in her head: *lost the one who held my hand, lost the one who gave a damn, he ran off with another man.*

Slumped on the sofa, she stared at the games on the bottom shelf of the bookcase. She wondered who'd play Scrabble with her now, all those lovely letters, all that possibility. Matt had suffered it on rainy Sundays, always willing to sit there and be beaten. She got the box out, spread the board on the coffee table and studied the last score sheet—she'd won, of course she had. She tipped the letters onto the carpet and filled the centre squares with "bastard". At first she felt rotten for doing it; she even looked around furtively. But the truth was it made her feel so much better; it was a release. So she added "ollocks" to the B and then "ick" to the D. She added "unt" to the C and surveyed her handiwork, straightening the tiles until they aligned perfectly. Satisfied, she slid the board along until it overhung the table. With one swipe of her clenched fist she sent it flying. Letters flew into the air in a dance above the airborne folding board and landed in a gibberish pile on the carpet. It was what Johnny used to do in his frustration at losing yet another game to Kitty. Boy, it felt good.

She knew things could be a lot worse: lost limbs, cancer, Parkinson's, and god knows Gill reminded her. But the confusing mood swings—one minute wanting Matt back, the next hating his guts—left her exhausted. She wished she could believe everything happened for a reason—that *this* had happened for a reason. Maybe because of knowing trauma so young, she couldn't.

'Remember that old woman in Hong Kong? That cheerful old woman with nothing who'd found joy in the simplest things?' Gill said.

'Well, you'd better send round a pig then and see if that cheers me up,' Kitty replied sarcastically.

'He's already left the building,' came her friend's lightening retort.

Kitty tried not to call Matt, she really did, but after several wines she clattered around for her mobile.

'You selfish fucking bastard. Hope you're happy now you cock-sucker.' She'd filled the message space with every insult that came into her drunken mind, spitting into the phone. Once she sobered up she stared in horror at how many times she'd called his number. He never replied and she didn't expect him to.

She made it to the canal early one morning. Wanted to see the scene of the crime— that's how she thought of it. He'd said that was where he'd met his *boyfriend*. According to Peter that was a lie too. They'd known each other from school. The park and the canal were probably where they met for sex, she decided. She weaved through streets, past parked cars with frosted windscreens, pavements glistening. It was cold but the crisp air felt good to breathe. The grass looked sugar-coated; it crunched under her wellies. She walked over a bridge to a clump of trees, so close together as if they were sharing a secret. She wondered what she was hoping to find; Matt and Kevin no longer needed clandestine meetings; and anyway, surely it was too early and too cold even for gays to get amorous? She cringed at having the thought but felt compelled to carry on. She stood with her gloved hands on her hips and watched the morning light start to filter through the branches. She spotted a ring of toadstools and next to it a discarded condom. She pictured Matt and Kevin going at it like animals. A scruffy fox trotted past on the other side of the water, gave her a sly look and carried on, unfazed. Kitty's breath huffed out like a cloud as she turned to make her way back with rage bubbling up inside her. Two magpies chattered overhead. One for sorrow, two for joy. *If only.* She passed the first stream of dog walkers whose pets looked around to spot her dog, their owners thinking her deranged for being up this early and in this weather without one.

She made her way home, sadder and none the wiser. The streets were filling with workers, heads down, pushing on, wanting the day over. She looked at her watch; she was going to be late for work. The atmosphere had changed in the bank. Her silly mistakes caused more lock-ins and although she hadn't confided in anyone about her situation, she knew colleagues avoided her and her coat of misery.

'You okay, Kitty?' Helen asked, but her concerned enquiry was brought to an abrupt end with Kitty's cold reply. 'Absoluuuutely fine.'

Some days Kitty just couldn't be bothered to get out of bed, couldn't think about ringing in with her excuses until it was too late and her boss's tone was terse. After her last absence she mentally made a note to see her GP, but then put it off for another day, another week. She'd no idea what she would say anyway. She wished she could just appear at the surgery and the doctor read her mind without her having to utter one word. She knew she needed something to ease her through the pain; her thoughts were becoming dark. She started to think she understood her dad's decision to kill himself. Suicide. *It's just an option,* she thought, and wondered if Johnny would have agreed. She thought she finally understood the impossibility of her dad's situation. His awful behaviour came back to haunt him; his cancer diagnosis must have felt like slamming into a wall. He'd only wanted to take charge of something that was hurtling out of control, she saw that now because she felt the same. She re-enacted meeting Matt, missing signs and poked at it like a rotting tooth. The thought of starting all over again made her feel she needed a lot of alcohol to get through.

One wet, dismal morning she dragged herself downstairs and filled the kettle with the intention of starting the day sober at least. She went through the motions of making a cuppa once the kettle rumbled to a climax and clicked off. But it offered no solace. One mug, one tea bag. She'd tried to keep a semblance of a routine but she was just falling through the months. Her mood swings were so severe some days she felt she was better off staying in bed. This morning she ignored the bottles of red calling her from the wine rack. She delayed climbing back into bed and catching up on the sleep that eluded her through the endless, restless nights. She headed from the kitchen into the room they'd grandly named their *office*. There was a desk, a dusty computer and a whole lot of paper, books and detritus lying around. On a shelf above the printer was a poem. She'd written it for one of Matt's birthdays and bought a wooden frame which she'd stained blue:

Skater
I try skating on ice.
Infinite circles spiral and hug
This cold surface,

Smoothly indifferent under blade,
Hushing my style, iced grit flies
From nothing scored.

Gliding wildly in pristine chill
I slice and drag this silent stage,
Diminishing in an instant.
I labour to impress again and again,
But I can leave no trace.

He'd unwrapped it, read it and looked uncomfortable, Kitty had thought at the time. Now she knew why—to Matt she'd been inconsequential and *had* left no trace. She laid the frame face down.

She studied the thirty or so framed photos hanging on the wall. Some big with white frames, others smaller with black frames; an arty idea copied from a magazine when she and Matt were nest-building. She searched for clues. In this one could she recall if he'd come straight home that day? In that one is that deceit in his eyes as he smiled at the camera? Who was he thinking of as he grinned in this one? Her? *Kevin?* Her eyes burnt into his for signs of the liar she now knew him to be. She slumped onto the chair in front of the desk, exhausted from the effort. She realised the photos were just random fragments of a story. They'd been chosen only for superficial purposes: the light catching his eyes, posed smiles. The truth would be in the missing pictures, the not so pretty ones or the ones not taken at all. This exercise only confirmed the total fool she'd been for loving, trusting and believing Matt. She hadn't seen that he'd been in search of his own rescue when they met. When you realise your rescuer needed rescuing, the fairy tale has ended. *I'll be the man you want me to be,* he'd said, but he hadn't said how long for. Kitty realised *she* had become the problem in their relationship. Matt would be patted on the back for coming out, *finding himself,* his new life a reason for celebration—while she tried to exist among the tatters. The post thudding onto the doormat and the letterbox slamming shut made her jump. She wasn't interested in seeing what was there; probably only bills and circulars, but it snapped her out of her reverie.

She walked back into the kitchen and tipped a shot of neat gin into a tumbler, swilled it around the glass and slugged it down. She could feel the liquid weave through her, making everything hazy and faded. She poured herself another measure and sunk that. She didn't have anything to keep a clear head for as the day stretched ahead interminably.

Her mobile rang. She wasn't going to answer it but saw that it was Gill.

'You okay, Kat?'

'No,' came out hoarsely.

'Want to go out for lunch?'

'No—thanks.'

'Can I come over?'

'I was about to go out,' Kitty lied.

Within seconds the doorbell buzzed. Kitty tripped over objects in her path: the hoover that was rarely used and now never put away, an overflowing bin of empty bottles and unopened post which she pushed to one side with her foot. Life's flotsam and jetsam with which Kitty felt an affinity; stuff once useful, now abandoned.

Gill was on the doorstep. She'd been parked outside the house when she made the call, Kitty realised. She took in the scene, the mess, the malaise, then turned her cheery face to her friend's miserable one. Kitty stood forlornly in her stained dressing gown. It gaped open showing a grubby nightie beneath. Kitty already regretted the loss of her solitude; she shouldn't have answered her phone. Not that it would have stopped Gill.

'Kat, get dressed. Let's go out for a bit.' Gill went into the kitchen to make herself a cup of tea, smelled the empty tumbler reeking of gin. She sighed as she washed it up. Before they left the house Gill asked Kitty for her car keys. Kitty gave them to her without a fight; she knew she was a danger on the road. She knew that much, at least.

They drove into town, parked, then headed for a café. Kitty stuffed her shaking hands into the pockets of her gilet and squinted at the bright day. Telling herself to buck up fell on heedless ears even though she knew she was short-changing her friend. This day she just wasn't in the mood to talk about anything despite Gill's best attempts to lift her friend's spirits with banal banter, avoiding any mention of *him*, avoiding confrontation.

'You watch that drama set in Hong Kong last night? The one I told you about?' Gill asked, bringing her steaming coffee cup to her lips.

'Nope.' Kitty let out an impatient sigh as she studied the froth on her cappuccino.

'Some great shots of Kowloon—and Ocean Terminal,' Gill persisted.

Before Kitty thought to bite her tongue, she spat out, 'Why would I want to see that? Just memories of another shit time or have you forgotten what happened to me out there? You with your wonderful memories. It's not like that for me.

Bloody jinxed I am.' Kitty felt her face flush red and turned away.

'I'm sorry, Kat—I was only trying to avoid mentioning *you know who.*' She reached out to rub Kitty's arm, but Kitty shook her off.

'We got bloody engaged in Hong Kong! I think he shagged someone in the toilet in that club we went to on our holiday! Didn't tell you that bit, did I? Nice new memory!'

'You can't keep dwelling on this, Kat. You have to remember the good times and move on.'

Kitty managed to keep her exasperation to herself until she couldn't any longer. 'Let's not mention that *wanker* again. He's the bloody great gay elephant in the room! *I can turn men gay,* how about that? What a skill!' Kitty looked at her friend defiantly and watched her expression change from shock to hurt.

'Oh, Kat!' Gill stood up and wrapped her arms around her friend as snotty sobs filled their corner and the café quietened as heads turned towards them.

Before Gill left she made Kitty promise to see her GP as soon as possible, even offering to go with her. They said their goodbyes. Kitty insisted on walking home saying she needed the air. She mooched around the shopping centre looking for nothing in particular but not ready to leave. She saw only colours and shapes wrapped in white noise. She knew she'd been horrible and had upset Gill. It had been a mistake to come out. She finally headed back home.

The house felt like a held breath. With each leaden step Kitty waded through the silent hallway until the effort proved too much and she plonked herself down onto the red rug. Misery rose up from her gut like a tsunami, tore at her heart on its journey and exited as a river of tears.

Hours later, slumped in the darkness half asleep, the roar from the boiler made her jump. Too weak to face going upstairs to bed, she stumbled with pins and needles into the kitchen. She fumbled in the darkness for the gin next to the fridge and collapsed on the sofa. She wouldn't have to get dressed in the morning, everything was in reach, no effort required. She unscrewed the gin cap and brought the bottle to her lips. She savoured the woody-sweet scent of pine before swigging the bitter liquid down ready for the burn. The television lit the room like a distress flare with one press of a button.

The next morning she woke gasping for breath. Her heart raced, her mind muddled from a drunken dream. She tried to grasp the detail but it seemed just out of reach. Her body tingled as if post-orgasm. Then it came to her. She'd dreamt Matt was there and they'd made love. His familiar frame had been on top of her. She could still conjure up the smell of his skin, musky and warm like a favourite blanket. She'd come while he'd held her. It had felt so good, so right.

'*Matt*,' she whispered until sobs racked through her and tears fell like persistent drizzle on a miserable day. She staggered into the hallway, shrugged on the first coat that came to hand, stepped into muddy boots and walked out of the front door.

FIFTEEN

A dull gull-grey sky loomed overhead. The air smelled of winter, the cold nipping at her face and bare fingers. She dug them into her coat pockets and walked in the direction of the surgery. Her eyes were shadowed and sore; she looked haunted and ill.

The minute her GP asked her what the problem was she started crying again. It was an age before she could actually speak.

'My partner left me—he—he's— gay—I'm—not—coping well.' Her gulps stuck noisily in her throat as she clumsily wiped away tears with her grubby coat sleeve.

The doctor wore his professional face, as she knew he must; Matt was also his patient. Did he already know he was gay? He looked at her. She stuttered in a lost, childlike voice that she didn't know how she was going to get through this. He fastened his stethoscope into his ears and listened to her heart. *Does a shattered one sound different to a whole one?* she thought as he breathed next to her face. He took her blood pressure. She sat there listlessly until the pump threatened to burst her arm and breathed again when the pressure subsided. He diagnosed severe trauma. He handed her the details of a Cognitive Behaviour Therapy course, a prescription for amitriptyline and a sick note stating she was unfit for work for the foreseeable future. He told her to be kind to herself, to give herself time and smiled reassuringly before holding the door open.

Clutching the pills from the pharmacy, Kitty walked back through her front door as if in a trance. She swallowed two of the tablets with a mouthful of gin and within the hour was out of her misery and in a deep sleep for the rest of the day.

Soon the drawer beneath Kitty's bed held a stockpile of amitriptyline. Its purpose was to aid slumber and buffer pain. The irony wasn't lost on her. She'd had little restful sleep since Matt left and was hanging with tiredness but felt she may need the medication in bulk one day—an insurance against further hurt. For the time being she managed without it. When she did sleep her dreams wove around Matt until she dreaded the return of night.

Suicide no longer frightened Kitty. These days she felt her dad had given her permission. Parents were meant to lead by example weren't they? Well, he'd shown her the way. She'd already attempted it—topping herself. When her darkest thoughts had closed in on her in the dead of another lonely night, had threatened to suffocate her, she'd reached down and retrieved the tablets. She'd meant it at the time. She'd copped out after swallowing just one sheet. Fourteen pills. She'd made a point of counting each blue dot as she'd knocked them back. Fourteen full-stops. The drink had kicked in before the tablets. She'd called Gill, laughing, crying and making no sense.

'S'at Gill? I've—I'm—' Gill had been there within minutes.

At hospital Kitty's stomach was pumped inside an hour. There followed a lecture from an exhausted doctor who'd handed her a sealed letter for her GP. Gill had driven them back to Kitty's where the evidence greeted them with a stark welcome—an empty bottle of Gordon's lying in a pool of orange vomit. Spin The Bottle gone wrong. Gill had watched Kitty's every move as she'd cleared up the sick and dropped the empty pill sheet in the bin. Kitty had watched Gill move about and thought of her suicide attempt as a practice run; fourteen commas.

'Failed again,' Kitty kept telling Gill in the endless hours of that morning. Her chin had rested on her hands as she'd hunched over the kitchen table, bought from Ikea with Matt.

'You're stronger than this, Kat. You've been through worse. You'll get through this.' Gill had hugged her friend who'd just stared blankly back at her. 'You *will* get through this. Everyone is here for you.' Gill had gagged as Kitty had watched her rinse lumpy bits of sick from the mop.

Kitty had wondered who *everyone* was. Matt had left with many of their friends, those remaining were too embarrassed to know what to say; in effect, her world had halved. No, worse than that—*everyone* had actually reduced to just Gill. Her work colleagues had sent flowers and cards but even they'd stopped contacting her since her regular sick notes. She'd let the team down.

The humiliation Kitty felt when Gill took her to an STD clinic had been palpable. She'd felt such a fool. An old fool. She'd been unable to ask Matt if he'd been having unprotected sex; the thought repulsed her. She just didn't need any more of those images in her head; one was too many. Gill had kept

221

on. Kitty had argued, but then given in—too exhausted to fight any more. Kitty felt sure the elderly doctor had done her professional best to conceal her surprise at her patient's circumstances. Before the detail had spilled out—*I slept with my partner but he told me he'd been sleeping with men*—Kitty had felt sure the doctor must have mentally asked herself if this one was going to be a really interesting case—urban sex orgies, S&M play parties, or just boring old shagging the milkman? Kitty was sure she saw the hint of a flinch when she was asked how long she'd been in a relationship with her gay ex-partner—her answer a measure of her own stupidity.

The doctor had handed her three long cotton buds with which to scrape her vagina and three tubes in which to place them. Synchronising the procedure in the ladies' had proved challenging; the weight of the situation so immense. The thought of having caught something—*HIV*—terrified her or even chlamydia or gonorrhoea come to that, and *did that last one even still exist?* she'd asked herself as she'd struggled to drag her pants down with one free finger and thumb. And the shame. She'd felt this maiming shame before. It reminded her of when she'd gone for a pregnancy test with her mum, except then she'd known the result before it had been confirmed. This was more like Russian roulette.

The wait for the results, like all results, had seemed endless. On nights she managed to drift off to sleep, Kitty had dreamt of her body covered in sores, eaten by a disease. A leper, with Carole's taunting laugh ringing out loud and clear. She'd felt a social pariah all over again.

A fortnight later the doctor's receptionist had asked her to hold while she checked her notes. Kitty had held her breath as she'd dug her nails into her palm, her life hanging in the balance. The air had been perfectly still except for the occasional whoosh of the boiler firing up in the kitchen. The morning sun had dappled the apple tree in the back garden. A pigeon had strutted beneath the bird table to peck the fallen seed.

'Hello, dear.' She'd been put through to the doctor. She detected a note of sympathy. She was sure the professional, no-nonsense tone had changed to kinder, quieter, concerned. She'd croaked a barely audible *hello* back.

'All three tests have come back negative so there's nothing more for you to do.'

Relief was sweet, but only lasted a day. By the next morning, Kitty's world returned only in shades of grey. She didn't have any diseases but she still didn't have Matt. The euphoria she'd felt after that phone call had even convinced her she could go back to work; however, within just twenty-four hours she'd absolutely known she couldn't. The thought of facing her colleagues or customers had made her heart race and her breathing shallow. She wondered if she'd ever have any energy again; the simplest tasks left her exhausted.

Sometimes she imagined herself going over to Matt's new place, beating at his door and yelling every obscenity at him, for all to know how much he'd hurt her. She imagined keying his car with pleasingly deep gashes or flinging something hefty through his front window. Sorry, Matt and *Kevin's* new place. Matt and *Kevin's* door, Matt and *Kevin's* kitchen window. But she hadn't. Yet. She knew the energy expended would only cause them a measly mess to brush up; a few sorrys to the neighbours for a rejected ex upsetting the cul-de-sac's peace and quiet. It was all replaceable, even her. It knifed her soul.

She tried to impose a six o'clock curfew. She wouldn't go out on bad days for fear of bumping into Matt; he, *they* only lived two roads away, and she couldn't trust herself as to what she might do. Other times she deliberately wandered the streets in the hope of seeing him, just to remind herself who this person was that had meant everything to her—that they'd existed.

Late one afternoon she was lying on the sofa toying with the idea of going out for a walk when her mobile shrilled into action. It was Matt! His name flashed like a warning sign at her. She hesitated for only a couple of seconds before pressing the green icon, as if in a trance.

'Hi, Kit.'

His voice stopped her in her tracks. It was like she'd forgotten it, but suddenly it was oh so familiar. She said nothing in case she was hallucinating; she barely drew breath.

'You okay? Would you mind—if—I came round for the last of my stuff?'

She waited and hoped he'd say he'd made a mistake, but there was no masking his happiness. His voice was upbeat. How dare he ask her if she was *okay,* as if he hadn't caused this whole sorry mess? As if he hadn't planted that final lurid sex scene in her head.

'No. I'm busy.' She didn't know she was going to say those words until they came out. She was busy on the sofa staring into space. Not busy at all really.

'Oh, could you possibly just put it in bags out on the drive then? Please?'

'I'll bring them over to you. Later,' she relented.

Silence.

And then, 'Oh, okay. I'm meeting Dad. But Kev will be here. Just ring the bell.'

Kev. He of the buff body. The not-so-new love of Matt's life, in her warm shoes, in her place—a ready-made home after he'd set off grenades in theirs. She couldn't find the words to reply so she clicked him off. She was still lying on the sofa, thoughts racing through her mind hours after the call.

She eventually roused herself to fetch his belongings which she'd already bagged up in their wardrobe. She thought about opening them, gouging the lot with scissors, leaving her mark, leaving a reminder that she was still here. Instead, she sat on the bed and looked around the room. After Matt left, Gill had helped her pin poems, jokes and mantras around the house.

'Kat. When you feel really sad, read these—walk around and distract yourself. If you really want, I could print off some T.Rex lyrics?' It took a while before Kitty engaged with what Gill had said. When she did, she was just in time to see her friend's wry expression.

'You're alright, I'm not *that* desperate!' And fleetingly Kitty felt her old self, the old them, and even managed a smile.

She recalled what had been on the bedroom wall before. She remembered it wasn't *that* long ago she'd wanted to lick melted chocolate from David Gandy's fit body. Boy, but he was hot. She'd seen him on a poster in M & S in his pants; the stretchy kecks that swaddle an ample package. They'd been shopping. Matt had noticed her lusting over the model and secretly ordered a calendar of him online. He'd unwrapped it with a flourish when it arrived. That same day he'd hung it on the wall at the end of their bed.

'Is this where you want it, princess? Is it straight?'

'Yep, great,' she'd laughed, and marvelled at the lengths her man would go to accommodate her lust for another man. She'd had no idea back then that Matt may have enjoyed waking up to those images: David simmering through the seasons. The pages were magically turned to the right month and never by her. She binned that calendar after Matt left. The model's sultry eyes had seemed to glower at her as she'd tied the knot in the black bin bag. But he had to go. The calendar was replaced with "He Wishes for the Cloths of Heaven", torn dramatically from the poetry book given to her all those years ago by Tom—another one who'd ignored the value of her dreams. They were her go-to words when things unravelled. Those beautiful words she'd read over and over long after Amy had gone. She'd written them on a card and placed it in the lilies she'd bought for her nan's funeral. She'd recited them to Matt; she'd read out all her favourite poems to him at the start. He'd enjoyed her reading to him back then, said he loved to watch her beautiful mouth move. This one had made him emotional. She'd given the lady at the Chapel of Rest a crumpled copy when she'd left her mum's ashes, Annie gently weeping by her side. She recalled carefully writing it out on golden tissue paper and pinning it to her dad's wreath. She'd watched friends and relatives stoop over and study it, then turn to look at her with such sadness in their eyes. Two years later she'd read it out at Annie and Bert's funeral. The words were so emotive. She wrapped her arms around herself in a tight hug and stayed like that until sleep silenced her sad thoughts and dreams in gold, silver and blue took over.

SIXTEEN

Becoming a recluse came easily to Kitty. She lost days, no longer certain of dates. When sleep proved elusive, sleeping pills become her constant companion once again and got her through where her self-disgust and loathing seemed partially hidden behind a gauzy haze. She slept while others worked. She stared, as if in a trance, at daytime television. She ate when she could be bothered and no longer acknowledged hunger. She drank when the fancy took her. The weight fell off. Her uniform of baggy jeans and threadbare grey jumper over a faded blue T-shirt grew looser. She couldn't remember when she last washed her hair and no longer felt repulsed by her reflection. There was no one passing judgement, no one telling her what she should do, say or feel. It had been easy fobbing Gill off when she was away—lying she'd been shopping or gardening or tidying up. The truth was, she'd retreated so far into herself she could barely see a way out.

Gill called around when she was in the country and Kitty heard her pleas, fearful she would do *something stupid* again. Suicide. *Suicide, pesticide, cyanide.* She'd know when the time was right, *if* the time was right. She'd hardly broadcast it; that was the nature of the beast. And besides, the pill stash was too depleted, her dire need for sleep had seen to that. Gill laid out clean clothes for Kitty to change into but always found them on her bedroom floor, untouched, when she next visited. She brought back jars of exotic bath oils from her travels in the hope Kitty might enjoy a rare soak, but found them gathering dust in the kitchen where they'd been opened under Gill's encouraging eye and then abandoned.

The sun rose. The sun set. It grew hot. It grew cold. Kitty slept, she read, she listened to the silence. She paced from room to room. She ventured out, hood up, headphones on and music blasting when thoughts crowded in. She kept her head down from the rain and cold, pounding onwards, oblivious to her surroundings. She did everything she could to shut down any chink of consciousness through which she might have felt her own vulnerability. She did stuff. She did nothing. She cried, and sometimes, rarely, she smirked. She smirked at the sardonic realisation when your life has nose-dived but actually you can still exist under the radar. In a half-life.

One morning she looked out onto a grey, dismal day. The murkiness was contagious; it matched her mood. It was as if she'd forgotten how to turn the lights back on. She crossed off an imaginary checklist. Today, like yesterday and the day before, she wouldn't bother washing her hair, didn't really need a bath and the clothes she'd worn for days would be fine. It cut down on the washing. She couldn't remember the last time she'd used the washing machine. Her lank and lack-lustre hair, gaunt and drawn face sometimes stopped her in her tracks when she caught sight of herself. She rarely looked in the bathroom mirror but sometimes she did it just to acknowledge that she was still here. She studied her eyes—bloodshot and sore—until the person looking back at her was unfamiliar. She wondered if she should venture out for supplies or just make do again. The effort involved in looking presentable eluded her; the energy not there to muster. She'd run out of milk a while ago and the bread had turned green.

This day she found herself pacing the sitting room, unable to settle. Next to the sink was an unfinished bottle of wine. Last night, with her belly sloshing with booze, she should have tipped the remainder down the plughole. But she hadn't, because she knew it left her with something to look forward to. She sunk it in one and thought about opening another. Instead, she decided to go for a walk. Needed a walk, needed a change of air.

Christmas was coming. Houses were strewn with coloured lights and maniacally flashing plastic icicles. The ritual of excess was upon them. The insistence of Yuletide cheer was everywhere, when cheerful was the last thing Kitty felt. Inflatable Father Christmases clung onto roofs and fat snowmen waved at her with their marshmallow arms. Twas not the season to be jolly as far as Kitty was concerned. Window ledges inside cosy front rooms were busy with cheery cards, just like the ones that landed on her mat. *Her Matt.* Her cards, however, ended up in the bin. It hurt to see their names together, *Kitty and Matt,* but she just couldn't find the wherewithal to tell everyone. She sloped on, ignoring the excited cries of children and the general anticipation of a week of gluttony, and presents destined for the charity shop.

Pretty soon the counting started, it always did when she went on walks these days. *One, two, three*—the rhythm comforted her and gave her a slither of hope that at fifty, one hundred or one hundred and fifty, she might spot something lovely. It often led to disappointment like a calcifying dog turd or an overflowing bin or sometimes just nothing. That's why she extended the counting until she *did* spot something, anything interesting, like a clump of snowdrops or a squirrel in a tree. It was also a ploy to stop her from making her way to Matt's street. However, this time every road she took she mentally calculated how to get over there—which paths to cut through—how much longer it would take. She knew she shouldn't. Several times she stopped, turned around but changed her mind again and carried on.

Minutes later she was standing outside Matt and Kevin's place. No tacky decorations hung from their gutters, just a tasteful holly wreath on the door. She stilled her shaking body by slowly rocking back and forth on her trainers; the motion calmed her while she worked out what to do next. Matt's car wasn't on the drive. There was no one home as far as she knew; there was a stillness about the house. The next-door neighbour appeared, led by an excitable Labrador on a lead. They both stopped and looked in her direction.

'Can I help you? Are you looking for someone?' the man asked kindly, the dog's tail wagging furiously at his master's voice. She wondered if she looked like a bunny boiler. She'd seen *Fatal Attraction* with Gill years ago; they'd laughed at that bit—Glenn Close with the bunny bubbling on the stove. Now Kitty wondered if she was turning into one.

'No. Thanks,' she muttered, hoping he hadn't detected the impatience in her tone. *Why do people always turn up just when you don't want them to?* She thought she should walk up Matt's drive and pretend to press the doorbell as the neighbour was now eyeing her suspiciously. Just as she took one step forward the front door opened and Kevin stepped out wearing black Lycra beneath a woolly cap. They made eye contact fleetingly until Kitty looked away, totally taken by surprise and starting to panic. For a split second she thought he was going to say something. And then he did.

'Hi, Kitty. Kevin Wilson.' He extended his hand to her as he came down the path, but she couldn't bring herself to touch it. The last time she'd seen him that hand had been on her man's arse. How could he pretend that they hadn't already met? Did he think she'd erased the memory of him and Matt shagging on her bed? She turned and walked stiffly back in the same direction she'd come, trying to stay composed. She held back the tears. *Not yet! Please let me get home first.* He called after her. She couldn't make out what he said for the screams in her head. She picked up speed and didn't turn around. *Breathe deep. You are safe and secure. Repeat.* She started counting. She barely made it down her avenue and through the front door when the hot, furious tears started. She cried until she thought her eyes were surely bleeding.

It was a while before she was calm again. She looked up Kevin Wilson on Facebook. She hadn't known his surname before. It was a common one, but she found him. She read he was an interior designer; he ran for charity, he played football and was popular, with over two hundred friends. *Of course he is*, she thought sarcastically. There were messages in Messenger which she couldn't be bothered to read. She tried to distract herself by looking at the opened page of a novel she couldn't remember the beginning of. She put it down. Daniel Powter's "Bad Day" played on repeat in her head, until she realised it was actually playing on the radio in the kitchen which she couldn't even recall switching on. A chirpy DJ suddenly assaulted her thoughts, so she leaped up and flicked the switch off.

Her mood was getting darker by the hour; she started to panic. *Options, Kitty, options,* she repeated slowly over and over in her mind, creating a rhythm, trying to order her thoughts. She unfolded herself from the sofa and climbed upstairs to the bathroom. She sprayed dry shampoo in her hair, dragged a slick of lipstick across her mouth and put clean clothes on from the last pile that Gill had left.

Then Kitty was walking into town. She could hear the cries of children playing in their back gardens before they were called in for tea. Closer to town the pavements were full of mothers and children heading home from after-school clubs and shopping trips, wrapped up in coats, artily tied scarfs and woolly hats. Happy chatter. *Bloody kids everywhere.* As she reached the centre, workers were leaving their offices and hitting the pubs.

She started at their old local—The King's Head. She stuck her head round the snug door to check there was no one there she recognised. Shiny, tacky decorations hung from every beam. George Michael droned on about Christmas last year, but the coast was clear. She ordered a bottle of merlot and one glass and headed for a table in the corner. She drank the first glass silently. She felt a warm glow after that and glugged down the second. Nought to New Year's Eve in just two glasses. She liked the sensation, the feeling of bonhomie, the thought that anything was possible. She needed the blurred edges right now. She liked the feeling of being part of the crowd and grinned at everyone around her. A builder in overalls at the bar with dusty hair smiled back at her. She got talking to the couple at the table next to her until she turned once again to tell them another amusing story and realised they'd left. Another bottle appeared in front of her plus another glass plus the dusty builder. He asked her about herself and she replied with amusing repartee, or so she thought, until she heard herself talking about Matt and started to cry. Then he was gone too.

That mechanism, that *Christ, I've drunk too much and I'm going to make an arse of myself* finally kicked in about 10 p.m. She gave herself a mental pat on the back for thinking about leaving before last orders in her pseudo sobriety. *I'm not one of those drunks who refuses to leave,* she thought. *I'm not the last sad soul whose glass is taken away with only the ring stains to focus on,* she told herself, and smiled smugly as she stared at the sticky table.

As she picked up her handbag she realised an unshaven man was sitting in place of the builder, staring at her. Kitty had no idea who he was or if they'd even spoken. He smiled at her and asked if she'd like another drink. His breath stank. They both looked at the empty bottle. When she looked back at his face again, she thought he looked just like Matt, with stubble. She wanted it to be him, she really did. A tiny chink of reality warned her she was on dangerous ground. She declined his offer and got up to leave, steadying herself with her hands along the wood panelling. She headed for the ladies', stumbled into a cubicle, dropped heavily onto the lidded toilet and rested her head in her hands. She closed her eyes to stop the spinning; her elbows slid off her jeans and she was jolted awake as the door next to her slammed shut. She knew she should get going before she really couldn't.

Outside, the cold night air felt harsh compared to the fug of the pub snug. She drew her coat around her, belting it tightly. She tripped off the pavement. An oncoming car blasted its horn at her; a delivery boy on a scooter waved his fist and swore at her. She waved back and decided not to cross the road after all. The crowds of student revellers barely glanced in her direction as she stumbled down the street. Pissed was the norm in those parts. She chuckled to herself as she looked for somewhere to sit to gather her thoughts; maybe even call a taxi. She rustled around in her bag for her phone. She spotted a tree to lean against and as she approached it, she noticed a raised paving slab. She made a mental note to avoid it.

'Are you okay?' She heard someone speaking as if miles away. Slowly, very slowly, the smiling face of a stranger came almost into focus, then his outstretched hand as he helped her into a sitting position. She was on the ground. Her head pounded and she could taste blood. She couldn't remember falling but now felt more disoriented than drunk. Everything juddered in her eyeline. The stranger asked where she'd been and was there someone he could call?

'No point,' she slurred, 'I don't have anyone. He turned *gaaayyy. Gotta BOYfriend!*' Kitty stopped her head from drooping to see if her words had registered. He asked her to open her phone. It took a few attempts for her to remember the password.

She must have nodded off because it seemed like only seconds later Matt and Kevin were hauling her into Matt's car. Yes, *Matt and Kevin.* She thought she must be dreaming.

SEVENTEEN

Kevin strapped Kitty into the front seat and placed her handbag on her lap. The car felt warm and comfortable, clean, like new. Matt climbed into the driver's seat. He smelled heady and dense. She peered at him through one slitty eye. When she was stone cold sober she'd kick herself for being drunk because she'd have enjoyed this scene so much more—him taking responsibility for her after the fact—after the relationship—after it was too bloody late. A good Samaritan had involved him in something he thought he'd left behind. Dirty laundry. All because he was still the "In Case of Emergency" contact in her mobile. In her sober state she'd question why she hadn't changed it, why she hadn't put Gill as her emergency contact. She knew why really. She still wanted Matt to care. As it happened he was a good choice. Kitty wondered who else in her contacts list would have been available on a Friday night. And sober.

They helped her into the hallway, one either side of her holding an arm. Kevin had her handbag on his shoulder. Kitty couldn't put the words in the right order to tell him it suited him, so she just thought it. Matt headed for the kitchen as Kitty struggled to focus on his familiar stockiness filling the doorway, so right in their house. She wrestled with her jacket as nausea pulsed through her. Kevin steered her towards the bathroom. She fell to her knees and clung to the toilet like a long-lost friend and vomited noisily. She vomited for most of the night until she found enough strength to propel her tired, sore body into bed. She fell into a deep, racing sleep. Her last thought was it was no thanks to Matt and Kevin she hadn't choked on her own sick and decided to tell Matt that when she next saw him.

Kitty awoke to a bright, spinning room and total disgust. Something had happened last night but she couldn't remember what. Her head pounded viciously. The alarm clock ticked too loudly. She hoped to god she hadn't slept with anyone or made a complete fool of herself. No. She still had her pants on. She vaguely recalled being in the car with Matt; how would he have known where she was? Kevin had been there too. Fractured images filled her head. Were they still here? The sheets were crusty with dried red vomit. Her hair had lumps in it. The smell re-awakened the nausea. She steadied herself on the edge of the bed and gingerly stepped over the plum puddle on the deep-pile sandy carpet. She skidded on the bathroom floor and her retches joined the morning birdsong for the next hour. After drinking thirstily from the toothbrush mug, she fell back into bed for several more hours' sleep.

The next time she woke, she lay motionless, just inside the net of sleep. Her head was still thumping. The smell of the room was putrid. She wondered if she was turning into a drunk. Or had she already become one? How long it would be before she started dragging men home in a sad attempt to replace Matt?

She knew she had to get up, clean up. She stared at the ceiling until she gathered enough momentum to slide off the bed. Her stomach was tender as if she'd been doing sit-ups all night. Her throat felt raw; retched raw. She felt wretched. Her memory of the previous evening was still hazy: dislocated snapshots of places, the ground beneath her face, broken conversations. She stumbled to the kitchen for coffee and found a note in Matt's handwriting.

Hi Kit, we stayed until you fell asleep. Hope the head doesn't hurt too much. Will ring later X. She cringed with embarrassment. Coffee was a bad idea; the smell made her feel like throwing up again. She tried to eat some toast but each bite refused to stay down. No amount of paracetamol eased the pain in her head.

The clean-up was slow and laboured, punctuated with further trips to the bathroom and mouthfuls of air gulped at the open window. She scraped chunks of sick up with the edge of a knife which revealed a bigger problem beneath. She mentally calculated it would probably be cheaper to replace the bedroom carpet because of the underlying stain but she'd got into a comforting rhythm by then. *Scrape, flick, rub.* She persisted until the stain surrendered to the caustic carpet cleaner, and bicarb sorted out the smell.

Lying in the bath, she found huge bruises on her body and a comb through her freshly washed hair revealed a lump the size of a tennis ball pushing through her roots. Even after a long soak in a blend of seriously expensive bath oils gifted by Gill, she could still smell and taste sick.

She turned on her mobile. It shrilled into life. There was a text from someone called Ed. Ed, she discovered, was the good Samaritan, the one who'd saved her from potential rape

237

and pillage and called Matt out. Forgive him, she thought, he knew not what he did. When she remembered telling him about Matt being gay, her shame was complete and she realised she was no different to drunk Dolly from the street party. With shaking fingers she sent Ed a text and thanked him for his kindness. She phoned Matt; luckily he didn't answer so she left a message curtly apologising and thanked him and Kevin for bringing her home. She was fine, she lied. The effort took it out of her. She retreated to the sitting room and slid down on the cool leather sofa and slept some more.

By 5 a.m. the next morning she could stand it no longer. Her head still throbbed. She squinted vampire-like in the kitchen light; even her ears felt raw. When she stood up, she swayed. She texted Gill. *Are you home, can I call you?* When her friend was home she usually languished in bed until after midday, because she could, because she wasn't travelling through time zones. Kitty knew her friend's mobile would be on during the night. Gill was nothing if not amenable to a constant flow of enamoured beaux whispering sweet nothings through the wee small hours when she wasn't working.

'What's up?' Gill asked sleepily.

The local A & E was busy with drunks, lonely old ladies and babies with suspicious rashes. They sat in amongst avid *Heat* readers and stared at the subtitles on the silent TV screen, avoiding eye contact with anyone; avoiding confrontation. Kitty fought the urge to flee; she'd hated hospitals since Johnny died: the smells, the awful gaping gowns and the bleeps of the serious machinery. She was told she needed a CT scan, an ECG and bloods.

Within ten minutes of their arrival her name was called. She kept her head down as she passed the sign declaring "At least a Four-Hour Wait". She was ushered into a room by a young nurse who took her blood and then into another room to wait to be called for the scans. Her level of fear increased with the speed of each summons, with each conversation, with each examination. Her condition was being taken very seriously. Her suicide attempt was mentioned twice. Her shame was big and raw.

Kitty waited for Gill in the cubicled observation ward afterwards. She glimpsed frightened, resting bodies behind half-drawn curtains and then Gill appeared. Kitty jumped up and clung to her, fearing the worst: fearing she'd done damage to herself, fearing she might die. Gill patted her on her back to stem the snotty sobs which were beginning to unsettle the bored staff. A strong cup of builder's tea arrived plus a round of thin white chewy toast which Gill encouraged Kitty to eat, despite Kitty's protestations. In the end, they shared it.

Over an hour later a Registrar aged about twelve, Kitty thought, pulled a chair up to hers until their knees touched. He gave her an intense look. *Here it comes, my death warrant signed and delivered by a boy who has his whole life ahead of him. Brain damage or potential sight loss caused by a drunken fall. How bloody pathetic. And especially at my age.* She wanted to be anywhere but here.

'I'm pleased to tell you, Miss Black, there is no lasting damage to the brain. You've suffered a hard knock to the head. You have concussion. It will take time to heal. I must ask if you make a habit of this?' Kitty flinched and stared at her lap. He obviously knew about her suicide attempt and probably had her down as a crazy. She actually wanted to leap over and kiss him; it really wasn't the news she'd been expecting.

'No, she doesn't but I'm always falling over when I'm pissed!' Gill attempted to lighten the mood. Kitty tried to stop the wide grin on her face and confirmed it wouldn't happen again. The doctor handed Kitty a letter for her GP, and left the cubicle with a sense of purpose and his open white coat flapping behind him.

On the journey home, Gill stopped to buy some milk. Kitty sat in the car and people-watched. Someone about her age stepped out of the hairdressers and strode down the road as if she hadn't a care in the world. Her hair shone in the cold, bright morning sun. Kitty could barely recall how it felt after a highlight, wash and blow-dry—it had been so long. She flicked down the passenger mirror and studied her lank locks, saw the strands of grey and got her phone out to call the salon in front of her.

'Yes, madam—two thirty tomorrow afternoon?' Between the thumps of her heart, Kitty said she'd be there.

Gill slid back into the car, dumped the milk into Kitty's lap and saw the mobile in her hand.

'What have you done, Kat?'

Kitty smiled at her. 'Dust my car keys off, Gill, I'm going to get my hair done tomorrow!'

Although the headaches and dizziness continued for another month, Kitty revelled in being given another chance. The relief was huge. The drunken fall had knocked some sense into her. She removed Matt as her ICE contact.

'Goodbye, Matthew Bright,' she said out loud to the listening walls.

EIGHTEEN

Kitty watched the seasons change and welcomed in a shiny, new year. By spring she knew she felt differently; knew she was over the worst. After regular fitful sleep there was a tingly sensation deep in her stomach which gently radiated throughout her body. Hope. Hope had replaced dread. It felt like shedding an old skin, her old life. She uncurled, saw shades of colour, smelled new life. She heard birdsong and watched nimble spiders in their dewy webs; the sun cast its spell in corners of the garden previously rotting and forgotten. The breeze began to smell of lavender and fresh cut grass.

She freed the garden of weeds, found crocuses pushing eager tips of purple, white and saffron through the lawn. Curled fern fronds unfurled their bright green leaves. She jumped as toads sprung from the shade. The rhythm of physical work comforted her and the earnt tiredness made for restful sleep. A blackbird followed her around most days, studying her with his beady eye, then flew off as dusk beckoned.

She found her smile again, noticing neighbours' concerned glances also change to smiles, and reciprocated their warm *hellos* having ditched the headphones delivering incessant dirges. The manic thoughts and noises in her head were now silenced. She'd fallen far enough, had broken enough, knew it was now time to put herself back together again. A piece at a time. Building a new life for herself after having no hand in dismantling the old one wasn't going to be easy, she knew, but at least now she felt she could make a start.

She shopped for proper food, hugged supermarket aisles, delighted in all the different brands; all that possibility. She bought colourful fruit and veg, organic meat and herbal teas and felt her body gradually return to wellness with meals that demanded time, love and care. Instead of seeing an interminable day stretching ahead, she noticed filthy windows, a "floordrobe" in her bedroom, magazines piled high, and was shocked. The kitchen looked like there'd been some fantastic party, with every surface covered in empty bottles, mouldy plates and dirty glasses. She set to, cleaning and tidying with an energy she thought was long gone. She went from room to room, picking up, and wiping shelves felted with dust. She could almost hear a collective sigh from anyone who cared about her.

Gill turned up to help. They talked as they worked. They lunched in the garden. They slipped back easily into their old closeness. Gill broached the subject of dating. She tried to persuade Kitty there was a stream of eligible men just waiting for the chance to take her out. Kitty thought it was probably Gill's cast-offs, but didn't say so. They laughed about their role changes: Gill had given up counting how many men she'd been with and Kitty wasn't sure she could actually sleep with one ever again.

She returned to work and enjoyed her colleagues' attention after a fleeting feeling of embarrassment. Helen and the rest of the females hugged her sympathetically, while her male colleagues smiled but eyed her suspiciously, probably in the hope she wasn't about to internally combust. Many complimented her on how well she looked, which helped enormously with her adjustment back into the real world. Her place on the till was like meeting up with a reliable, old friend. The drawer to her right holding all the familiar notes and coins warmed her heart; the smell of copper was as comforting to her as the smell of baking bread.

Returning home after her first week back at work, Kitty flopped on the sofa and reached for her iPad which immediately alerted her to a new message.

Ping.

She keyed in the code and opened Messenger.

Katherine Black! The bewty who broke my heart! Broken heart emoji.

'Bloody hell!' Kitty gasped. She hadn't expected that. She tried not to be offended by the spelling mistake; and in any case, a warm feeling was spreading through her body. She read the message several times then clicked on his Facebook photo just to make absolutely sure it was him. The iPad Gill had bought her for her last birthday had opened up a whole new world for Kitty. She spent hours on it when she wasn't working. In a lonely moment several weeks ago she'd trawled the site looking up almost-forgotten people, renewing friendships of old. She'd even found her old schoolmate, Amy, after her surname came to her in the early hours one morning. But this message was from Paul. Paul from Scarborough. Her first boyfriend. His face had popped up in "People You May Know". It had taken her breath away the first time she saw it; years had passed between them, but she hadn't been completely convinced. Except for those eyes—those gorgeous eyes had given him away. Instead of committing to friends' statuses she'd messaged with, *Hi! Are you the Paul Scott from Scarborough I knew in 1971?*

She enlarged his profile photo. His wavy dark mane at sixteen had been replaced with a polished pate. A chubby, tattooed fifty-year-old looked back at her. She was about to respond immediately but stopped to think it through. She'd learned that from CBT: no knee-jerk reactions. She wondered if it was a good idea to churn up the past. She didn't want any more drama. But the fact was *she* had reached out to Paul, *she* had felt lonely, *she* had wanted to know what had happened to him. *Paul! I can't believe it's you.* she messaged and added a thinking emoji before pressing send.

There was no immediate response.

She flicked back onto his Facebook page. He had a partner, children and grandchildren. His wife (she spotted a wedding ring) looked the opposite to Kitty. She was tall, blonde and looked relaxed and happy in every photo. She had benefitted from Paul's kind and caring nature; *she* hadn't, she reasoned. She noted that Paul's son was the image of him as a teenager, and saw similarities in the grandchildren: laughing on fair rides, waving from café tables, doing handstands on the sand. There was a picture of Paul in army uniform and she wondered if it was a fancy-dress party, but he wasn't grinning like he was in the one wearing Superman gear with a fag in one hand, a can in the other. His profile told her he ran a car sales business. When she knew him he'd spent a lot of time driving them or peering under bonnets with only the legs of his blue overalls visible. And stealing them, of course.

She checked her messages again, hoping.

Nothing.

I see your love of cars has stayed with you, she wrote. No emoji—she tried to act cool and unconcerned, although her heart was thumping and the exhaustion of her first working week had magically vanished.

Yes my son Nathan and I run the bizness together, but I didn't finish my apprentiship after you left. I went off the rails a bit, Kit, he replied an hour later.

I wondered why your letters suddenly stopped—I guessed you'd found a new girlfriend.

No! It was years before I met anyone else. Can I call you?

Kitty put the device down and went to the kitchen to make a cup of tea. She slowly reached for a mug, tossed in a tea bag, and lingered while it stewed under the spoon. She plopped in milk and rhythmically stirred clockwise. She took a sip and felt the hot liquid in her throat. She closed her eyes. She heard another message arrive.

Please give me your number Kit. I have so much to tell you.

'Oh, god,' Kitty muttered and wondered what she would say to him if he started asking questions. Did she tell him everything that had happened, did she tell him some of it, none of it?

'Oh, sod it,' she finally said out loud, then banged in the numbers.

07786140277. There. It was done.

The second she'd sent it she regretted it. She grabbed the remote and flashed it at the television. The mobile in her bag in the hallway sprung into life. She didn't move a muscle, just kept staring at the muted gardening programme. Eventually her phone went quiet. She waited as the ringtone alerted her to a voicemail. Only then did she move and start to breathe regularly again.

'Hi Kit, thanks for giving me your number. I'll try again later.'

She replayed it twice. She couldn't believe it was Paul. He sounded like his dad. She switched off the mobile and headed back to the sofa. An hour later, dozing in the dark with the television off, she opened her eyes to the ping of another message alert on her iPad.

Kitty, please speak to me. It's great to be in touch with you, there's so much I want to tell you. I've left you a mrssage on your phone.

She clicked the television back on and stared at it. Paul seemed keen and her thoughts turned to him as a young lad: impetuous, a speed freak with an attractive swagger. So much had happened in the intervening years. She was a different person now; she *had* to be.

Sorry, Paul. Just as you rang, my neighbour popped round. Let's talk tomorrow. She watched as Paul's picture dropped down alongside her text. He read it then went offline. She retrieved his voicemail and added his name and number to her contacts.

The next day, she was catching up with housework when Paul rang.

'*Kit!*'

She tried to remain calm and took a deep breath in. Her heart thumped violently.

'Hi Paul, it's great to hear from you—I'd been searching on Facebook for a while and then you appeared. How are you?'

'Okay—well—no—not so great, if I'm honest. These last couple of years have been— pretty rough. My wife, Jules, died. Cancer. I miss her so much. I keep busy with work. Don't think I'll ever retire. How about you? The last time I saw you was in Peasholm Park.'

Kitty was shocked about Paul's wife, sad that he'd suffered trauma in his life but if she was honest, she felt something else too. She could hardly believe she was in touch with him after so long. It felt surreal. Somewhere, deep inside, she also felt put out—jealous even, that he'd chosen a life without her.

'I'm so sorry to hear about Jules.'

'Thanks. It's been grim.'

They talked for a while. Kitty offered him sympathy for the wife he'd found later in life and had obviously been devoted to. He talked about his grown-up son, the grandchildren he had—three girls and a boy. And then the questions started.

'I've seen your photos on Facebook. You were so gorgeous when I knew you. You still are. Couldn't believe my luck when you agreed to go out with me! What've you been up to, Kit?'

'Still the charmer, then? Well—left for sunnier climes, exams, work, stuff. Wondered why you stopped writing?' She threw the question back in his court. He hesitated.

'I have a confession, Kit.'

She sat up, 'Go on,' she said, intrigued.

'My world fell apart when you left—I got done for the cars again.'

'God, Paul.'

'It was a long time ago. We were kids. I've since paid the price.'

'What do you mean?'

'I was so upset when you left—I was nicking cars most nights, got pulled in by the cops and ended up in Skipworth Borstal again. You knew I'd been there before we met? They finally let me out on recall but I couldn't get a job—I was still angry—at—losing you. My mum and dad tried to get me back on the straight and narrow. They got me playing my trumpet in the band again. It was Christmas. After doing the pub rounds one night I stayed on and drank myself stupid.'

He told Kitty that in his drunken state he'd staggered down the wrong side of Falsgrave Road with his top off, playing his trumpet and stopping the traffic. She stifled a chuckle at the image, sucking in her lips in an attempt to stifle a guffaw. It was so him. The police kept him in overnight to sober up then sent him on his way the next morning. Except, as they'd handed him his belongings, they'd also handed over a box wrapped in Christmas paper, tied with a big golden bow. He'd found his mangled trumpet inside. The desk sergeant had smirked; Paul thought he'd done it, and belted him across the head with it. He was back in Skipworth by the afternoon, served another three months; couldn't face any more. He was given the option of staying on for another nine months or joining the Services. He'd joined the army. His dad had been relieved, said it would make a man of him; his mum had been heartbroken.

'When was that?' Kitty asked, barely breathing.

'Umm—September 1974 by the time I was drafted to Ireland with the regiment.'

She went cold. And quiet. She closed her eyes and fireworks exploded behind the red lids. She wanted to end the call. Images of Amy and the mother and baby home flashed through her mind. She couldn't find the words to explain what had been happening to her then. She repeated how great it was to talk to him and made the excuse that she was meeting a friend and had to go. She wasn't, but she really couldn't talk to him anymore; his words had shocked her. The timings had shocked her more. While he'd been setting out on a life-changing journey to unimaginable dangers, she'd been having Amy. She'd no idea how he'd react to the fact she'd given birth to an illegitimate child, and so she wasn't going to risk it.

She poured a glass of wine, pulled down the kitchen blinds to the darkness outside and caught a glimpse of herself in the reflection. She thought about how far she'd come. She'd been badly let down, had survived so much trauma, was still here despite some agonisingly low moments. But was she ready to tell her old flame everything that had happened, opening herself up again, making herself vulnerable? She spent the night mulling over her mixed-up thoughts.

The next evening she went to the pub with a group from work. Tensions were high as the auditors were in all week; it was a strain being on your best behaviour all day every day, but the manager demanded it. A drink was just what they'd all needed. It was late when she got home but after grabbing a snack from the fridge, she made a bee line to her iPad and flipped it open to messenger.

Kit, some photos of your old house, 15 Walnut Grove, drove past it earlier. Speeding car emoji. There was a line of images.

'*Jesus.*' Kitty put her plate to one side.

15 Walnut Grove. She'd forgotten that had been their address in Scarborough. So much had happened after, it had been squeezed from her memory. She was moved by Paul's gesture and the fact he even remembered where she'd lived.

There were four photos. She really hadn't given this house another thought since they'd left all those years ago. She looked at the three-bedroomed semi perched above and looking down over Scalby. A laburnum tree stood in the garden—the view from Kitty's bedroom window—and the subject of a prize-winning murder story she'd written when she'd first started at Scarborough Girls' High, encouraged by Mr Moore. There was a photo of the back of the house and Kitty noticed the cellar door was a different colour—red. She was sure it had been green back then.

The next image she studied was the street sign "Walnut Grove". She'd passed this many times as a teenager and it had usually filled her with dread, wondering what state her mum would be in—sober, drunk or even dead. She remembered the strong smell of cat pee from the hedge behind the sign— she now knew it to be boxwood. She saw the steps leading to the bottom of the road below. Twenty-eight in total with a handrail running down the centre and a sign stating "Leading to Walnut Grove". She definitely remembered those steps. She and Paul always parted there after their goodnight snogging session and she'd count each step on the way up to her house in an effort to calm herself.

The final photo was of her in school uniform at fifteen years old. She was smiling at the camera. There was a jewelled clip in her hair holding back her fringe. Her hair looked greasy; she'd angry spots on one cheek and she was wearing a too-pale lipstick. Her pleated skirt was rolled up to just beneath her knicker line, and where her Clarks shoes should have been were yellow clogs. *Yellow!* A roll of bracelets adorned the wrist that coyly pushed her hair back. At the time she'd thought she looked the business. *What a state,* she now thought.

OMG Paul! That last pic's dire!

You look luvly, Kit.

Paul sent her another photo. It was of him sitting astride the gun of a tank looking fierce in army fatigues with war paint on his face. She recognised him only from his eyes.

What was HK like? Emoji wearing shades ended his sentence.

Kitty started typing. *I messed up too! I missed you so much and fell pregnant to the first person who showed an interest. He raped me! YOU SHOULD HAVE WRITTEN, you selfish fucking bastard!*

Then she pressed delete. She now knew why he hadn't been in touch, but it felt good to see those words in black and white, if only for a few seconds.

Hot and noisy and a million miles from Yorkshire. Here's a photo of me.

The picture was faded and was taken by Gill from her balcony showing a young, slim Kitty who was looking up at Gill.

What a stunner! You've obviusly had a good life, Kit. Did you ever look for our stars? A trio of twinkling stars winked at her.

He remembered. This had more of an effect on Kitty than it probably should have; it felt like basking in warm sunshine.

She didn't respond to him immediately but looked at the photo properly. Life *was* pretty good then because she'd met

Gill. She'd missed Paul terribly especially when neither he nor his parents replied to her letters, but she'd had to eventually accept it was over between them.

It was really great, Paul, it was another world—and yes, I often looked for our stars.

They messaged for several weeks. He recounted his time in the army, how it changed him, turned him into a killing machine (didn't take much training he said, he was as angry as hell). His mum had been distraught; his dad couldn't have been any prouder. He asked Kitty about returning to England: when, where, what? At first she was cagey. She filled in the gaps with schools and jobs. Not a word about Amy. Nothing about Matt. When Paul spoke about Jules he talked so tenderly, so lovingly. Kitty made the connection between their loss of innocence: his to the army and hers to Tom and the mother and baby home. She could see they'd both lost loves. She and Paul had lost each other before anything had really begun.

Soon the time came when Kitty was no longer afraid to tell Paul the truth. She'd mulled over it while she served customers, while she watched television, while she bathed. In fact, it dominated most of her thoughts. She'd reached a point where she needed to tell him what had really happened to her. She'd reached out to him, needing a friend, and she wanted this renewed friendship to be based on honesty. Feeling a rush of confidence, she called him.

'Hi Paul. I've been thinking long and hard about this. I've something to tell you.'

'Kit! You don't have to tell me anything you don't want to. It's water under the bridge.'

'I do, Paul.'

And she did. Paul stayed silent as she talked about Tom. Then Amy. Then Matt. She heard him inhale. She heard the break in his voice when he offered her sympathy. She heard his reluctance when she ended the call. It was as if a great weight had been lifted from her.

She slept the best sleep in ages that night, dreamless and restful. She was walking on air the next day when Paul called and they arranged to meet in a month's time. In fact, the thought gave her goosebumps. He said he'd be happy to travel down country but Kitty had insisted on travelling up to Scarborough; she'd often wondered what it was like now. She was so happy to have Paul as a friend, but it did make her wonder where it might lead, if anything would come of it. She'd read somewhere that first love was the measure of all that followed. They'd met at such an impressionable age. Losing him the way she had, with no word of explanation, had meant she'd never quite got over him. They had unfinished business. Anything could happen.

They met on a blustery Sunday in the calm of the Grand Hotel's bar. It had recently been refurbished, and the plush burgundy carpet felt soft and luxurious under her new tan wedges. The elderly barman asked her what she'd like to drink and Kitty decided a coffee was probably a good start, then thought about coffee-breath, and ordered a lemon and ginger herbal tea instead. When he returned with a steaming bone china cup and saucer, Kitty told him she'd lived here as a girl. They both looked out to sea. He said the amusements were still there but Jaconelli's ice-cream was long gone; *kiddie fiddler,* he said, giving Kitty a serious nod before returning to the bar. Kitty surveyed the harbour and South Bay. She'd never been inside this hotel before but had always looked up at it from down below—impossible to miss this Victorian landmark, shining gold in the sunshine. She could've chosen from several modern places to stay in town but had kept coming back to this one on her iPad. In the end she'd booked a room for two nights, giving her time to explore.

Kitty fiddled with the sugar tubes until one split in her sweaty hand and spilled white crystals across the wooden table. She picked them up with the pad of her index finger and flicked them down by her side. When she clapped her hands together too loudly to dust all the sugar from her sweaty palms, a well-dressed couple enjoying red wine looked over at her, questioningly. She smiled apologetically at them and pulled her phone from her handbag, staring at it as if engrossed.

'Hi Kit.' Paul stood next to Kitty and grinned. Kitty looked up into the eyes of the person who'd stolen her heart as a young girl. Those darkest brown eyes flecked with cinder toffee were now lined and bloodshot. She stood and they embraced warmly, their bodies touching, her heartbeat pulsing. She noticed a stud in his left earlobe. She wondered when she'd grown taller than him. Had she kept on growing after they'd parted? He'd been a giant to her all those years ago. His distinctive leather flying cap and greatcoat had been replaced with a bald head, a jogging top and his once trendy flares were now old man slacks. And he had a shifty look about him; his youthful twinkle had become a steely glint. She realised he must be thinking the same of her. Her shiny long hair had been replaced with a middle-aged manageable bob. Her clothes were classic and comfortable. Her once youthful tight bum no longer peeked cheekily below revealing hotpants—they drooped way too far beneath her sensible M and S knickers. They were both older, no longer the kids they were. But for all of this, deep inside her it felt like a swarm of bees.

They sat down. The barman took their order of a beer and a wine. They talked. Kitty described her sight-seeing trip to her old house earlier that day. She'd walked up through town—now pedestrianised, past the Market Hall (which still sold big bags of cinder toffee), and up past new coffee shops and tattoo parlours. While she said this she tried not to look at Paul's hands. As he'd raised his drink to his lips earlier, she'd noticed a tattooed letter on each of the stubby fingers of his right hand. They were spidery letters, home-made probably. It had taken her a while to work out the word until she realised there was another letter further down on his thumb. At first she'd thought they spelt "leper" but then she'd realised they actually said "rebel".

She told Paul how she'd carried on up to Alma Square and had spotted the very rundown Victorian hotel she'd stayed in with her parents before departing for Hong Kong. She remembered how elegant it had looked back in the 1970s but thought it had now been turned into flats and was scruffy with grimy windows and discoloured net curtains. Paul said the whole square had been turned into social housing. Kitty had walked past the Odeon and onto Falsgrave Road, looking left over to the station, which looked exactly as it used to. She'd passed their old doctor's surgery, the one her dad had made her walk two miles to when she'd been doubled up in agony with appendicitis. Her mum had pleaded with Bobby to drive her to the GP.

'What is this? A bloody conspiracy? It's probably *women's problems,* you all milk it!'

He'd said he wouldn't waste the petrol but would walk with her. With the pain and cold air she'd struggled for breath and by the time they'd reached the main road, the searing pain in her right hip made her limp. When the building had finally come into view, Kitty had felt like she was no longer inside her own body. The doctor had examined her and announced she needed to go straight to hospital as her appendix was about to rupture. He'd said it would be quicker for her dad to take her in the car rather than wait for an ambulance; speed was of the essence. When Bobby told him they'd walked, the doctor glanced at the notes in front of him and said, 'You made this poor girl walk miles in this state? What's wrong with you, man!' And he'd brought his own car round to the entrance and carried Kitty onto the back seat as Bobby quietly slunk into the front. She'd spent ten days in hospital after having her appendix removed. She had just one visit from her parents and a big card handwritten by her form teacher and all her classmates which she actually found very touching. Recalling this memory had left Kitty feeling weary, so she'd stopped for a coffee and pictured Paul drunkenly playing his trumpet down the middle of the road with his top off.

Continuing her journey, Kitty had turned right onto Scalby Road. The old council flats where there were nightly fights had gone and in their place were new houses with tiny gardens full of children's toys. The off-licence was now a betting shop, flanked either side by charity shops; there was also a pharmacy and a funeral directors. The area had an air of neglect with overflowing bins and dog turds. Heading up Osborne Park towards their old cul-de-sac, Kitty felt her guts clench.

By the time she'd reached Walnut Grove, she'd calmed herself. She'd stood in front of their old house and looked towards her old bedroom window and saw a brightly coloured blind and teddies lining the window-ledge. A wind chime hung in the laburnum tree and tinkled in the breeze. The garage door lifted from the inside and a young woman came out backwards pulling a pushchair. Kitty turned to go but not before smiling at the little boy waving at her from the pushchair.

'Hi there, can I help you?' the mother asked, smiling broadly.

'No, no, it's okay,' Kitty replied, scanning the windows and pointing towards the house. 'I used to live here a long time ago, just came to see it.'

'I've just got to collect my daughter from a friend's but I'll be back in twenty minutes or so—would you like to come in and have a look when I get back?'

Kitty declined, thanked her and said she was meeting a friend. She skipped down the steps where she and Paul had snogged and headed back to the hotel knowing she'd exorcised a whole load of bad memories.

Paul squeezed Kitty's knee and said he was glad she'd done the journey before his expression turned serious. He looked into her eyes and asked her why she'd stopped writing to him. She told him she'd waited ages and ages for a reply from him, but nothing had come. His eyebrows arched in surprise when she said she'd written to his parents asking why he hadn't replied.

'I *did* write to you, Kit! From Borstal. I asked you to wait for me to sort myself out and then I'd be there for you when you returned to the UK. My parents didn't mention any letters to them. Mind you, they were so bloody ashamed of me for ending up in Borstal.'

'Oh my god,' was all she could say. Her thoughts raced. Her parents must have hidden that letter from her. They'd probably thought she'd settle down to her studies without any interference from him. *Well that backfired.* She'd ended up in far more trouble with Tom.

'You thought that I'd forgotten you. Just like that? You were the one I thought of when I was in Afghanistan. The army turned us into—killers, Kit. You had to hold on to everything you believed in. A day didn't go by where I didn't think of you. These things— change you.'

And she could see how it had changed him. His eyes darted about, as if seeking danger. She could see he was uncomfortable. She reached over and held his hot hand. They ordered more drinks and talked about old friends. Timbo had got his life together, had the nicest wife, six children and many grandchildren. Paul had met his wife, Jude, at his local; she'd been the barmaid. They were both in their thirties by the time they'd married. Kitty asked about his lovely mum and dad and they hugged when they discovered each other's parents were dead. Over fresh drinks they reminisced about the mad, fun times they'd enjoyed back then: the cars, the escapades, how close they'd come to having sex but hadn't.

Whether it was the effects of the alcohol or just the mention of sex, Kitty felt a roaring hot flush and undid the three buttons of her jersey. They caught each other's gaze again only this time Kit saw longing in Paul's eyes. She grabbed for his hand. They both stood up and headed for the sweeping staircase just outside the bar. By the time they reached room

613 they'd broken into a run and were laughing. Kitty flung the door open, lay back on the bed and Paul was on top of her in seconds. Their kissing had moved on from all those teenage Jackie tips; there was an urgency there now that no longer had to be stopped. Kitty tore at Paul's clothes and when he stood up to remove them properly, she whipped her knickers off in one deft, tipsy move. Paul smiled down at her. His erection jutted out from beneath his beer belly. He slid on a condom and gently entered her. They moved rhythmically to the tune of their lust. Kitty felt she would explode with excitement; it had been so long.

'Oh, Jules,' Paul murmured. Kitty stopped and opened her eyes. Paul's weight pressed down on her. She wriggled to get more comfortable, and huffed as she did so. Paul leant on his elbows and looked at her through dazed eyes, realising something was wrong. Within seconds his hardness shrivelled and slid out of her.

'Sorry, Kit—was I squashing you?' he asked, oblivious to calling Kitty by his dead wife's name.

'It's okay, thought I had cramp for a minute there.' Kitty tasted the sourness of the wine in her mouth, smelled the beer on Paul and tried to block out the cheap stud earring glinting at her.

'Really sorry, Kit. Try again?' But they both knew the moment was lost. An embarrassing silence fell until Paul struggled up from Kitty and reached for his big Y fronts on the burgundy fleur de lis carpet. Kitty gathered the jacquard bed throw around her, suddenly aware of her lumpy bits, and erupted into a fit of giggles.

'What?' Paul said, losing his balance as he tried to put his socks on.

'This was a bad idea, Paul! We always were friends and we should stay that way. Let's blame the booze. Fancy a bit of sight-seeing and some dinner?'

They eventually parted. They hugged and reluctantly turned away from one another. They promised to keep in touch. And they did. As friends. They'd started as friends and were continuing as friends. Way back then they'd both wanted to be lovers but the timing hadn't been right. It was the way things were. They'd loved each other but their lives had taken different paths; they were different people and there was no going back.

NINETEEN

'Online dating's the answer,' Gill said randomly one evening as they sat at a table in Gill's favourite French restaurant—Per Se. Gill was wearing a shot silk ochre dress. It fitted her beautifully and shimmered with hues of blue and copper when she moved. It brought out the deepest shades of her lustrous auburn mane. Kitty marvelled at her friend. Her friend who once had no dress sense whatsoever. The airline she worked for had groomed her into elegance. She always looked well turned out these days, even in jeans. On her phenomenal salary and with no commitments she could afford the best. The cost of her shoes alone would buy a complete outfit (including a coat) for Kitty. Like Kitty, Gill hadn't married but only because she didn't want her amazing social life compromised. She was out most evenings when she was in the country, enjoying expensive meals in fancy restaurants all paid for by an entourage of wealthy men, eager just to spend time in her company. Kitty thought about how they'd started out on the same trajectory but had ended up in very different places.

The owner of the eatery came over to take their order. Kitty was always impressed when Gill spoke another language, confidently and fluently. *This is what she was learning while I was being stupid with Tom.* Kitty was so proud of her. But Gill's idea of Kitty finding someone online to date was a curved ball.

'Why would you even suggest that for me when it's something you'd never do?' Kitty asked, trying to keep her tone mock indignant.

'I have! That's how I met two lovely blokes. Still see both of them—plus the pilot from the last long-haul.'

'Jesus, Gill! How come you end up with a menagerie of men who appear to satisfy your every whim and I pick one, just one to spend the rest of my life with, and he turns out to be bloody gay?'

Gill snorted into her glass.

'Did I turn the fucker gay?' The wine was kicking in now.

'Of course you didn't Kat—look at you, you're absolutely gorgeous and don't even know it anymore. You settled for Matt. It was the timing—a perfect storm. You were still broken, so vulnerable when you first met him, still hating yourself for getting pregnant and giving up Amy. You were in love with the idea of love. You could have had no idea what he was up to.'

'You've never said this before.' Kitty's voice was getting loud.

'Because you haven't been strong enough to take it. You are now. I want that friend back that was full of life, always laughing, always up to something. I miss her.'

Kitty didn't have to remind Gill that she'd recently got *up to something* with Paul (what *were* you thinking? Gill had

262

said), and look how that had ended. She reminded Gill it had been a big step to meet up with him. It had taken guts.

'Oh come on, Kat! He was a rogue, a loveable thief and you've lived in separate worlds since. Back then it was different, you were a teenager pushing boundaries.'

'My life was shit, Gill! He made it all okay.'

'I know, Kat. I'm not trying to marginalise any of it. You've shown resilience that most people can only dream about. You've come through so much. But I also remember that girl. You're made of even stronger stuff and you need to move forward just that bit more. It could be the best part of your life ahead of you now, you know.'

'But, Gill—all I've ever wanted is to find someone who can give me the love I need—is that really too much to bloody ask? It's all I've ever looked for and yes, I need it probably because of the shit home life I had after Johnny died, or maybe I was just born weak and pathetic! Whatever the reasons, it's beginning to feel like I don't deserve what I've been looking for. I thought Paul might have been the one had we stayed in Yorkshire but I realise now we were young and were finding our way. Tom promised me love, raped me and then disappeared and Matt was sleeping with men behind my back! For fuck's sake!'

'Kit. You *do* deserve what you're looking for and you *will* find it, but it may not be where you think it is. You have unfinished business with your daughter—*that's* your priority now. I know you! You won't rest until you've found her and until you do, you're not open to the love you're looking for—all that lovey-dovey domesticated claptrap, frilly apron kind of shit.'

Kitty tutted and raised her eyes skywards but knew that everything Gill was saying came from a place of love. She knew her friend was right. She'd settled for a safe haven with Matt, somewhere to hide from her pain—losing Johnny, her drunk mum, her abusive dad and that bastard Tom—it had been a refuge, but it had backfired in the end. In all the years of turmoil, her friend had been there for her, always supportive, wherever in the world she was. Kitty knew she hadn't reciprocated that friendship as well as she could have. She guessed Gill must have suffered heartache along the way but had chosen not to dump it on Kitty. Her heart swelled for the one constant in her life, and promised herself she would be a better friend.

'Am I being pathetic?'

'If I say you're sounding a lot like Dolly, does that answer your question?' They both chortled with laughter and clinked glasses.

'One other thing,' Gill said as their starters appeared. 'How about moving, Kat? A fresh start.'

'No way. There's too much stuff to sort out and it opens a whole can of worms financially with Matt. He'll want his pound of flesh.'

'That's why I think you should move in with me.'

Kitty was surprised. Not in a million years had she expected Gill to suggest this. She thought it through. Some days she still felt trapped in the house, sliding up and down the emotional scale of hating Matt for what he did and then just wanting his car to pull up outside. There were still too many reminders of him; it had become a shrine to her fake life with him. It had taken Gill several attempts to get her out for this meal. There really wasn't much to think about; Kitty knew Gill's offer was a gift.

By the end of the three courses, Kitty graciously accepted her friend's offer and they celebrated with another bottle of wine.

'Yay! It means we can go out together more,' Gill said. Panic crossed Kitty's face, so she followed it up with, 'We can play lots of Scrabble and I'll beat you!'

'Yeh, right!'

Online dating. That decision took Kitty a lot longer. There were several false starts with a resolve never to return. It was a whole new world. She'd had no idea how many hours you could waste scrolling left because a man's ears turned you off, or you thought the teeth behind those closed lips would be rotten. Initially, Kitty had been against meeting men this way; she'd felt it smacked of desperation: no shared history, no friends in common, no way of knowing if they were chancers. It was open to reinvention—axe murderers in sheep's clothing. She thought she must know enough male friends to find a single one to go out with without resorting to strangers. She trawled through a mental list one day, but drew a complete blank—they were either married, gay or revolting. Gill and Sheila from the bank had persisted and recommended sites to her. She'd thanked them but politely declined, imagining boozy failed trysts just like with Paul. Everyone had so much baggage and she more than most, she feared. She knew she couldn't compete with girls of today— all big boobs, rubber lips and flicky eyeliner. She couldn't be what she wasn't and she didn't need a man-child. On the phone a few evenings later, she told Gill it was a no-go.

The next evening Gill breezed in, her heavy curls swinging behind her and a bottle of expensive red in each hand which she thrust at Kitty in the hallway. 'Time to survey the goods!' After a couple of glasses of wine and handfuls of peanuts she declared, 'Synchronise iPads!' She whisked hers out of her soft leather bag and Kitty reached over to the coffee table for hers. Gill's eyes glinted as she turned to smile at Kitty, as if to say *strap yourself in!*

They started with "Love Bytes", the latest dating website that everyone seemed to be talking about. Kitty was reluctant to commit and hesitated when it came to completing her profile.

'I've no idea what to put, Gill—it's only going to attract crazies. If I say something as innocuous as liking pottery, they'll think I like having my tits rubbed!'

'Well, do you?'

'What? Like pottery or having my tits rubbed? Neither, really,' Kitty said, and they burst into giggles.

'How about—you look like a stallion, your sunken face is like a galleon, clawed with mysteries of the Spanish Main?'

Kitty looked at her friend blankly. 'What?!'

'Oh come on, Kat! How could you have forgotten your favourite song of all time?' Gill grinned maniacally at her.

'Fuck's sake, bloody Debora!'

In the end they settled for simplicity, making Kitty sound like the girl next door with no grand mission statements and uploaded a sweet photo of her after editing Matt out.

They simultaneously looked at profiles, taking it in turns to read out heights and hobbies, punctuated with guffaws and leery comments. They discounted more than a dozen through poor grammar (they couldn't help themselves) and earmarked a few possible maybes as they huddled over Kitty's device. Their faces lit up like children unwrapping presents beneath a shimmering Christmas tree.

Flirty conversations followed with men who, in unguarded moments, revealed they were unhappily married or even happily married and just looking for a quick shag.

Gill reached over and flicked each of those aside with a satisfied swipe. Kitty couldn't be absolutely certain, but she was pretty sure Dave, her musician neighbour, was on there. He wore a cap pulled down over his eyebrows and his goatee was flecked with silver. He must have moved from the area ages ago and the moody goth obviously hadn't been a keeper.

They whittled the maybes down to a cheery two—Rob and Craig.

Kitty spent far too long over-thinking the outfit for her first date with Rob. She settled in the end, after an excited Facetime chat with Gill, for her best jeans, pretty blue top and tan boots. She felt comfortable and still looked like herself after discarding dresses and skirts from the back of the wardrobe that made her look like she was trying too hard.

Outside the designated pub—chosen because it wasn't her local—she strategically parked her car ready for a speedy getaway. Just in case. She walked through the lounge and followed signs to the terrace as arranged. Couples nestled at tables beneath dusty speakers blaring tinny seventies music, but the atmosphere was good, it was building, it was Friday. Everyone was keen to draw a line under the working week with the help of gin, house wine and beer on tap.

Outside was noisier with groups of overalled labourers competing for the funniest line and office girls shrieking with laughter in their capsule clothes. Kitty scanned the sea of revellers, wondering if such a rowdy venue had been such a good idea after all. And then she spotted him—Rob. She knew it was him. He'd already asked her online what she'd like to drink and she'd said *sparkling mineral water please, I'm driving.* It was there in front of the empty seat beside him. He was at least fifteen years older than his profile photo. His greasy hair was thinning and in a comb-over. His neck was blue with tattoos which had been covered by a polo neck in his photo. Kitty hesitated and was about to turn around when he stood up and waved her over.

'Hi, you must be Kitty. I'm Rob,' he said in broad Mancunian and as he smiled he revealed discoloured, misshapen teeth, and Kitty knew she could never kiss this man. He had nose hair and dirty fingernails that could never hope to venture near her. *And what about the Irish heritage he'd mentioned in his profile?* she thought. What about that wavy dark hair she'd seen? What about a bit of bloody luck for once?

She stayed for as long as it took him to start slagging off his ex to say she should have gone to the ladies' on her way in; she was bursting. She excused herself and once out of his sight, broke into a run towards the car and sped away without a backward glance. Back at home she phoned Gill and told her what had happened.

'C'mon, Kat—you know the saying about kissing a few frogs along the way, right?'

Kitty could detect a stifled snigger and retorted, 'Gill, there was NO way my lips were going anywhere near his, he was AWFUL!' They broke into laughter until Gill nearly choked and told Kitty not to give up. Kitty went onto the site to block Rob and checked if there'd been any interest that day. There was a message from someone called David. He was very good looking in his photo, dark hair greying at the temples, and sparkling teeth beneath a sexy smile—not that that was anything to go by, she'd learned. His profile said he had his own marketing company and was divorced with no children. She decided to give David some more thought and then sorted through her emails. She caught her breath as she spotted one from Matt, expecting to feel a wave of hurt—or anger, but her emotions remained steady. She was calm as she read:

Hi Kit, I hope all is well with you. Kev and I were wondering if you'd like to come round one evening—we'll cook. We'd love to see you. Matt. X.

Kitty's first thought was *no bloody way! Definitely not.* But when she thought it through she decided that actually, it might be a good thing. This might be the step she needed to prove to herself and the world that she, *they,* had survived and moved on. She replied, *Hi Matt, that sounds good. I'm thinking of moving in with Gill so once that's done I'd love to if the offer's still open? Kit.* She pressed send and exhaled. She was proud of herself for accepting his invitation, for having come this far and for making the decision to move out of their house. It all felt right to her now.

Matt replied the next day. *Hi Kit, that's great and I'm pleased you're moving in with Gill. I've contacted a solicitor to remove my name from the deeds so the proceeds go to you. I'm really settled with Kev now. I know how I turned your world upside down. You don't deserve further stress. We're sorted and business is great, Dad's finally retired and I run it now. Let me know when you're ready and we'll set a date for that meal. Matt. X.*

Kitty closed her iPad and let her shoulders drop from her ears. It was a relief that they wouldn't be doing battle over the house. He'd created a shield of lies, maybe protecting her from the toughest of truths, or maybe protecting himself? Maybe both. They'd been together for such a long time, they'd meant so much to each other once and Kitty hadn't wanted his lies and deceit to be the overriding memory of something once so strong. Now she could remember the happy times she'd had with the handsome, shy man she'd spotted all those years ago when she was a new, young teller in the bank, instead of doing battle through solicitors.

Later that evening she went back to David. He was online. She was about to ask him what he was looking for in a relationship but he got in first. *Hi there, lovely. I've been hoping to chat to you. You caught my eye. What brings you to online dating?* She liked his style. They messaged into the night. They decided on an evening date. Kitty told Gill who insisted she would take her and collect her this time.

'If anything goes wrong, Kat, text "H" and I'll be there.'

'"H"? Is that for "halitosis", "horrific" or "hospitalised"?'

'"Help", doughnut.'

Kitty pulled out the stops for this one. She decided from their easy online banter they were going to get on. His answers had ticked all the boxes: he liked weekends away, cinema, going for walks. He was solvent and owned his own house; boasted his car was top of the range, although Kitty had no idea what it was even when he told her, which he'd laughed at. He seemed to have the GSOH as described on his profile.

Gill called round to find Kitty flinging clothes out of every cupboard. Finally she decided on a clingy black wrap dress and heels. Gill gave a wolf-whistle when Kitty stood in front of her, breathing in and craning her head to see the back view in the mirror. She thought she could get away with it so long as she didn't eat too much; she felt too excited to eat anyway. Gill wished her luck and reminded her about texting.

Kitty had to adjust her eyes as she stepped into the

dark bar; the atmosphere was sultry and sophisticated. She spotted David sitting on a stool. His eyes were fixed on his mobile phone screen. It gave her the chance to study him before he noticed her. Good start— he had hair just like his photo. It had been a recent picture. *Phew.* He was wearing a linen jacket, smart jeans and expensive shoes. He saw her and greeted her with a kiss on each cheek. His aftershave was musky and his hand on her arm sent tingles up her neck. His teeth were beautiful. *God, he's gorgeous.* And she prayed she hadn't said that out loud. She was a bit taken aback when he ordered a bottle of white wine and two glasses without even asking her what she'd like to drink, but went with it.

They settled into a cosy corner. The place was beginning to get busy. Jazz played softly in the background; there was an excited buzz. That is, until David's nasally whine started. He talked about his job, his car, his money, until Kitty realised she'd barely said a word. When he wasn't talking about himself he leered at her; he could barely contain his dribbles, or his hard-on. Kitty gave him the benefit of the doubt and decided he was nervous; *she* was, that was for sure. She kept adjusting her dress, wishing she'd worn trousers, but still he continued to leer which added to her unease. She started to tell him about her job in the bank but was interrupted by him launching into tales of his latest skiing holiday. She complimented him on his tan but he barely heard her as he animatedly described his skill in the sport: the harder slopes, the most expensive gear, the best après ski. He mentioned money again and then his preferences in women. Kitty flinched at one point, hoping she'd mis-seen but she was pretty sure he winked at her.

On and on he went until Kitty started to squirm in her

seat, wishing he'd shut up. Her tight dress was now really uncomfortable. She thought about a lovely warm bath. At home. David's mobile rang and he took the call without apologising for the intrusion. He leant back in his seat, crossing one leg over his other knee and talked too loudly to the caller. She began to think the call had been staged to impress her. Boredom kicked in. She swigged her drink. She spotted his expensive watch, looked at his groomed nails and then stopped in her tracks. On his wedding finger was a white mark. A white mark where a wedding band had been— recently—she was sure of it. She snorted out loud but he didn't notice. So much for being divorced three years ago. *Scumbag.* She pulled her mobile out of her clutch bag. *HHH!*

She stood up and, putting his mobile to his chest, David said, '*Sorry.* Work. Can't manage without me.' He tutted and raised his eyes in mock helplessness.

Kitty pointed in the direction of the ladies', but he'd gone back to his call. She teetered on her heels towards the exit and out into Gill's waiting car thinking, *I'm too old for this shit.*

'Bloody hell, Kat! That didn't take long. I thought something dreadful had happened. Think I've probably got done for speeding. Didn't go well, then?'

'Complete and utter knob.'

During her lunch hour the next day, Kitty collected packing boxes from the removal company and fixed a date, deciding to market the house once she was settled into Gill's. That evening she started packing up. Gill had left on another long-haul trip and Kitty was glad because she knew she must do this by herself. There were albums of photos she just couldn't resist flicking through; she couldn't stop herself.

The pages of the first album fell open on a large photo of the whole of St Gilda's Convent. It was dated 1962—she would have been six. She was sitting cross-legged on the ground on the far left of the front row. Her best friend, Amy, was two rows behind. Mother Superior stared sternly from the centre of the front row. Kitty's stomach lurched. She stared at the girl she was, so young, so vulnerable, so innocent. She thought about the bullying at that school—pupils *and* nuns—feeling sad that people could be so cruel. But those had been good days, comparatively. Whatever the day brought then, she'd go home and wait for Johnny to get back so she could follow him around and immerse herself in his world. His energy and fun seemed to keep everyone buoyant back then. The memory of his grinning face and his guttural laugh filled her eyes with tears, so she closed the book. The next one in the pile saw the tears slide down her face as she looked at her dad handing her an ice-cream he'd queued ages for in Parson Park. It had become a ritual every time they'd gone there during the summer; it was as if he'd been trying to make up for all the treats she'd missed out on after Johnny had died. Her mobile sprung into life. It was Gill.

'Hi, Kat! How's the packing going?'

'Fine, thanks,' Kitty lied, and wiped her wet face with the back of her hand and tried to stifle a snotty sniff.

'Come on, Kat. You can do this, right? This will all be for the best. Trust me.'

And she did. She packed the albums into a box, threw in the framed pictures of Matt, once hanging in the office and then relegated to the cupboard beneath the bookshelves, and secured the box with tape. She wrote *PHOTOS* on the side with marker pen and pushed the box into the dining room. As she brushed out the cupboard, a glint caught the corner of her eye. Something tiny and shiny was pushed up under the right-hand door. She flicked it out with her finger, blew off the dust and could hardly believe what she'd found. Matt had made her the most beautiful daisy clip-on earrings with opal petals and an amber stone in the centre when they'd first got together. Not long after they'd moved in they'd been invited to friends of Peter's for dinner, excellent customers of Bright's, and Kitty had dressed up and worn the earrings. They'd got home late; Matt had lit the fire and put music on. They'd pushed the sofa back, kicked off their shoes and danced to "Green Onions", the title track of Matt's favourite album. The earring must have come off during the dancing. To Kitty, those earrings had symbolised hope, of outrunning the storm of her youth, a new beginning. She'd been distraught when she couldn't find it; they'd hunted high and low but with no luck. She cleaned it off and matched it up with the other one in her jewellery box.

A week later and the house that Kitty and Matt shared was a mere shadow of its former self, the white expanses once again revealed, stark, endless and marked, the soul dismantled. Kitty was leaving all the furniture behind; she'd sell it along with the house once she was ready. There was no rush, she told herself.

She stood in the hallway, intending to leave but not quite able to take that last step out of the door. This house had known her dreams, her happiness, her sorrows. It had seen the storm catch up with her again. It had been her sanctuary *and* her prison. She'd laughed and cried in it, drunk vineyards of wine in it, sobered up and started the numbing process all over again. But there was nothing keeping her here anymore.

It was time for it to be filled with someone else's memories, happy ones, she hoped. Maybe even children, a possibility with the size it was, and her heart gave a familiar throb at the thought. The removal men finished loading up their van and said they would see her at the other place in about fifteen minutes. They were already outside Gill's detached house by the time Kitty whispered a hoarse goodbye to her old home and closed the front door quietly behind her. The borders of lavender stroked their farewell as lovingly as they'd welcomed her all those years ago.

Once her belongings had been off-loaded, Kitty searched for the box marked *IMPORTANT STUFF*, and pushed it into her new bedroom. Gill had freshened up the walls with a pale grey paint and a new duvet set of peacocks in rich turquoise and orange. Co-ordinated cushions rested against the headboard. In the wardrobe were satin-covered hangers, each tied with a little heart, so thoughtful of her dear friend. She unfolded the cardboard top of the box and pulled out the blue suitcase. She'd lovingly emptied the contents of the red vanity case her nan had given her. It was so worn in places but she just couldn't throw it away. She kept it in a cloth bag inside the suitcase. She hadn't opened the suitcase for a while—everything become too raw after Amy turned eighteen and no word.

She tipped out the items of both, moving a brown envelope from the suitcase to one side. She placed her Scarborough Lucky Duck, the engagement ring Paul had given her, the ceramic hedgehog from that cracker next to the rabbit, and matinee jacket on her bed. She rubbed Johnny's suede marble pouch and laid it down. Next to these she placed her mum's small box of jewellery, her glasses in their worn burgundy case and the red shoes. She placed her mum's Lucky Duck next to her own. She placed the photos of Amy, Johnny and her and Gill in Hong Kong on her bedside table. She studied the one of Johnny. He was leaning against their white pebble-dashed garage. His denimed left knee was raised. Brylcreemed hair shone above the turned-up collar of his leather jacket; his thumbs were hooked through his belt loops. He looked so cool. He stared sultrily at Kitty; ash threatened to fall from the cigarette hanging from the corner of his mouth. Along the white border at the bottom of the photo was written *James Dean 1964* in Johnny's scrawl. Johnny had borrowed the camera from their dad's desk and shown eight-year-old Kitty how to take the picture. He'd wanted to give the pic to his latest pash—Sylvie on the deli counter at Tesco's. Kitty had struggled to put her fingers in the right place.

'Fuckin' 'ell, Kit! Just click the bloody button!'

She'd tutted at him as she always did when he swore, then clicked the button a second before the back door had opened and their mum called them in for tea. The cigarette had fallen to the ground and was under Johnny's winkle-pickered shoe in one deft move; he'd popped a Polo mint in his mouth and winked at Kitty. In the end he'd kept the photo, said it was too good to give away. It had leant against the conch shell on his chest of drawers. He'd broken up with Sylvie a week later. Kitty placed the photo next to the others on her bedside table. She put her dad's Seiko watch in the middle of the display on her bed and laid her own little Timex next to it. She set the chain and crucifix from Mary over her mum's jewellery box. She re-read her dad's last note and put it under his watch. She picked up a small piece of yellowing plastic. It was a tiny baby-sized wristband with *Amy Black 10 November 1974* written on it. Her fingers traced the edge of the band as she remembered how small her baby had been, how she'd clung to life. She looked at her most treasured belongings for a while and carefully put them away again. She reached for the brown envelope. Inside was a letter from the Adoption Contact Register. That lady *had* got back to her when Amy had turned eighteen, but it hadn't been good news. They were very sorry but Amy hadn't been in touch with them. Kitty knew every word without actually reading it. She closed the case and stored it at the back of her new wardrobe. *New home, new start*, she thought, and went to put on the kettle.

With Gill's encouragement Kitty was soon back on the dating site. There was a wink from someone called Andy. She couldn't believe her eyes. Partially disguised by a fedora dipped below one eye was Andy Barker. His profile clearly stated he was divorced. Kitty hadn't seen or heard from either him or Jane since her split from Matt; she'd assumed they'd stayed friends with him and that had hurt. Andy had been promoted and transferred some time ago to another branch of NatWest. Kitty sent him a message saying *hi*, joked about *this dating lark* and wished him well. Nice bloke and everything, she thought, but not for her. Craig was keen to meet; he was the last one of the trio her and Gill had earmarked. Kitty chatted online to him for an hour and arranged a coffee in town with him the next day. Before she settled down in bed she took a last look at her iPad before switching it to silent. There were over ten messages from Craig, ranging from *Can't wait to meet you* to kissing teddy bears and hearts floating up to the sky. Kitty smiled and looked forward to meeting him.

Craig didn't turn up the next day: a no-show.

'You've been ghosted, Kat,' Gill said matter-of-factly on the phone.

'But he was dead keen! He sent me flowers, teddy bears and hearts for weeks! I looked a fool in that café waiting for him for over an hour!'

'Kat. It happens. Some people like to play those games. It didn't cost him anything—nothing he sent you was real.'

'And that's exactly what I don't like bloody about online dating!' Kitty said indignantly.

'I bet if you try to find his profile now it won't be there.'

Kitty was still in the High Street; she was furious he hadn't turned up. She marched into the Boars Head for a glass of wine to calm her anger. She trawled the dating site and, sure enough, Craig was nowhere. He'd ceased to exist. Was this how some men got their kicks? She vowed to stay off online dating forever.

Within a week Kitty found herself on the sofa in the dark, Gill at her side, poring over a lit screen as if deliberating over a favourite chocolate.

They found Jack sandwiched between two no-hopers.

'Such a good, reliable name,' Gill said, and Kitty sniggered and said she sounded like Miss Marple. *Probably a manic-depressive with false teeth*, Kitty thought, but if first impressions were to be believed then this one did seem to have something about him—a cheeriness, a sparkle even. And, if his profile wasn't pure fiction, they did appear to have much in common: both had been out of long-term relationships for some time, both liked walking, reading and listening to music—except his specified reggae. He was two years younger than her. *Oh well*, she sighed over his music taste and read on. He had a good job, was taller than her and had his own place.

'Send him a wink,' Gill encouraged her.

'Are you kidding, Gill? He'll start sending me dick pics and he'll think I want sex with him on the first date! No bloody way.'

'Oh my god, Kat! Listen to yourself! You need to get back in the saddle. Just go for it.' Gill sighed loudly for effect.

Unbelievable, Kitty thought. *This* from someone who'd previously run into the sea to escape the opposite sex. But she did it anyway and Jack replied with a virtual bunch of flowers. They messaged and made each other laugh. Jack seemed to have a good sense of fun about him. During her lunch hours at work they communicated with heart emojis and GIFs. They exchanged phone numbers so they could talk before meeting. After that previous date with the Mancunian accent Kitty was taking no chances.

Days passed. When Jack called it caught her completely unawares.

'Hi Kitty, it's me. Jack. We met online.' As if he needed to remind her who he was.

'Hello, Jack,' her voice quivered. She'd practised saying this several times to avoid the "hijack" thing, but she still sounded nervous. Then they both spoke at the same time and apologised at the same time. Kitty decided to shut up. It was then he asked her out.

'I'd love to,' came out before he'd finished asking.

She gave him the name of her road, said goodbye and let out a loud '*Yesss!*' before she realised she hadn't clicked her mobile off. But the minute she'd said it, she no longer wanted to do it. But she'd committed. For days her emotions were all over

279

the place and she came so close, several times, to cancelling and would have had it not been for Gill's persistence.

The day of the date arrived. Kitty knew it was too late to cancel now; any excuse, other than near-death, would sound lame. And anyway, she hated letting people down. She decided to go ahead—*it's only one date*, she told herself. She didn't have to see him again after that; even Gill told her there was no pressure—she'd never have to see him again if it didn't pan out. She had no idea what to wear, especially as she'd got it so wrong the last time. Gill came upstairs and helped her get ready after almost an hour of Kitty pulling dresses and tops on and off in a fit of self-loathing.

'Keep it simple. Keep it *you*,' she said.

Kitty didn't want to try and look younger than she was—that really smacked of desperation—but she didn't want to look frumpy either. Finally, she settled on her jeans and favourite top; no tight dress this time and no high heels. They heard a car. Gill asked what make Jack drove but Kitty had no idea, she'd forgotten to ask. Gill said the one that had pulled up at the end of the road was silver and had a fin on top. 'What? Like a basking shark?' Kitty said as she ran over to peek from behind the curtain. They watched him look anxiously around. Was he doubting his decision to come? Kitty was about to voice her doubts for the millionth time but Gill pushed her towards the stairs and wished her luck.

Kitty watched Jack's face light up as she walked self-consciously towards the car. He got out to greet her. Unfolded, actually—his legs seemed to go on forever. His shoulders seemed as wide as a wardrobe, strong and reliable. There was sincerity in his eyes. His dark eyes. Kitty felt herself melting as she slid into the passenger seat and breathed in the smell of him, thrilled by the unfamiliarity of a new person.

They spent the evening talking and laughing as if they'd known each other for years. There were no uncomfortable silences. He lifted their locked hands at one point and kissed her knuckle. So tender, it made her catch her breath. The shock of intimacy made her realise how much she'd missed it. It felt good. She liked the laughter, the ease, the possibility. Everything seemed to change in Jack's presence: colours became more intense, the air fresher, everything clearer. His energy and enthusiasm were infectious and the best bit was he looked at Kitty as if she were a beautiful flower. She found herself twirling her hair when he spoke to her. She felt like a girl again.

On their next date they drove to the beach. They walked along the deserted sand as a storm brewed; seagulls swooped and squawked. The sky was gunmetal grey. The wind grew stronger, blowing Kitty's hair around her face and making her eyes water. The tang of seaweed whipped about as waves dashed angrily into the cliff edge. It was hard to see where the sea ended and the sky began. Kitty heard thunder rumble in the distance and urged Jack back to the car. He held her close and, placing a finger under her chin, lifted her face to the sky.

'Feel the rain on your face.'

She jerked her head as lightning forked across the clouds. His words flew away with the wind.

'What are you afraid of, Kitty Black?'

She hesitated then admitted, 'Thunder and lightning, actually.'

The way he said her name. The way it sounded in his mouth made her pulse pound. He made it sound like poetry.

He kissed her on her lips, making them tingle. They ran from the sand onto the pavement, dodged puddles and laughed like children all the way back to the car. She would never have believed that at the age of fifty she'd be back on the dating scene and enjoying herself. She'd thought she'd be with Matt forever—until death did they part. But now here she was having fun with this lovely man called Jack. Kitty and Jack.

TWENTY

Armed with a bottle of merlot and a bunch of yellow roses, Kitty stepped out of Gill's car and looked towards Matt and Kevin's front door.

'Ring me if it all goes tits up, Kat. I'll come straight away.'

Kitty walked up the path to the house, breathing in deeply, exhaling slowly. She no longer wanted to hurl bricks through the window or shout obscenities from the garden. Instead, she pressed the doorbell and hugged Matt warmly when he appeared wearing an apron of a bikinied lady with big breasts. He looked relaxed and happy. The smell of cooking was inviting.

'Hi, Kit. Come on in, it's great to see you. You're looking well.'

Kitty chuckled and thrust the flowers into his chest before walking along the hallway in the direction he nodded. She already knew the layout; it was similar to their old house. What surprised her were the colours and the artwork—bold and striking—just the way she liked it. Kevin was waiting in the sitting room. A muscle flexed in his jaw as he probably wondered if she'd bolt again—or throw up. She held the wine out to him.

'I'm relying on you not to let this get messy, Kevin.' Kitty winked and then hugged him. Muzak played on the stereo—no memories rekindled here before dinner. On the shelves were photos of Matt and Kevin. Kitty spotted the silver "K". The silver "K" that had never belonged to her, and with that the reminder that Matt hadn't either, but her heart didn't miss a beat. Books about gardening, cooking, theatre and exercise leant into one another just like Matt and Kevin did when they sat together on the sofa as they enjoyed a pre-dinner glass of wine. Matt looked at Kevin the way he'd once looked at her many years ago. Kitty felt happy for them.

'So how are you, Kit? How's work? How's Gill?' Matt asked.

'Good, thanks, still love the counting house and my lovely little old ladies! Gill's still flying around the world and—uh—sends her regards.'

'Good to hear, although I don't believe the last bit!'

'No, I made that up,' Kitty said, smiling over her glass.

Kevin disappeared, then returned and offered her a square turquoise plate with smoke salmon hors d'oeuvres artistically arranged, and in his other hand was a clutch of cute napkins. The napkins were decorated with seahorses. She took one and reached for three of the fishy delicacies, hardly needing further urging. The next plate Kevin appeared with was tiny quails' eggs finely dusted with celery salt, a favourite of Matt's, Kitty recalled.

'Did you do these, Kevin?' Kitty asked, popping one in her mouth.

'Yes, I did the fiddly, important stuff,' Kevin said, turning and grinning cheekily at Matt.

'Please tell me you got the bought ones from M & S and didn't have to mess around boiling and shelling these.' Kitty reached for another.

'They *are* from M & S, actually—there wouldn't have been enough room for me *and* Delia Smith in the kitchen, as I'm sure you know, Kitty!'

'Still enjoy cooking then?' Kitty asked Matt.

Matt nodded over to the cookery books on the shelf. 'Yep, Kev buys the recipe books and I make the magic happen.' He looked lovingly at Kevin who placed both hands on his heart. Matt chuckled and went pink.

The meal was a feast with salmon, prawns, cream and a lemon cheesecake deserving of a heart attack. Although Kitty missed Matt's cooking, she didn't miss the extra weight that had hugged her hips for far too long.

'So,' Kevin started, as the three of them sat stuffed and happy around the table, unable yet to move themselves back into the sitting room, 'you seeing anyone, Kitty?' Kevin asked. She knew it was bound to come up this evening; was surprised even it had taken this long.

'Actually, I *am.*'

Matt and Kevin looked at her, waiting.

'I've met someone online. His name's Jack.' She reached for her mobile in her pocket and scrolled through her photos until she came to one taken at the beach. They passed her phone between them, studying it like two schoolboys looking at porn.

'Mmm, not bad,' Kevin said, looking up at her and smiling.

'I'm happy for you, Kit,' Matt said, sincerely.

The rest of the evening passed pleasantly with talk about holidays, the jewellery business, Peter. Matt and Kevin held hands and Kitty didn't lurch at Kevin with a broken wine glass demanding he unhand her man. She didn't linger in Matt's embrace on the way out or tell him to stop being silly and come home. Nor did she feel sad about the years they'd been together. Good times, bad times, happy times, sad times. Those times were all now just part of life's rich pattern, re-affirming her resilience and his coming out—becoming the person he was meant to be, no longer having to disguise secrets with shyness. Kitty had never had to hide from who she was, never had to pretend to be someone she wasn't—all her crosses to bear and mistakes had been out there for all to see. They'd made her who she was today and for part of that journey she'd loved Matt with her whole heart and he'd cherished and cared for her in his way.

Gill was waiting in the car outside at gone midnight. Kitty hugged both men warmly and thanked them for a great evening. She waved to them as she climbed into the car. They blew kisses to her, arms entwined as one from the doorway, silhouetted by the pink hallway light. The evening couldn't have gone any better and Kitty gave herself a virtual pat on the back.

Kitty and Jack slept together for the first time and fireworks exploded. Literally. It was November 5th and they'd decided on an evening in. Gill was away with work. For weeks now neighbours had collected cardboard, crates and any other detritus found lying behind composts and piled them high ready for a bonfire in the park at the end of the road. Posters appeared in shop windows and on lampposts;

Kitty could feel the excitement building. She'd never been one for standing in the freezing cold, flinching at fireworks. In fact, she'd never been one to stand in the warm and watch them either. In Hong Kong on Chinese New Year, apart from the dancing dragons, the constant gong-banging and incessant firecrackers were sure to bring on a headache. But she enjoyed the anticipation of this night and had watched the bonfire build earlier, culminating in a rather macabre grinning Guy Fawkes wearing a floppy red felt hat, reputed to belong to the local gossip.

Outside, Kitty and Jack could hear children's squeals as families made their way to the event. Indoors they enjoyed a warming chilli with jacket potatoes, drank prosecco and cuddled on the sofa. Bangers and rockets boomed and whizzed outside their window as Jack's tongue became more insistent. The curtains lit up from the bigger blasts. Kitty dragged Jack down on top of her as she slid onto the carpet. Fleetingly Matt's face came to her. She froze. *Matt who ran off with another man,* she reminded herself, making the image evaporate. She felt her body might explode when Jack touched her; it was as if parts of her were coming back to life. When she climaxed, her whole body shook and buzzed as if she'd been turned inside out. She'd never felt anything like it. Jack's post-coital tenderness was something she'd never experienced. He dropped a kiss on her shoulder.

'Happy, Miss Black?' he asked her with such gentleness.

'Very, Mr Meredith.'

It felt so good to have a warm body next to hers, to feel wanted, needed. She felt herself falling for this sexy man whose sense of humour brought out the best in her. He made her laugh, and that counted for a lot. Jack was full of life, compelling, and his dark eyes lit fires in her belly. They'd exchanged so many confidences but she hadn't yet told him about Amy. He'd confided in her about his marriage, how it had failed after their son died at just five years old from a massive seizure; he'd never wanted another child, it was just too painful, but his wife had and it had torn them apart. He'd cried uncontrollably as he'd told Kitty. He described the heartbreak of burying his parents together after they contracted food poisoning on a once in a lifetime world cruise which he'd encouraged them to go on. He even revealed the fact that he'd survived testicular cancer and could still remember the shock he felt at the diagnosis, the rawness of thinking he was staring death in the face. So Kitty knew he'd already lived a life that had embraced pain and suffering, she knew he'd empathy, but she still held back from telling him about Amy; the stigma was always there. She lost sleep worrying about how to put into words she'd had an illegitimate child and then would wake feeling she was worrying over nothing; times had changed.

The next time they met Jack asked her if she was okay. He said she looked exhausted. She made an excuse about work. He hugged her, saying he'd take her for a meal somewhere, anywhere she liked. And that was the moment she chose to let it all tumble out.

'I had a child when I was a teenager—he was a married man—I gave her up for adoption.' She watched his expression closely, waiting for a change, waiting for the disgust. Silence. He pulled away from their embrace. He started to say something, pursed his lips and looked down at the ground. Tears pooled in her eyes. She waited.

'Please say something, Jack,' she pleaded. He lifted his head up to the sky. She saw tears drop from the corner of his eyes; his face looked pained.

'Can't believe this, Kitty. My child died, it nearly killed me—and you—you—just give one away, just like that because you made a—a—*mistake?*'

'No! *No!* It wasn't like that, Jack—I was ra—' But he hadn't heard her and was getting into his car. He swung the steering wheel furiously, manoeuvred out of the space and sped away. Kitty stood there watching the end of the road long after his car had disappeared from view. With a heavy heart, she turned and made her way back to her car.

She didn't shed another tear when she relayed the day's events to Gill, despite Gill's exasperation. She listened and made all the right noises in all the right places but deep down she knew she'd wasted more than enough time and energy on mindless distractions. She deleted her profile from "Love Bytes" as Gill continued to persuade her that not all men were morons. By bedtime Kitty's resolve was unbreakable.

After rushing home from work the very next day she set about finding her daughter. If Amy still hadn't contacted the Adoption Contact Register then she had to find her another way. Her head spun at the realisation she'd never thought to search for her on Facebook; she was sure to be on there, wasn't she? Working on the slim chance that Amy had kept her name with her adoptive family and not married, Kitty punched in "Amy Black" and pressed search. Her heart missed beats when twenty or so possibles came up, of which over half had profile photos. She trawled through each and every one for any sign of familiarity or identifiable area in Devon. One Amy Black lived in Exeter, but on closer inspection the detail revealed she'd originally come from Birmingham, but that was the closest she got. Then realisation dawned. Of course her daughter wouldn't have kept Kitty's surname, she would have taken on her adoptive parent's name.

During her lunch hours she began to make phone calls. She discovered the mother and baby home was now a Care Home, but they gave her the name of someone involved in the administration. That person gave her information concerning records recovered from the premises on closure and added children's Adoption Case Records were meant to be retained for a minimum of one hundred years after the Adoption Order. She intimated to Kitty that that probably wasn't the case with this place as other enquiries had revealed missing papers. Kitty hoped with all of her heart that Amy's records still existed. She called the Adoption Contact Register and passed on every detail she'd collated, catching her breath when she was told not to give up. If Amy contacted them, they would be in touch, they said. Kitty jotted down all details of the phone calls she'd had and placed the notepaper inside the brown envelope and back in the suitcase. She took one last lingering look at all the treasured items inside before closing the lid, wanting the next time she opened it to be to gather some of them to show Amy. Every day after work Kitty rushed home to see if there was any post. On really impatient days she phoned Gill to ask if there were any letters for her so that disappointment didn't greet her at the door. It got so that Gill didn't wait for Kitty to ask the question, she just said, 'Nothing today, Kat.'

Weeks passed. Kitty became convinced her daughter didn't want to see her. While serving customers she went over and over her time with Tom, berating herself for being such a bloody fool, hating the state she'd gotten herself into.

Some evenings she couldn't face going straight home after work; instead she paced supermarket aisles, finding solace in familiar foods in numbered aisles, order in the stacked shelves. On sunny evenings she sometimes sat in the park, the sun warming her face as she tried to block out children's laughter. Gill sometimes popped up with a bag of chips and they'd sit on a bench and watch the sun disappear. Or they'd go to the cinema where Gill knew Kitty could just sit and think, never taxing her about the film, knowing full well she hadn't taken any of it in.

Then one day a letter plopped onto the doormat. It sat there until after Kitty finished work, went to the supermarket and walked the park until dark. It was a relief to escape the blustery evening as she was propelled through the door, side-stepping a line of post. Banging on the hallway light, she bent down to sift through takeaway and double-glazing flyers, a letter for Gill which she placed on the table, and one addressed to her. It looked official; the font was serious, meant business. She tore the envelope open. It was from the Adoption Contact Register. She screwed her eyes shut not daring to read the bad news. She mulled over the possibilities until she could bear it no more. She held her breath as she read the words *your daughter has recently contacted us, we are in receipt of all paperwork, we can now put you in touch with each other.*

Kitty thought she might explode. She couldn't believe that her biggest wish had come true and was contained here in these words. She closed her eyes again and this time savoured the joy she'd felt when she'd first held her new-born daughter. She said a silent prayer. It was as if all the bad times, the losses and the dross had been sloughed away.

She'd waited for this ever since that day in 1974 when she'd watched two strangers walk away with her world and Sister Jude had comforted her. Years and years of wondering, wanting, needing. She called the number on the letter within minutes of reading it. She texted Gill who called her back. They laughed and cried together.

'Oh, Kat! You've so much to tell each other. Lives lived and all that. Are you taking photos with you?'

'I'm taking a whole load of bloody stuff,' Kitty said.

Kitty sits in an artisan coffee shop. Waiting. Her shoulders are rigid with tension. She brushes fluff off her jeans, straightens the collar of her jacket, looks at her nails. She has a good view of the street outside, but bursts of rain have brought out umbrellas, shielding people's faces. The smell of roasting coffee adds to her light-headedness; her eyes dart about. The milk steamer screeches behind the counter. She clutches her big brown leather handbag to her. It holds a packet of tissues for the tears she knows she will cry plus some precious items from the blue suitcase. She traces the stitching on one handle with her finger and prays this meeting will go well, that there will be no long silences—or even worse, recriminations. She'd thought long and hard about what to bring; she didn't want to overwhelm Amy, but it might be her only chance in showing her daughter how much she's loved. She'd had to run back into the house to retrieve the photos of her and Gill, Johnny and Amy from her bedside table.

She looks down at her watch and then across at the door. She's oblivious to what's going on immediately around her, aware the coffee shop is busy, but doesn't see the detail or hear the conversations. The anticipation is delicious and disturbing all at the same time. She has held on to the hope that someday this moment would arrive. Now she can barely believe it *is* happening. She wonders if she should go up to the counter and get two coffees but doesn't want to presume. And besides, she's had so much caffeine since waking in the early hours that she now has palpitations. Her thoughts race: if she waits to get the drinks how much precious time will be wasted on queuing? She stays in her seat. Then, as she grabs her purse to buy the drinks, her mobile buzzes. Her heart pounds as she reaches for it. There's a text. *Oh god. Please don't say she's not coming.* It's from Gill. *Good Luck, Kat. X.* She shrugs her shoulders up to her ears and drops them in an effort to relax.

The door swings open, ringing the overhead bell. A girl wearing a navy mac, black boots and a handbag across her shoulder is blown in. Kitty tenses. The girl lifts her hand in greeting and smiles at an elderly lady in the corner. Kitty slumps back down in her chair. Minutes pass, the sun comes out, and she studies the dust motes hanging in the air. The man at the table next to her asks for her pepper; she passes it to him and almost misses the next ring of the bell. As if in slow-motion, she turns. She sees a woman step into the café. She's wearing jeans, a navy jacket and a burgundy silk scarf knotted at the neck. Kitty knows instantly she's her daughter. She's a younger, much better version of herself. Amy's grin threatens to out-do the sunshine streaming through the café's blinds. She knows who Kitty is and looks straight at her. Despite the carefully applied make-up, Kitty stands and greets Amy with a tear-smeared face. Amy rushes over and hugs her.

'Hi Mum. I'm Debbie.'

293

ACKNOWLEDGEMENTS

Thank you to the following people for helping to turn my ramblings into something real:

Troubador Publishing – in particular Beth Archer for her positivity and patience.

My Clevedon writers' group – Andrew, Alistair, Chris, Nick et al for their constructive feed-back and good company.

The 2018 BSU MA Creative Writing cohort, especially Chris, Vik and Irene for dragging me kicking and screaming to the end of the course; for all those wonderful hours spent at the Methuen and Flemish Weaver.

Jo Nadin for inspiring and encouraging me.

Tricia Trott for her friendship and all we have shared, then and now.

Suzy Frost for keeping things real and always being there with an open bottle of wine.

Finally, my family for their generous support. In particular Eliza - for her boundless enthusiasm, loyalty and joy, an absolute star and I wouldn't have got this far without her.